# Kathy the Good Samaritan

## Robert Bennie

*Authors*
On Line

**Visit us online at** www.authorsonline.co.uk

An Authors OnLine Book

Text Copyright © Robert Bennie 2009

Cover design by William Russell ©

ISBN 978-07552-0483-0


Authors OnLine Ltd
19 The Cinques
Gamlingay, Sandy
Bedfordshire SG19 3NU
England


This book is also available in e-book format, details of which are available at www.authorsonline.co.uk

*With my best wishes*

*Robert Bennet*

*For Daisy, for her patience and fortitude in keeping me writing.*

# Contents

# The Characters Involved

POSEIDON (P) – Marcus Lorenzo –The strong chief leader of the Triumvirate clan, who is a racist towards Jews and is also a ruthless individual who buys and sells antiques as well as drugs to various places throughout the world.
He lives in Hamburg (Germany), also has a flat in Paris and Monte Carlo.

HADES (H) – Mario Lorenzo – A brother of Marcos Lorenzo – Another co-leader of the Triumvirate clan, He is a very wealthy person who lives in America and dislikes Islam.
He recruits and initiates the members of the clan from all around the world and also deals in antiques and the main dealer and supplier of the drug cartel.

CEREBERUS (C) – The Hon.Nicholas Pitman – (nephew of Duke of Chardminster) Who is a Playboy living in England and is a dealer in antiques and drugs, and the co-leader of the Triumvirate group in England.

Gerry Giovanie – An American Gangster, known as Gee.Gee who lives in Las Vegas U.S.A. and dislikes Jews and Islamic people.

David Hogarth – Ex. R.A.A.F.Pilot and working for the Australian Security Service

Kathy Goolaburra – . Now working for the Australian Security Service.

Mark Broadbent – Chairman and Chief executive of the Charleston development Corporation and also the Deputy C.I.A.Director, Chicago division

Melinda Broadbent – Wife of Mark Broadbent

Richard Crossley - Head of Intelligence (MI 6)

Penny Williams – Sister of David Hogarth and married to Guy Williams with two young children called Rachel and Nicola

Nancy Oldfield – A Newspaper reporter for the "Daily Tribune" which is owned by her father Lord Oldfield.

Wendy Willerbey – A very close friend of Nancy Oldfield and the daughter of Lord Leslie Willerbey,

Lord Leslie Willerbey – Who, when he retired, was made a Baron for his work as Chief Financial Officer with a Life Insurance Company

Susan Pitman – Youngest daughter of Duke of Chardminster) and who is also a friend of Nancy Oldfield.

Jeannette Pitman – Duchess of Chardminster.- 2nd wife of the Duke of Chardminster and the stepmother of Susan Pitman

The Hon.Andrew Ashley-Grove – Son of Lord Ashley – Grove. A deputy head of Intelligence branch of M.I.6 and a friend of Nicholas Pitman

Bruce Robertson – Ex American Army air force pilot and also a C.I.A.Officer –
Who is a friend of David Hogarth.

Pierre Bouverie – Owner of the motor yacht "Pricilla"

Harold Phillips – A Police Chief Supt. and member of MI6 who drinks very heavily and steals drugs to offset his financial problems caused through his drinking. Is also a double agent for the Triumvirate

Paddy Foulds – With his blood brother Sandy Foulds, they operate and manage the "Nick-Nick" gang, who specialize in big bank robberies and are also the main dealers in drug distribution in England.

Luigi Muraditori - Head of Mafia in Milano

Commander Charles Bryant - Head of Special Branch of the Met. Police.

Wing Commander Mike Taggert - R.A.A.F. and a senior member of the Australian Security Forces and attached to the U.N. Security Force.

Abraham Filligoti - Head of the Mossad (Israeli Secret Police)

DGSE = Direction Generale de la Securite Exterieure , represented by an agent called Henri Fouchard
(France's foreign intelligence service)

DST = (France counter-intelligence agency)    Direction    de    la
Surveillance du Territoire

Elysee & Renseignements Generaux Intelligence is the gathering arm of France's national police

Mossad = The secret service of Israel.

# CHAPTER 1

## (Kathy's Family)

It was 1922 and Irene and Robert Goolaburra were living near Camperdown about 35 miles outside of Melbourne in the poorer part of the district that was allocated only to coloured people. Irene and Robert were both lightly brown skinned and fairly poor, they had been married for 5years and were living in a very old ramshackle house that had no electricity, and had candles to light at night and a small scullery and an outside lavatory. One morning they were sitting down at a table in their very small kitchen having their breakfast discussing their future when Irene began to cry a little, they were both honest people who were very proud of their upbringing and being religious they were also proud that they attended the local church every Sunday. It was because Irene had been unwell that Robert looked at her and said "Are you feeling a little better and are you still concerned over what the doctors have told you?" The tears were now running down Irene face as she said "I'm sorry Robert, but after the operation I've had, I can't stop thinking that after all the trouble we have been through, we can never have children and I did want to have a baby by you. One that we could both love and watch grow into a good human being, but I know this is impossible, and I'm upset because I believe it is because we are considered by the white people to be unsuitable human beings because of the colour of our skin. We go to church regularly and believe in God, but I cannot see what good that does us because we have not had the best of luck. What with some of the white folk saying that we are not acceptable to them because we are of a different colour and also demanding you have to work hard to earn money, having to do the menial jobs in the mines just to earn money to enable us to buy food and pay the rent, it seems to me as though life is not worth living."

Robert fairly exploded at her saying "Now stop that talk. You

1

know that we are just the same as those white folks. We breathe the same air as them, and like us, they were born a child from God regardless of the colour of their skin. So stop thinking we are something different because we are not. You have to remember that some of those white folks have to do the same work as me because like us they are also poor. You and I are normal human beings with a different coloured skin, we eat the same food as them and those people who think they are different to us because we are of a different colour are wrong. We are human beings, and you should always remember what the vicar is always telling us, that everyone, no matter what colour their skin, whether they are white, black, brown or yellow, we are all God's children and I don't want you thinking or saying anything different to that again. Now stop that crying and I will make you a cup of tea."

Irene stopped crying, looked at Robert as he rose to make the tea. It was while he was making the tea she was thinking and feeling very grateful how he had looked after her all the time she had been very ill, then when he gave her the cup of tea she smiled at him and said "Robert I'm sorry for my outburst I just get a little frustrated at times."

He said "Don't worry honey I understand how you feel, now I wasn't going to tell you, but when the doctors told me what they were going to do to save your life it was while they were operating on you, I went to see Father Sherbrooke, and I told him the doctors were performing a hysterectomy and you could never have a baby. He knew that you and I wanted to have a baby, and he told me not to worry, and he then told me the full story of the Aborigine plight of how, many, many years before we were born, the Australian authorities had taken the Aborigine children away from their parents and separated the brothers and sisters from each other and sent them away right across the country."

Irene began to cry again and cried out saying "How could the authorities be so cruel and wicked to take away the children from their parents and separate brother and sister from each other" Robert interrupted her by saying "Now stop that crying because you have to remember that all of this happened many years ago, and it is only recently that people are beginning to talk about it and they have been told, and we have been informed, that neither they, nor us, will be punished for talking about that suffering, because something is being done about it and the situation will eventually be solved."

2

Robert stopped talking to drink his tea and as Irene made herself comfortable in her chair Robert again began speaking to her, "Father Sherbrooke told me that in those earlier days of years, and years ago, the Aborigine people were separated from the white people and were not allowed to mix with them, but they could work for them and after many, many years had elapsed, some beautiful young Aborigine girls began to have babies by the white men and he said he can remember your mother wasn't as dark skinned as most Aborigine people are. He said she was a lovely Aborigine girl with olive coloured skin, and he remembers her being married to your father, who was white because his family had some time in the past originated from one of those mixed relationships, and his family had no objections to your parents getting married. This is why you, and I, are olive skinned and it was because I told him I knew nothing of my grand parents, he also told me about my parents and said that they had originally come from somewhere near the Rocklands reservation and had also come from mixed relationships". Before Robert could say anything else Irene interrupted him "Robert what is all this leading up to?" He looked at her with a nice smile on his face saying "Well I hope this will be a nice surprise and you will not be too upset by what I'm going to tell you." Robert looked at her and was still smiling as he said "Father Sherbrooke said that if you want a baby you could still have one, because he knows of an orphanage that has unwanted babies of mixed relationships. He said that he was recently told of a white woman who has had a baby by a man whose colour was slightly black and the colour of the baby is olive skinned, but the parents of the white woman will have nothing to do with their daughter because the baby is by a black man, and therefore she must put the baby in the orphanage. Father Sherbrooke says that if you would like to go there, he is certain you will find a baby who you will love, and if you want to visit the orphanage he will make the necessary arrangements and alert them that we are going to visit them."

Irene looked at Robert for a few moments before she said "Robert I know I shouldn't tell you this but I have always known the feelings of the white people around here and their feelings towards people being of a different colour to them, because when I went to school I was not allowed to sit, or play with the white skinned girls, and I was never invited to their homes and they tend to treat us as though we are different and not a normal human being. At first it used to upset me because I felt as though I was different to them and I only went to the homes of the girls who were lightly coloured, then eventually as I grew older I began to realize that I am the same as the white people because I am a human being but with a slightly coloured skin." Irene stopped for moment then said "At first I just put it down to their ignorance and to their snobbery, but then I did begin to hear of the troubles of the dark skinned Aborigine's of years ago and sometimes of the fights between them and the white people, but being young I didn't want to get involved or persecuted, so I kept quiet and never spoke about it." Robert had by now reached a point of where he could no longer wait, because he interrupted her as he quickly said "I have been thinking of what Father Sherbrooke said and I have coupled it with what you have been through. Would you like to adopt a baby and before you answer I want you to know I would like you to have a baby even if it is through adoption because I know you will be a good mother?" Hearing Robert say that made Irene feel very happy and she said " Robert I want you to know that I do love you very much. I shall always remember the day we first met and how nervous you appeared to be when you asked me to go out with you and I will always remember the look on your face when I said yes. Now having been married to you for all these years I would have liked to have had a baby by you, and if you are asking me whether I want a baby and start a family, the answer is yes, but not for the reasons you could be thinking of. The baby we have must be desired and loved by both of us and to all intent and purposes the baby must feel as though it is ours and ours alone, and there is to be no thinking or talking of colour, race or creed." With a big smile Robert said "I love you very much as well and I agree entirely with what you have just said, and I'm also pleased that you married me because you have made me very happy and I am ever so pleased you are beginning to think like me, because what you have just said about the baby is what I believe and I also believe that we can offer the baby a nice happy home and if we are lucky enough to have one, it is ours and belongs to us alone."

The following day they both went to see Father Sherbrooke and when they had told him what they wanted to do, he spoke to them for quite a long time asking them all types of questions, but it was the manner they used in answer to his questions that made him realize that they were genuine in their desire in wanting to adopt a baby. He was ever so pleased with them and he told them that he would make all the arrangements for them to be interviewed and he would let them know where to go to the orphanage. Two weeks later he visited them again and told them that he had made an appointment for them to be interviewed the very next day, and they were to go to the Christian Church orphanage that was situated just outside of Melbourne near Geelong.

They were very excited hearing that news and being financially poor they didn't care that they had a long way to go, but knew that they would get there somehow. However they were feeling confident knowing that Father Sherbrooke had told them he wanted them to visit him when they got back, because he wanted to know if they had been accepted. The following day they put on their best clothes even though they were of a poor quality and shabby, and because of the long journey they left home very early. They waited over 30 minutes for the local transport, and when it arrived it was a very old ramshackle vehicle with solid wheels and wooden seats. They knew that on its journey to Geelong it stopped at various small places to pick up more people the same colour as them. They were told that when they could see Lake Corangamite and then after a few more miles they would be near the orphanage that was in an isolated spot, just outside of Geelong. The whole journey took over three hours to reach where they had to get off the vehicle, and then holding hands together, they walked along a dusty side road wondering what the orphanage would be like and how they would be received. They eventually reached a big old red brick building with a large courtyard that looked very forbidding and they stood still while they looked at the notice on the wallboard that read "The Christian Church Orphanage".

Very nervously they opened the big gates and walking slowly through the courtyard they went up eight steps to the front door, and with a great deal of trepidation they rang the door bell that made a mournful chime. When they entered the building they were shown into a small room where three ladies were sitting at a table waiting to interview them. Seeing them Irene at first thought they looked very formidable, but those ladies began by asking both Irene and Robert a number of questions in a haughty, yet inspiringly    encouraging manner that gave both of them a glimmer of hope, with the main question being "Why do you want to adopt a baby?" After they had answered all the detail questions, and after they had answered the main question, they were told to wait outside in the other room while those three ladies decided on their verdict. Whilst they were outside waiting, Irene held Robert's hand and whispered "I m praying very hard that all will be well for us." When they were called back into the committee room they were both feeling very nervous and worried fearing they would be refused permission, but the Chairlady told them that the committee were satisfied that they would be suitable people to foster a baby and they were told that it would take another four to five weeks before they would be informed when they could come to collect and take a baby home and then it would be approximately another twelve months before a court of law decided whether they could adopt the baby. They left the orphanage feeling very pleased and when they eventually arrived home, they visited Father Sherbrooke and told him the good news.

Three months later they received a message from Father Sherbrooke that they were to go to the orphanage the following day and to wear their best clothes because the time had come for them to collect a baby. That morning they went full of apprehension and worry and when they arrived at the orphanage they were shown into a room and told to wait. About five minutes later a door opened and a lady appeared with a very small baby in her arms, wrapped in a shawl.

The lady looked at them and then holding the baby out towards them said "Would you like this baby? It is a baby girl and only six weeks old, and she also has had a full medical examination and has been cleared by the doctors and is therefore in a perfect healthy condition, or would you like to choose another one?" Not knowing, or understanding that they would be called upon so suddenly to make such a big decision like that, they looked at each other and without looking at the baby they both immediately replied "Yes please that is the one". The lady looked astonished because she said "Wouldn't you like to look at the baby, or look at some other babies before you first decide?" Irene replied "If I was giving birth to a baby I wouldn't be able to look at the baby first to see what it was like and then say I don't want it would I? I would have to accept what God has given me, so today is just like me giving birth to a baby and I'm very grateful that God is allowing me to have this baby." The lady was amazed at Irene's answer and looked at Irene and she immediately knew that the baby was going into good hands and handed the baby to Irene, who, when she looked at the baby saw it had light brown skin. The baby smiled, then Irene saw there was a small bible with a small cross and chain lying on the shawl, but before Irene could say anything the lady disappeared to go into another room leaving Irene holding the baby and when the lady came back she was holding a paper file and she asked Robert and Irene to sign for the baby.

It was after signing the forms, that Irene asked about the bible and the cross and chain, and was told that the baby's mother had left them for the baby. On hearing that lady talk about the baby's mother, Irene began to cry and tears began flowing down her face, because she felt she knew how the baby's mother must have felt at not being able to look after her own child. When they had completed and signed all the necessary papers they left the orphanage feeling very happy with Irene carrying the baby, but as they walked slowly away she suddenly stopped in a frightened manner she exclaimed "Robert we have nothing ready for the baby. We have no baby food and no cot for her to sleep in so where is she going to sleep tonight?"

Before Irene could say anything else, Robert said "Stop panicking we'll soon sort these problems out when we get back home, because the first thing we do when get there, is to go and visit Father Sherbrooke and show him the baby and thank him for the first edition to our family." When they reached the home of Father Sherbrooke he invited them inside and after a long talk he looked at them and said "I do realize that a year is long time to wait, but when the twelve months is finished and you hopefully have legally adopted the baby, would you like me to baptize her?" They both looked at each other and in unison said "Yes please" with Irene adding "and I would like her to be baptized Kathy." It was then that they told him that they didn't have a cot for her to sleep in.

Knowing that they didn't have much money to spare, Father Sherbrooke immediately said "Do you know I am always saying that God surprises us in many unusual ways, and today is no exception, because it is very strange that today someone came here and has given for the Church fete, this a tropical cot." He was holding it up for them to see.

Then he carried on speaking "It is in good condition and very clean with a zip-up netting covering and is perfectly bird proof and I can think of no better couple to have it, now would you like to accept it?" They both looked at each other and at that moment they both realized that their problem of finding somewhere for the baby to sleep had been solved, and Irene turned to look at Robert and said "Aren't we a very lucky couple." Robert had tears in his eyes as he nodded his head in agreement with her. Being very grateful and very pleased to accept it as he gave it to them Irene said to him "Would you please thank the person who gave you this cot, please tell them that we will look after it and we are certain that Kathy will have many peaceful nights

7

sleeping in it, and if they ever pass our house they will probably see Kathy asleep in the cot when we put the it in the garden in the sunshine."

It was 6 months after collecting Kathy that Irene suggested to Robert they go and see Father Sherbrooke to try and adopt another baby as company for Kathy. Knowing that they were a very poor family Father Sherbrooke suggested to them that they wait a little while, because the local work situation was very hard and the wages were bad and he suggested that when work begins to get better the prospects for them adopting would also be better. It was after the railway line between Adelaide and Alice Springs had been completed that working conditions began to improve and Robert was now fully employed and working harder and longer hours to enable him to get extra money. During the all of this, they loved and looked after Kathy and she began to grow into a lovely young child. Every time they took her out people would stop and say to them "Isn't she a lovely baby" and this made Irene and Robert feel so very proud. They were very happy having Kathy with them and as the months went by, they were nearing the time for them to go to court over the adoption. One day they were discussing the forthcoming court proceedings of the adoption of Kathy when Robert said to Irene "I don't care what you have just said about that court, because if they say we are not good enough to adopt her as our child after caring and loving Kathy as we do, I can tell you that I love her very much and I shall fight them all the way to prove to them that we are a loving couple and good enough to be her parents." When the day arrived for them to go to court they were apprehensive and very nervous and Robert was very quiet hardly saying a word to Irene and it wasn't until after they had signed the adoption papers and had a certificate proving that they were the legal adoptive parents that Robert began to relax and then he kept smiling at Kathy all the way home. Over the next few years everyone around them knew, and could see that they had become a very happy family with their child and were very good parents to her. Every Sunday they would go church and afterwards they would go for a walk in the nearby fields and Robert would say to Kathy "Kathy you know the stories I tell you at bedtime about Brer Rabbit well he lives over there" pointing to a large cluster of trees then he said "and he lives there amongst those trees with his friends." Kathy laughed. Every evening Robert would sit besides Kathy's bed and tell her fairy tales, but most nights she would ask him for the story she liked most of all about Brer Rabbit who had his friends and the pygmies, but one evening after she had asked him to tell her about Brer Rabbit he said "Kathy I have another nice story".

Robert looked very serious at her then said "Kathy I would like to tell you another story about a little girl and she is a very special little girl" and as Kathy snuggled down he began "One day a lady went to the doctors and said she wasn't feeling very well and after the doctor had examined her he told her she was expecting a baby. This made the lady feel very excited, but when that lady told her parents she was expecting a baby they were not happy because she was not married and they said when the baby is born she must put it in a home for unwanted babies." Robert paused to look at Kathy but she was now wide awake listening to him telling this story and he began speaking again "Now you must remember that before that lady went to the doctors your mummy also went to the doctors and she had to have a serious operation and after the operation your mummy was told that she could never give birth to babies" Hearing Robert say that Kathy began to have tears in her eyes but he was still talking "One day Father Sherbrooke visited us and told mummy about a home where there were very young babies who didn't have a mummy or daddy." Robert paused to look at Kathy and seeing she was wide awake he carried on speaking "and mummy asked him if she could go and have a look at those babies and Father Sherbrooke replied of course you can. Well it was about a year later that Father Sherbrooke told mummy that he had made all the arrangements for mummy and daddy to go, because if we wanted a baby we could go to that home and look at the babies and probably bring one of them back with us. When we arrived at the home a lady said to mummy would you like to go into a room and look at all the babies we have in there, and as she opened the door we could see many babies in their cots and as we walked along looking at all the cots one little baby lifted up its arms" Robert stopped talking and lifted up his arms to show Kathy how the baby did it then he said "Mummy reached forward and cuddled that little baby and held it in her arms, then mummy said to the lady, this little baby has chosen Robert and I to take her home to be her mummy and daddy could we have this one please? The lady looked at mummy and seeing the baby was looking and smiling at mummy, she said yes we could take her home." Robert was very close to tears when he finished the story but as he tucked some clothes around Kathy he said "You know Kathy that little baby was you" but as he said that, she put her arms around him and said "I thought it was me and I love you and mummy very much, goodnight daddy" He kissed her goodnight and he went away feeling very happy he had told her that story.

As she began to grow older she became very pretty and most of the time she would be singing in a childish way lovely nursery rhymes and their lives were very happy. It was because of her fascinating personality that some people called her a coloured precocious child, but others found her alluring charm very attractive and she became well liked. One day she asked her father why there were no white children in her school, at first he found it very hard to explain, but compromised by saying that it was because all the children in her school were much brighter than the white children.

Kathy knew that he was not telling her the real reason but thought it wise to wait to find out the truth when she was older and somehow she also felt it wise not to ask anyone else that question again.

Then came the great financial crash and the American Wall Street Slump that caused a great economic depression throughout the world with people and institutions withdrawing their money from the banks that ruined the banks causing them to close. Many small working class firms went into receivership and the ordinary working class man could not find work, causing greater hardship to them. It was during this great depression that Robert and Irene's luck began to get worse because it was during the very bad winter that Robert became ill, first with pneumonia, then this developed onto consumption and his health gradually deteriorated until eventually he died. Being very poor, Irene was finding it very hard to get food and help Kathy and it was as the months went by that Kathy, who was too young to understand the economic depression, missed her father very much and his death began to upset her. It was because she missed him at evening times when she went to bed, she would remember when he would sit by her bedside and make up lovely stories of animals and fairies and then one evening she remembered the story of the little baby girl, and it was due to the absence of Irene being out most of the day that she began to realize that the reason her mother was out looking for a job was to help look after her.

One day Kathy began telling her mother that she could feel the presence of her father around her. Irene began to worry and tried to help her but she didn't know how, because she was worrying how to earn money to buy food and pay the rent and she knew that time was very precious to her, and it was very important that she had to obtain some kind of work and then one day she heard of a position and applied for it and eventually she managed to obtain work as a housemaid working for a white couple living in a large house not far from where they were living. Irene worked from 8.30am until 6.30pm every day and she knew that the work she was doing was very tiring and the pay was small and after working a long hard day she would have to go home and cook a meal for herself and Kathy, but she kept her house reasonably clean knowing she would have little time to look after Kathy and this made her become worried because she still had little time to take Kathy's mind off of her father's death.

When the big economic depression eased throughout the world, life became a little easier for people like Irene. She was struggling very hard to get Kathy interested in reading, as well as studying other subjects and it was because she persisted in her efforts telling Kathy that she didn't want her to become a housemaid, that Kathy eventually began to take a great interest in reading and studying. Kathy knew that her mother was working very hard and was beginning to look very tired when she came home from work, so Kathy began to help her mother by cleaning the rooms and tidying up the house and occasionally getting their meal ready. It was when she was ten years old and because her mother kept telling her that she had to get a good job to obtain a good position in life, so she tried very hard and began to show great promise by studying other subjects. As time went by it was because of this improvement, and despite the colour bar that existed between the white and the coloured people, she was able to show to most of the teachers at the secondary school she was attending, that she had a very good academic brain.

At her school it was noticed, that despite of her colour, she was an outstanding pupil and her exemplary academic standard was of such a high standard, that some of the teachers spoke to each other and those who knew Kathy well knowing of her lovely disposition, and disregarding the colour bar that existed around the area, began to be very keen to help her progress to a higher academic standard.

One day Irene was speaking to Kathy and explaining to her that she was unable to earn a higher wage and because of the shortage of money, she suggested it might be a good idea that during the school holidays, Kathy should go to see Father Sherbooke and speak to him to see if he could find her a small part time job. Irene had heard that the local children's refuge home was looking for someone to look after the small children. When Father Sherbrooke heard of the difficulty that Irene was facing, he was very good and he helped Kathy obtain the small part time job at St Francis refuge home for unwanted children that had nuns looking after children. When Kathy arrived at the refuge home she was introduced to the Mother Superior who showed her around the small complex and explained to her the duties she was expected to do. Kathy was surprised to see some small animals that were in a small compound where some very small children were stroking and feeding them. Kathy asked the Mother Superior why the animals were there and the Mother Superior said "St. Francis is the patron saint of animals and therefore we thought it only natural that we should have a few small animals here to help the children understand how to treat animals." Although it was only a small wage Kathy obtained, she knew the money would help her mother with the financial outgoings. In the refuge home there were children aged three up to six years of age whose mothers, couldn't or did not want. Having the same colour skin as the children they accepted her and being a little older, she was able to join in the games with them and afterwards she began telling them short animal stories similar to the stories that her father had told her, and because she also began singing nursery rhymes, she soon became a great favourite with the children. At the end of the summer school holidays it was time for her to leave to go back to school and the children were very sorry to see her go, but she promised she would go back to them every time she had a school holiday and she kept that promise to them.

When Kathy went back to her school, she found that the teachers had eventually managed to get her into another higher educational school, and it was while she was at that school she underwent some traumatic periods of bullying, but thanks to the help of a white teacher called Mrs Viner, who one day found her crying in a small room, she was helped.

When Mrs Viner entered the room Kathy was crying but stopped immediately and wiped the tears from her face. Mrs Viner asked Kathy what had happened to make her cry, Kathy very slowly replied "It is some of those girls who are white coloured, who with their taunting and nastiness is making me very angry and frustrated. I cannot help the colour of my skin and therefore I'm called a coloured girl, but I can't retaliate because I know of the colour problem and knowing the seriousness of the problem that exists between the white people and the black people, I have been thinking that even if I passed my exams and was offered a place at university I wouldn't take it."

Mrs Viner also knowing of the colour problem in the area as well as in the country as a whole nodded her head, because she was against the colour bar and she knew that some bullying had taken place with other colored girls during this term and she was certain it had happened to Kathy. Mrs Viner then asked another question "Have any of these white students used physical violence on you?" At first Kathy looked a little frightened and was slow to reply before she said "Oh no, but what they have done is to remove the laces from my shoes and plimsoll's, then it's all their little digs at me being coloured and calling me funny names like Darkie, Blackie and Gollywog that upsets me most of all." Realizing Kathy's true feelings Mrs Viner said "Kathy you must realize that some of these girls here are very ignorant of the facts of life. They do not understand that people cannot help the colour of their skin, nor of the dialect in the way they talk. Now I suggest to you that you must always remember that if you wish to make a success of your life, I'm afraid you will have to accept these little setbacks and when you go out into the big wide business world, you will have to forget the ignorance of these stupid students and also the ignorance of many people who do not understand, or realize, that everyone is a human being, regardless of the colour of their skin or their religion, because everyone deserves the same respect." Kathy was listening to Mrs Viner to what she was saying, but when Mrs Viner looked at Kathy she thought that from the look on Kathy face that Kathy had not understood the meaning of what had been said, so Mrs Viner said in a rather strong voice "Kathy are you really sure you understand what I am telling you?" Kathy began nodding her head in agreement and was about to speak, but Mrs Viner was still not convinced, quickly stopped her by continuing saying "I would like you to remember that you must have the courage to forget the ignorance of those students and the ignorance of other people."

Then for a moment she stopped talking and looking at Kathy she said "Kathy I am sorry that you have experienced some very bad behaviour from some of the girls in this school and I deplore their actions. Now I feel that you should know of the meaning of courage and a very good example I can offer you is of the courage of an English woman who loved flying aeroplanes who said she wanted to fly to Australia, but the male fliers at her flying club just laughed at her and advised her of the dangers that existed on such a long flight that had never before had even been tried by men. However on the 5th May 1930, that was when you Kathy was a very small young girl, this young woman called Amy Johnson, took off from Croydon airport, which is in England, and flew all alone in a very small plane called a Gypsy Moth and after stopping at a few refuelling places, she flew all the way to Australia and on the 24th May 1930 landed safely at Port Darwin in the Northern Territory, which is, as you know, a very long way from here."

Mrs Viner paused, smiled to look at Kathy, who was sitting there with her mouth open and a look of wonder and disbelief on her face. Seeing the look of wonder and disbelief on Kathy face Mrs Viner began talking again "Amy Johnson had to fly across the Timor Sea and the engine of her aeroplane was behaving very badly, however she landed safely at Port Darwin. It took her 19 days and nights to fly from England to Australia and it took a great deal courage to do that all alone, especially for a woman who, after she defied those male airmen who had told her it couldn't be done solo, let alone by a woman, showed them it could be done. So Kathy, you can see by the example set by Amy Johnson that by courage and determination, whether they be a man or a woman, a person can achieve most things so now if you put your mind to it and forget these stupid student jokes, you too can achieve anything you wish to do" It was after Mrs Viner had finished speaking that Kathy said "Thank you Mrs Viner for that lovely explanation I do feel much better now and I do understand what you have said and I really do believe I now know what I have to do when I have studied and hopefully have passed my exams and have the courage to succeed."

It was due to hard work and determination, that within two years, when she was eighteen years old, she graduated with a higher National certificate. Mrs Viner who attended the local church every Sunday was pleased to see Kathy there and they spoke to each other. It was during the following weeks after a Sunday morning mass, that Kathy explained her various problems to Mrs Viner, who after listening to them was able to help her overcome a number of them including the colour problem and especially Kathy's troubled feelings concerning the death of her father and it was due to this talk that Kathy agreed go to university. Within a few months, she realized that she was being ignored and found that many of the university white students, both male and female, disliked coloured students attending the same university as them, so she decided to keep herself isolated from them by studying very hard. It was from one of the books, from the university library, called *"The little black boy"* by William Blake that she read the Songs of Innocence and after reading it many times she put it to her memory and one day began to recite one of the poems,

*My mother bore me in the southern wild,*
*And I am Black, but O! my soul is white;*
*White as an angel is the Australian child,*
*But I am black, as if bereaved of light.*

It was because she had a lovely figure and was generally very good looking that on several occasions, even though she was coloured, the male white students tried to date her, but she knew from the remarks she had overheard and their attitude towards students of a different colour, that all they wanted was to satisfy their sexual desires. This made her determined to make them, and other people, understand that the colour of the skin of a person did not matter and she thought about this subject very strongly. Through her studies she began to realize it was only the distinctive character and qualities of a person that actually counted. It was due to this outlook, and her attractive personality, that later she began to be noticed again by the male students, but she remembered what her parents had taught her. Then she remembered the story Mrs Viner had told her of the courage of Amy Johnson and then also remembering the poem from the *"The little black boy"* she recited the poem and it made her realize that what ever colour she was, we are all God's children and this kept her faith in her Christian beliefs.

With Kathy at university, Irene was still working at the big house for the rich white people when one day she picked up a newspaper and read that in Sydney there had been dawn to dawn celebrations to celebrate the first landing of a white settlement led by Admiral Arthur Phillip in 1788 against the local hostile aborigines, and it was due to this landing by him that through the stages of prospecting and the gold-prospecting days, that had made Sydney one of the largest cities of the British Empire. She also read that the celebrations were called the pageant of Australia's *'March to Nationhood'* and had taken place in Sydney harbour, which had been brilliantly lit, and more than one million people had witnessed the celebrations that had lasted for three days. While reading that item of news, Irene began thinking of the aborigine children who had been taken away from their parents and she felt sorry for them and then she thought about the gold-prospecting days and began hoping her fortunes would change, but illness overtook her.

It was due to Kathy's keen interest in languages and the taking of extra subjects in foreign languages, that she was able pass her exams in Psychology and Languages and obtained a full degree with honours. It was just after getting her degree in Psychology and Languages, that it was announced over the radio that Great Britain had declared war on Germany and Australia was also at war. Then Kathy heard that her mother, who had been very ill, had died. She was devastated and felt very lonely and went to see Mrs. Viner, who seeing Kathy was very upset and hearing of the death of her mother, told Kathy of young children who had lost both parents and were at a local orphanage and needed help, because they were very lonely. She advised Kathy to go to the orphanage and to offer her help. At first Kathy didn't want to go, but as Mrs.Viner kept talking about the children's loneliness it reminded Kathy of the loneliness she was experiencing and began comparing the loneliness the children were having, and gave it a great deal of thought. She went there and was able to start work, and to her delight she was given a small group of children to talk to, and began telling them stories and sometimes singing to them. Kathy had a nice singing voice and the children loved listening to her sing, then one day she had a small group of children aged four to seven years old, and while she was telling them a story about a boy and girl who were very lonely and had no home to live in, she began to sing a song called *Underneath the spreading chestnut tree,* she made the children copy the actions with her, and this pleased them, so she continued telling them the story about the lonely boy and girl who found many friends with the animals who lived in the forest. She told them about the small animals like squirrels, rabbits and small cuddly bears, who at night when the little boy and girl went to sleep, some of the owls, squirrels and birds kept watch, while the cuddly bears kept the little boy and girl warm and safe by sleeping with them in the long undergrowth. It was during another story when she began singing *Old Macdonald had a farm* and again she made the children make the noises of all the animals while they were singing with her. At the end of the singing they were all laughing and singing, but she made them be quiet, telling them that they must think positively and remember that somewhere in this big world there is always someone who wants a small child and that person could soon be calling for one of them. The children clapped their hands and thanked her for such lovely stories, but just before she left the room she said "Now I will tell you another story because you all must have courage".

She began to tell them a story of the courage of a little girl who wanted to be a ballerina, who had been injured through the rubble caused through a big earthquake that demolished her school, and she was trapped in the rubble of the classroom with some of her school room friends and though she had lost one of her legs, she still managed to find the courage to dig a tunnel through the rubble to help free her friends.

When Kathy left the orphanage, she felt that by the action of the children, that everything she had told them had been very fruitful and she also felt pleased that from the time she had been with them they would never forget her or her stories, and it made her feel sad knowing she would never forget them, because she was joining the RAAF. It was then she began remembering what Mrs Viner had said about courage and determination and she felt that by Australia being involved in the war against Germany and Japan and volunteering for the RAAF she could emulate the example set by Amy Johnson.

It was because she had obtained a degree in psychology and foreign languages that after her initial training she was posted to the Intelligence section and during the war she was posted to various places gathering intelligence. It was due to this type of work that eventually she became well conversant with the subject of security, and having this knowledge of security, together with her attractive personality of always treating everyone with the utmost respect what ever their rank, that she was noticed by many senior people in the RAAF. At the end of the World War 2 she was sent to investigate the atrocities committed on the Australian prisoners of war by the Japanese during their capture. Before she left, she was told that the Japanese Foreign minister, called Togo, had given a formal assurance that although Japan was not bound by the Geneva convention it would apply it *mutates mutandis* to all American, Australian, British, Canadian and New Zealand prisoners of war and by this understanding Japan was morally bound to comply, but in any event the Japanese were formally bound by the Fourth Hague convention of 1907 and it was pointed out to Kathy that if any Japanese Officer, or any other Japanese official were charged with atrocities to the prisoners, they could not maintain that the Geneva Prisoner of War Convention of 1929 did not apply to them. While being informed of these regulations, she was shown a facsimile of the instructions sent to all Japanese commanders by Tojo the Prime minister. When Kathy read the full letter, she was devastated by its contents that stated of the inhumane treatment that should be given to the prisoners. After she had read the letter she was told that she was being sent to the island of Borneo of the Indonesian Islands where there had been a number of prisoner of war camps that had been retaken by the Allied forces in September 1945, after the Japanese had capitulated.

When Kathy and her team from the RAAF arrived at one of the camps, she found a large number of Australian prisoners of war and they were in a very bad state of health. Speaking to some of the prisoners she found they had been had been badly treated by the Japanese and forced to build an aerodrome under very harsh conditions. It was during those interviews that besides obtaining the information she required, she managed to help some of them with their disabilities.

Then she began to be noticed by many other people in the camp because she was behaving in a good Samaritan manner to every class of person of whatever nationality. While attending to a soldier called Captain Theobald who was in a bad physical condition and who looked like a skeleton, (who unbeknown to Kathy was a Chaplain) She was told by him that one of the Japanese guards, and an old man, was under arrest being charged with murder, who had unbeknown to his Japanese superiors treated all the prisoners, including the Australians, with kindness and he asked her if she could help that Japanese soldier. Having listened to the whole story of that Japanese soldier's kindness to the prisoners over a period of two years, she asked one of her staff who was a senior fellow RAAF woman to accompany her, to see if she could speak to the American Colonel who was in charge of the liberating forces that had reached the camp. When she met the Colonel she began remembering the moment when she first arrived at the camp and while she spoke to him he was pointing to the Japanese prisoners saying, "Look what those bastards have done to our men, they don't need a trial. You know what I would like to do, I would like to kill the lot of them right now." When she spoke to him of that particular Japanese soldier's humane work towards the prisoners, her plea fell on deaf ears because he was adamant and rejected her plea for clemency, but she persisted in her pleas and eventually the Colonel began to get irritated with her talk of clemency. However unbeknown to him or Kathy the prison camp tannoy system had been left switched on and everyone throughout the camp was listening and could hear the conversation between the Colonel and Kathy. It was due to Kathy's persistence in pleading for clemency that the colonel became irritated and shouted at

18

her in his southern American voice "Now look here ma'am I've had enough of your talk of clemency towards those yellow bastards and I don't like coloured people like you talking to me as you are doing............" Kathy immediately interrupted him "Oh I understand what you are now saying, that because I'm brown skinned and the Japanese is yellow skinned we are different from you, so will you please answer this question Sir, what is the colour of your skin?" The Colonel literally exploded and shouted at her in a more American southern accent "I'm white and bloody proud of it" but before he could say anything else, Kathy interrupted him again saying "Colonel it's not the colour of ones skin that makes a person whole. It is how they behave and treat other human beings that counts most of all." When those in the camp heard Kathy words, they all cheered like mad. However just before that moment the Colonel was remembering the time a coloured American officer had risked his life to rescue him when he was slightly wounded, then he heard the cheering and he relented and apologized to Kathy saying "I will reduce the charges against that Japanese prisoner." When the Allied troops heard of her efforts with the American Colonel, they thanked her because they had heard that Corporal Hideki Suga had his charges reduced and it brought much joy to them knowing that the true brutal captors would be executed and would pay for their crimes. The American Colonel was watching and smiling when she and her fellow workers were about to leave the island, because in his hand he had a letter, signed by the Chaplain, stating that the troops knowing of Kathy's Samaritan work to them and to Corporal Suga had been of a true Christian Samaritan and they wished it to be recorded.

When Kathy and her fellow workers were leaving the camp, the troops, together with the Chaplain, all cheered and wished her and her colleagues a safe journey home. It was the detailed reports of her compassion and her Samaritan work, that senior people, who thought very highly of her, decided she would be the right person to help them in another special operation. Shortly an opportunity arose when a position was offered to her, the duties explained and was told the position was still attached to the RAAF, she accepted. Within a short period of time she became very knowledgeable in her work and it eventually helped her to obtain reasonable position in the Australian Intelligence Security Services, (AISS).

Kathy travelled with small groups around the different parts of the southern hemisphere, and while doing this work she always kept her faith in the church and when ever it was possible she went to church services. It was after a short period of time she began to realize that some days when she was alone certain things were happening around her that concerned her. These events made her feel her belief in life after death was becoming very prominent. Even though she had a degree in psychology, she still couldn't understand, why these occurrences were taking place and why her belief in life after death was so strong. She then experienced another visitation and became very concerned, thinking she was suffering from a mental health problem and was pondering what to do about it. One Sunday while visiting her local church she met Mrs. Viner, who was very pleased to see her and decided to relate her fears to her. Mrs Viner advised her to see Mr Theobald the church minister.

Meeting the vicar, Mrs.Viner quietly whispered to him Kathy's problems and he, knowing that before Kathy had joined the RAAF she had been a good member of the church, he also knew of her tremendous help at the local orphanage, and of her work at St.Francis refuge home for children, he said to her "Kathy I am quite ready to help you if you want me to do so?" She didn't know what to say and said "Father I am at a lost for words because I do not know what Mrs Viner has said to you" The vicar, had been a prisoner of the Japanese in Borneo, and unbeknown to Kathy he had seen and had experienced the good Samaritan work she had performed during her investigation work of the prisoner of war camps, and particularily when she had visited his prisoner of war camp. He looked at Kathy and knowingly said "I have been told that you have a problem and I know of the good work you performed locally and also when you were in the RAAF during the war years, and unbeknown to you, everybody who has come into contact with you have said you were a good Samaritan," then to her surprise he said "Kathy I am going to read to you a short passage from the Holy book of Luke that refers to the 'Good Samaritan" and he read to her:-

*A Lawyer stood up to test Jesus and said "Teacher what must I do to inherit eternal life?" He replied "What is written in the law and how do you read it?" The lawyer answered "Love the Lord your God with all your heart and with all your soul and with all your strength and with all your mind, and love your neighbour as yourself." The lawyer was told "You have given the right answer; do this, and you will live." But the lawyer wanting to justify himself asked "And who is my neighbour?"*

*Jesus replied "A man travelling from Jerusalem to Jericho was attacked by robbers who stripped him of his clothes , beat him and then left him for dead. Now a priest came along and when he saw the man on the floor, the priest crossed over to the other side of the road, then along came a Levite who also passed by on the other side. A Samaritan riding a pony came along and seeing the injured man, bandaged his wounds and poured oil and wine on them, he put him on his pony, took him to an inn and took care of him. The next day the Samaritan gave two denarii to the innkeeper saying "Take care of him and when I come back I will repay you whatever more you spend" Jesus asked the lawyer "Which of these three do you think was the neighbour to the man who was attacked by the robbers? The lawyer replied "The one who showed him mercy" Jesus said to him "Go and do likewise"*

Kathy was enthralled hearing that piece of scripture read to her and was about to thank the vicar when he, after looking at her face thought he could detect from its features some doubt, and in a deep resonant voice asked her "Kathy do you really understand why it has been read to you?" She quickly replied "Yes I think so Father" the vicar spoke again saying "I read that piece of scripture because many of us know of the good work you did with those children, and I know the ex prisoners of war consider you to be a good Samaritan" She was amazed at the vicar knowing of that work, then the vicar looked at Mrs Viner, and looking at Kathy with a smile, waited a few moments before speaking. and said "From what you have told me about the spiritual visitations you have experienced, I am led to believe that you have Extra Sensory Perception, commonly known as E.S.P." he paused again and began to explain to her what was meant by E.S.P. then suddenly he stopped and laughing said "I feel as though I am teaching you how to suck eggs" Then he said "In my congregation there is a man who is a psychic medium and although some of the congregation believe this person's talent is a gimmick, I have been told on many occasions by some other members of the congregation that they have visited this psychic medium and they have found it very rewarding." The vicar looked at Kathy and suggested she should speak to this medium, and if she agreed he would make the arrangements and promised he and Mrs Viner would be with her, Kathy was reluctant to go, but as the minister began to explain things it persuaded her.

The vicar then said he would contact the medium and arrange a visit that was agreeable to all three of them. Eventually they accompanied her on her visit to the medium. At that meeting, the medium asked Kathy many questions and she answered all of them very truthfully and then he gave a small demonstration of his psychic power. Everyone was impressed and it was from that demonstration that they all felt contented and relieved and from the comments made to her, she also knew she was not suffering from delusions from those visitations she had been experiencing. She felt very relieved that she didn't have a mental health problem, and was told by the psychic medium and by the minister that all she was suffering from was her strong belief in life after death, and she should feel very proud that she had the ability to have knowledge of life after death.

It was as she walked away from that meeting with the minister and Mrs. Viner, they were all smiling and feeling very relieved telling her that she was again returning to her normal happy self and she should be able to continue with her Intelligence work in the RAAF that she felt satisfied. Just before she left them she said to Mrs. Viner "I am ever so pleased and relieved that I spoke to you about my experiences and for recommending me to speak to Father Theobald" then turning to the vicar she said "Father I shall always remember that verse of scripture from the Holy Book of Luke regarding the Good Samaritan's work." The vicar blessed her and said "God bless you and may He be with you with all that you do and Kathy I thank you for your work just after the war, and I feel sure that whatever part of the world your work takes you, that with God's help you will always be a Good Samaritan to everyone." She was mystified by his remarks and after saying goodbye to the vicar she turned to Mrs.Viner and said "I would like to thank you for helping me with what I thought was a problem, but I know now it isn't a problem anymore"

# CHAPTER 2

## (David Hogarth)

David Hogarth was very keen to fly aircraft. He lived with his parents Stephen and Mary Hogarth in a nice house in Geelong just outside Melbourne. Stephen was a bank manager and Mary was a teacher of English at the local school, they had a daughter called Penny who was a nurse. In 1939, when England and its Dominions declared war on Germany, that meant that Australia, being one of the Dominions, was now committed to send men to assist in the fight by sending servicemen to England. David wanted to join but was too young, but on December 7th 1941 when Japan attacked Pearl Harbour and the United States of America had declared war on Japan, the Australian government knew that as Japan was now committed to fighting the U.S.A. it was also invading colonies belonging to Great Britain and its Allies, and Japan could also attack Australia. This caused Australia problems, because besides sending Servicemen to assist Great Britain in its struggle against Germany it was also sending servicemen to fight the Japanese, and it knew it had to have enough servicemen to defend itself. When David heard of the Japanese attack on Pearl Harbour, being of the age of 18 he volunteered to join the RAAF and after being trained as a pilot in the RAAF, in 1943 he was sent to England and after training at various O.T.U. aerodromes, he was eventually posted to a squadron at an aerodrome at Marsham Heath that had Lancaster bombers. It was because he had been flying on operations over the German occupied countries for a long period with the same crew, he had formed a close relationship with his crew and he also had a strong close friendship with his Canadian navigator Jack Donoghue.

One day because of the bad weather over England and the Continent, flying operations that had been planned for that evening were postponed until the following evening. The following day having performed the test flying of their aircraft and having time to spare from flying, David asked Jack if he would like to accompany him to see some of the local area. After leaving the aerodrome they walked to the local village where they visited a couple of pubs and it was while they were in the "Drovers" pub that they spoke to some of the local people, who told them of the mystery and unusual circumstances connected to the local village church. This conversation intrigued them and having finished their drink and said goodbye to the locals, they were outside the pub when David said to Jack "Would you like to go and visit this unusual church?" Jack was very quick to reply "Yes please. I am interested in history and I was very impressed by what those locals said and I would like to know if it was true, because what they have told us about it, seems so unreal."

When they reached the church and were walking through the church grounds they could see that the church looked very old and were just about to comment on it, when a man stopped and began speaking to them. They learnt from him that he was one of the Church Wardens. When they told him that some of the local people had told them of the mysterious events and happenings connected to the church, he laughed and agreed to show them the church.

When they were inside, they both noticed and mentioned to the Warden about the Church's unusual layout. He began to explain and show them some more of the unusual things, as well as the outstanding beauty of the church, and explained that part of it had been built in the Saxon period two or three hundred years after the Romans had left Britain, and he added that it was believed the church was built in 680 AD. The Warden then went on to say that it was not known how the church had survived as a centre of continuous Christian worship for all this time. When Jack asked the Warden "Has this church been extended from its original building?" the Warden replied "Yes. It was a much smaller church than it is now and no one has ever found out why it was extended or why it was built where it now stands, and why it has survived so long. Some historical researchers have stated that it is definitely an Anglo-Saxon church and although the aisles or side chapels have gone, the main west doorway with its balcony above was replaced in the tenth century, and some other historians believe it may even have been King Offa's church and may have possessed a relic of Boniface who was a Devon saint martyred in Germany in 1754. However most historians agree that in the district around the church, there had been a royal residence and knowing these facts it is suggested that the church was a Mercian royal church". He paused then he went on to say "Many theologian scholars who have visited the church have suggested it was built because it was a suitable centre to spread the Gospel to the heathen natives of Mercia, which was at that time, the middle kingdom of England. The reason why I have mentioned this is because I have noticed that one of you is from Australia and the other from Canada." David and Jack were very pleased to have met the Watden and felt privileged to be in such a lovely church. .He then showed them some Roman Tiles in portions of the church tower and as they were about to leave, he said "When you are outside, I suggest you look at the Saxon Eagle head made of stone which is just above the Norman porch that you have to go through to get out and may I also suggest when you are outside that you look at the church tower because there is a piece of gold strip in the tower wall that local superstition believes, was placed there to prevent the decay of the church."

When they said their goodbyes and offered their appreciation to the church Warden for such an interesting and enjoyable few hours, he suggested that as they walk through church grounds they look for a tombstone with the name of Mabel Flitch and added with a smile on his face "You may find that interesting as well." As they walked slowly making their way out, they were looking at the names on the tombstones when they saw one dated 1764-1789 of a young woman whose tombstone had a rhyme engraved upon it *"Here lies Mabel Flitch who was burnt at the stake for being a witch"* They stood there talking of her unusual death and discussing her death at a very young age and then they began comparing her death with their chances of living, then David said "That as each day comes along our flights over enemy territory are becoming more dangerous and I believe it must have been like that for Mabel Flitch, who must have been living a dangerous life like us". Just as David was speaking, the vicar had come out of the church and as he went to go past he stopped. It was now getting dark and the evening shadows were beginning to show, they were surprised he stopped and spoke to them.

They began to ask him questions about Mabel Flitch, though at first he was reluctant to talk about her because he had heard them discussing their own slim chances of living. However it was when Jack Donaghue said to him "Father, my friend David and I have just been discussing her death at a young age and we have agreed that we hope that there is life after death" then with a big grin on his face he said "and it is because we are looking for a good piece of luck, because we are hoping she can hear us saying how sad we are over the sad ending to her young life." Hearing Jack say those kind words about Mabel Flitch and knowing that they, like many other young men, were sacrificing their lives every day fighting against a bad foreign regime, the vicar smiled at them and said "The ancient records of Mabel Flitch state she was a young woman of 25 years who was said to have been able to help people with illnesses through spiritual contact, but because the gentry in this area thought her help was witchcraft, they said it was unlawful and she was arrested, charged with witchcraft, found guilty and was burnt at the stake. The local people who believe in the old folklore say their ancestors related the good deeds Mabel did to their kin folk and they have handed all this information down to the present day generation and this of course has caused a mystique over whether it was true what Mabel did. However like you I do believe it was terrible way to die but I am pleased that she could have truly believed in Christianity and the Almighty."

As he went to leave, the vicar with a smile on his face said "Oh by the way some of my congregation have told me that during the dark nights that as they have been passing her tombstone they have seen her ghost, so look around and you both may be lucky yourselves tonight. Good night lads and good luck." When the vicar had departed they were standing discussing whether there was life after death and within a few minutes they were both laughing when David said "Let's hope that if ever we are in need of help when we are over Germany, a ghost will suddenly appear and help us to get home."

It was as they were walking away from the churchyard that Jack solemnly said "David when the vicar was talking to us and we were standing near Mabel Flitch's tombstone, I am sure that something, or someone, was standing close to us." David stopped walking and looked startled and then to Jack he said   "Jack thank you for mentioning that, because I have just been thinking how I was going to tell you that I had a similar feeling, but I thought I wouldn't say anything to you because you may have thought I was going mad." Jack just laughed and said "David, I'm glad you also experienced that strange feeling because I too was also beginning to think I was going mad." They were still laughing and talking about that incident when after a short walk they eventually came across another local pub and went in and without saying anything about the church to anyone they had a drink, then seeing the time was 4.30 pm they quickly made their way back to the aerodrome.

Later that evening, after they had been to the briefing room and told their target was to be Berlin, they looked at each other knowing of the great gun defence around that city and were apprehensive of their chances of return, then after receiving the weather forecast over the target area and what the weather would be like when they returned, they departed to board their plane.

While they were flying over Germany David noticed the weather was beginning to deteriorate, very shortly afterwards Jack informed him that the weathermen had just reported that there was thick cloud over the target area and there would also be heavy rain storms with lightening. Over the target area the gunfire was very severe and after dropping their bombs their plane was hit and received severe damage and knowing the plane was in a bad condition David asked Jack for another course home to try and miss those rain storms. While they were flying home on three engines, David was silently praying that Mabel Flitch would help them, then as they neared the French coast he had a strong feeling that she was close to him, suddenly Jack said to him "Skipper you will never believe this, those met boys say our 'drome is fog bound and we have to divert to Downham Market where they have FIDO." David knew that Fido was a system where tubes of fuel were placed along at each side of the runway to give flames that disperses the fog to give a flare flight path. As they approached Downham Market aerodrome David again had that feeling of Mabel Flitch standing beside him and though the plane was badly damaged and flying on three engines he landed the damaged plane safely between the lines of flames. After he had told Jack he had felt the presence of Mabel Flitch he silently vowed he would never reveal to anyone again his beliefs in ghosts, the supernatural or his belief in life after death. Shortly afterwards with the war in Europe being over and after being transferred back to Australia, David decided to remain in the RAAF, but because the Americans had bombed Hiroshima and Nagasagi with the Atom bombs and the war with Japan had finished, he found life in the RAAF so boring he resigned and decided to study for a degree.

A few years later it being summertime, David, who with his blue green eyes was still a good looking fair haired young man, was visiting his sister Penny and her husband Guy Williams at their bungalow that was situated quite near the Blue Mountain National Park. The reason he was visiting them was to see the new home they had purchased after their marriage and because it had been a hard three years of study he also wanted to go for walks in the solitude and peacefulness of the beauty of the National Park and to relax after passing his degree in Physics and Law. He was also extremely delighted that because he loved flying he was going to tell them he had been accepted to rejoin the RAAF. David was nearing his 26th birthday and he loved walking in the countryside and he knew that during his stay at their home he would be able to enjoy the scenery and the walks he had missed during his long studies.

The next day he decided to go for a walk alone and with the sun shining brightly in a lovely clear blue sky, it was while he was walking through the lovely countryside along a narrow pathway he was looking at the sky and the long contrails of planes flying very high, and he was thinking about the RAAF and then thinking of Mabel Flitch, when suddenly he slipped and fell to the ground, then he felt as though someone had put a hand on his shoulder to stop him falling further over the edge down the steep hillside that had plenty of hard granite rocks lying around. He lay there for a few moments just thinking and as he began picking himself up he suddenly had a uncanny feeling that something unusual had happened to him, he looked around and seeing nobody nearby he made his way home.

When he got back to Penny and Guy, because he thought it silly, he never mentioned the uncanny sensation he had when he fell, but he did tell them the news of his degree and also of him volunteering for the RAAF again, and they were very excited and took him out to a nearby restaurant to celebrate. Over the meal Penny said to David "Haven't you found yourself a girl friend yet?" David was embarrassed and began to laugh as he replied "No I've been too busy studying and really and truthfully, you know I love flying and studying very hard to obtain my degree, I just haven't had time for girls." Guy said "Well the degree is a lovely surprise and you haven't told us when you are likely to be recalled to join up." David said "I do know, and this again is one of the reasons why I wanted to come here to see your new home as well as its lovely views, because when I leave here at the end of the week, I shall report to the RAAF office in Sydney to collect my travel warrants, then I am off to start my retraining and I've signed on for five years and hoping that everything will go to plan."

It was Sunday the day before he was due to depart and they all went to church and it was during the church service that David, who was listening intently to the sermon being given by the minister, he

28

suddenly felt a strong feeling as though someone was sitting close to him, he looked around and found no-one was there except no one near him was his sister and her husband. Suddenly he began thinking of Jack Donaghue and thinking about Mabel Flitch and then of wartime flying days and then he heard the minister say,

*"Love your enemies and do good,*
*Be kind to the unthankful,*
*Forgive and you shall be forgiven.*
*Remember that the blind cannot lead the blind*
*Otherwise the blind could fall into a ditch"*

David sat there listening to those words and was thinking of that moment of the wartime trip when he had that strange feeling of someone helping him flying a badly damaged plane on three engines and landing in thick fog, then he thought of the incident of walking through the countryside when he fell and he remembered that strange feeling of again someone helping him, and he began saying to himself "I wonder if Mabel Flitch was there to help me and of course hearing that verse of scripture, I can see I have a lot of things to think about now that I'm rejoining the RAAF and also thinking of that sensation of someone saving me from falling over the edge of that steep hill and I find myself I'm again thinking of Mabel Flitch so I do believe my life and views will probably be very different to what I have been used to." The following day David left his sister's home and as he walked towards the RAAF office he was still thinking about the words the minister had spoken when suddenly he met Tony Wright, who had been a fellow student at his university. With both David and Tony being slightly older than the other students, he and David had become good friends. David said "Why hello Tony, fancy meeting you. Where are you off ......?" but before David could say anything else Tony answered "Since I received my degree I......." David quickly interrupted him saying "You've got your degree as well. Why that's wonderful, I got a B.Sc. what did you get?"

Tony quickly answered "The same as you, a lovely B.Sc. This is strange meeting you again and I'm sorry but if I didn't have to go somewhere special, I would invite you to come and have a drink with me to celebrate" he paused and began to laugh, and said, "but being out of work I've volunteered to join the RAAF and unfortunately I'm just going to the RAAF office to collect my travel warrants" David could hardly conceal his jubilation as he said "Tony you will never believe this, that's where I'm going, because I've also volunteered and I am rejoining. Oh boy this is great, the two of us joining the RAAF together and let's hope that we can be together." At the RAAF office they found that they were being sent to the same aerodrome. During their initial training they formed a very strong attachment to each other and at the weekends, when ever possible, they both went to church every Sunday. One day Tony was told to report to the Squadron Adjutant and informed that he had failed the pilot course. He immediately volunteered to train as a navigator and was accepted, and posted to another aerodrome where he eventually passed all the exams and gained his navigator wings. David however had been posted to an advanced pilot's course being retrained to fly jet powered aircraft, which he eventually passed obtaining a 1$^{st}$ class proficiency printed in his flight log book and posted to a squadron flying jet fighters, but due to his very good flying acrobatic skills he was posted again but this time to No.115 squadron, known as the 'Blue Streak' squadron, which was noted for its flying performances at crowd displays. Eventually he found that Tony Wright had become a member of the squadron and they renewed their friendship that grew stronger than before. While David was attached to the squadron, his flying skills and his personality made him a favourite with his fellow pilots, especially with the women in the RAAF who were always keen to be seen out with him.

Unbeknown to him his proficiency had been noticed by Group Captain Gerald Thomas the Station commander, who eventually began to have a deep influence upon his future. It was David's quiet mannerisms and his excellence in his flying abilities that attracted him to Gerald Thomas, because whenever David was sent on special flying missions, even if it was a hazardous one, he never complained or moaned about the trips he made or the flying displays he had missed, and he always had a boyish and impish smile.

One day he was called upon to make a trip that tested his goodwill. It was a bleak day with heavy cloud when he awoke that day and after he had his breakfast he was unexpectedly told to report to the Squadron Leader's office. On entering the office, David saw Squadron Leader Mike Taggert standing looking at a map of the Pacific Ocean. Mike Taggert turned and said "Good morning David I'm sorry to get you up so early in the morning but Flying Officer Andrew has reported sick. I do know that what I am about to say is going to disappoint you, because I know you were going to have two days leave but with everyone else being on other duties, I'm afraid I have no one else to take his place and I have had to cancel your leave."

David felt deflated and upset because he had arranged to meet a young, pretty RAAF lady officer and on telling Mike he had made that arrangement, Mike said "Don't worry David, I will tell her you will not be able to meet her and knowing her, I know she will understand."

At first David was very disappointed at having to cancel his arrangement and also knowing that the flight was to a far eastern country where he had to fly to a remote island in the Pacific Ocean that had been occupied by the Japanese during World War Two, but unbeknown to David this trip was to collect five secret agents of the Australian Intelligence services. It was a trip that also eventually made David again think seriously about his future in the RAAF.

When he had been told the destination, and the length of the journey and how many people he had to bring back, David felt deflated especially with the type of plane he was going to have to fly, because it was not a jet plane that he was used to flying, but a plane powered by two Wright Cyclone engines with a maximum speed of only 246mph. He knew that station flight section had only one plane, that was an old twin engine Lockheed Hudson with a range of 1,700 miles that could carry a number of people and could fly the required distance with a full load of petrol, at an economical cruising speed of 170 m.p.h. and he remembered he had flown one of these planes during W.W.2. Realizing that he would need a navigator, he asked who was going to be his navigator, Mike Taggert replied "We only have Flying Officer Tony Wright available". David smiled when he heard that news and it changed his mood because he was pleased, knowing that Tony was a good navigator.

Just after leaving the Squadron leader's office he met Tony and they were both happy to be flying together and they began to discuss the flight route. David said to Tony "If we can fly at an economical speed of 170mph, I know the plane has a range of 1700 miles, that means it's going to be roughly a eight hour flight. What do you think of that?" Looking at his maps Tony said "It's not going to be an eight hour flight because I can tell you it's going to be roughly a 1000 mile flight to that small island in the Pacific Ocean, and if we fly over the Arafura Sea and the weather is kind to us and we don't have too many deviations, I feel sure that the trip will only take about 6hours, but we must therefore ensure we have full load of fuel for the outward journey and I think it would be a good idea if we can find out if they can refuel us on the island for the return journey." Having made sure that those on the island could refuel them, they made their way to station flight to board their plane, but just as they were about to board their plane a messenger run up to them and gave Tony the latest weather forecast stating that there could be bad storms in the area at about the time they were due to land. The message also stated that the Japanese had built the runway on the island during the war and as it had not been used since the end of the war, it could be in a bad state of repair.

When David heard that news, for a moment he was at lost for words, then he said to Tony "Tony that's all we wanted to hear isn't it? I'm not worried about the bad weather or flying this type of plane but what is worrying me, I'm used to flying jets and I am fairly new to the squadron in comparison to some senior officers with more experience than me in the squadron who are also quite capable of flying the 'Hudson', and I keep saying to myself. I had that lovely WAAF Officer to meet, why did the Commander have to pick me?"

Tony burst out loud laughing and said "Oh David you are such a fool. Don't you realize you are younger and your flying ability is much better than the others, and you can be trusted not to take a risk. You should also remember the Squadron Leader is a good judge of character of his men and I'm certain he'll keep the WAAF officer happy for you." David was very embarrassed hearing Tony saying those things and said "Tony thank you very much for those kind words I'm sure they are not true, but all same it was nice of you to say such nice things, and I hope the Squadron Leader doesn't keep that WAAF officer too happy. Well I suppose we had better get into the plane and get started"

Shortly after taking off, David was talking to Tony about their briefing and said "Those meteorologists really get me upset, first of all they tell us about weather for the outward journey, and for their return journey, but they don't warn us of the bad storms in the area where were we are going to land until were are boarding the plane and then they say there are a possibility of storms. I can remember during the war, many times we were given a weather forecast before we took off for a raid and when we get to the target the weather was different and then when we returned to base it was foggy". David sighed saying "Those planner's don't seem to do their job properly and it's just our luck, storms and more rain." To ease the boredom during their flight

David told Tony about the unusual experience he had with his Canadian navigator in the churchyard and how they had both experienced a strange feeling and he asked "Tony do you believe in life after death?" It was after a long discussion that Tony eventually said "I really haven't given it much thought but I suppose I do believe in life after death?" They had been flying for about five hours and they noticed in the far distance that the clouds were looking very thick David asked Tony to work out another route to bypass the heavy clouds and then said "With that sunset looking hazy, those storm clouds could be the storm we've been told about." Within a few moments Tony returned and said "To miss that bad looking storm, I will get you to divert from our original course, to 208 degrees N, and then after twenty minutes flying I shall ask to you to come back on to our original course. By doing this it will only add another 150 miles on the length of the journey, and with luck, we should be over the island about 15minutes later than we should be. Are you happy with that?" David nodded his head as he looked at those big heavy clouds ahead, and then shortly he began flying the new route given to him by Tony.

David found that even though it was raining hard and they were in thick cloud, flying the plane wasn't too bad. A little later Tony asked David "How many people are we having to bring back with us?" Before David could reply he was trying manfully to hold the plane steady from the sudden severe buffeting from the very strong wind and heavy rain. David replied "Hang on a bit it, it's getting a trifle rough handling the plane at the moment" then about five minutes later he said "I think it could be five people but I wasn't told who they are, and why they have to be collected by us, hopefully one day we will be told. By the way, this strong wind is buffeting us from the North West, I hope you have taken this into your calculations, because I'm still flying on the course you have set me and I don't want to be off course"

Tony was grinning as he spoke to David "Don't worry skipper, I'm watching you and plotting the course all the time and I have included in my calculations the strength of the wind because I estimate it to be 35 miles mph which is a about Beaufort force 6 or 7, and I also estimate that we should be over the island within an hour and we can start dropping down to a respectable altitude and hopefully beneath these clouds and into less buffeting." David quickly looked at Tony laughingly saying "Oh we are using the Beaufort scale are we. You are a clever old navigator aren't you?" After thirty minutes Tony said to David "Ok skipper drop down to two thousand feet and even though it is raining hard we should be able to see the island."

David brought the plane down to two thousand feet, but couldn't see anything and he asked Tony to look out to see if he could notice any landing lights. Then he began speaking to a local air traffic control and then he heard through the bad static on his head phones, a foreign dialect voice trying to speak in English "This is Banktu air traffic control who are you? Repeat your call sign, I say repeat your call sign" Looking at Tony and pursing his lips, David drew a deep breath and spoke into his mouthpiece and repeated his call sign, a few moments later they saw a small flame appear, then a few more flames began to appear, then another row of flames appeared opposite the others, forming two lines of flames, David suddenly exclaimed "Bloody hell they are using kerosene flares and that I assume is the flare path we have to use." Hearing that Tony said "How do you know that is kerosene flares?" David quickly replied "I remember during World War 2 when I was flying Lancasters in England we had to land at an aerodrome called Downham Market, where they used a contraption called FIDO, which enabled planes to land in thick fog, but I don't care if there's no fog, or if I'm wrong, because we must land, so we are going in." Getting into position they lowered their undercarriage and turned towards the flames and as their air speed decreased they got lower, the rain and wind was buffeting them very badly, and when they were near the ground they could observe two rows of flames in a straight line that they assumed was the runway. David said "At last. By the way Tony I hope you said your prayers last Sunday, because those flames are being blown at right angles and it is making judging the middle of the runway difficult. So hang on to your seat belt because here we go."

It was as they were flying into the flare path that David began to feel that someone was near him and thought it strange but he took no notice of it and concentrated on flying the plane. He could see the flames were blowing close to the fuselage on one side of the plane, then expecting the plane to have a heavy bump when the undercarriage touched the ground, but all they heard and felt was a squelching sound of water and due to the state of the runway there were many heavy bumps. As they went between the flames David decreased the speed of the aircraft by gently applying the brakes and parked the plane in a vacant landing bay. A strong wind was blowing when they parked the aircraft and it was raining and it being very dark they could just about see a building not far away, but to get to it they had to walk through long grass and by the time they reached the building, their feet and clothes were very wet.

Then above the noise of the wind they thought they could hear gunfire in the distance and when they eventually went into the small single floor brick building, a small dark skinned man spoke to them in very bad English with a strong dialect, hearing that voice David suddenly realized that this was the person who had spoken to him from the flight control. David said to him "Where is the Flight control?" the man replied in very broken English "This is the flight control." David was amazed and then looking around and across the darkened room, he saw a small radio set with microphone and a headset. After short pause, David decided to ask why there were no runway lights, but at that moment a very beautiful young, lightly brown skinned, woman with a petite body and dark smiling eyes, of about 28 years of age came into the room and hearing David question she replied in perfect English "You should consider yourselves very lucky, because about half an hour before your request to land came through, we had a most terrible monsoon, the rain was so heavy it put the main generator out of action."

She paused for moment because of the look of astonishment on their faces, then with a smile on her face she continued "and for some time we didn't have any electricity at all, but after short while, we managed to get a small generator going to operate the radio set, but it was not strong enough to feed all the equipment including the landing lights, luckily we had the FIDO (Fog Intensive Dispersal Operation) system that we used to light up the runway to guide you in." Hearing her giving such a detailed description of the cruel conditions the station had to endure during the storm and how they managed to light the Flare path and also her knowledge of FIDO, David replied "Thank you very much for that report but where on earth did you learn all about FIDO?" She was still smiling as she replied "I joined the Australian air force 6 years ago and during my training I was for a short period trained in a medical section, luckily for me on our course we had an old wartime instructor who, when we were taught how to treat patients for burns, he also taught us about those burnt by the FIDO system." She paused for moment because she felt that the word FIDO had shocked them then she began speaking again "We didn't know what FIDO was until he explained the system and showed us how to operate it, but we didn't think we would have to use it since FIDO is not used in many places, so it was fortunate that my knowledge how to work it, came in very handy today." David could see she was giving him a good smile and immediately sensed that she was no ordinary medical person, when she suddenly said "I have to leave you two for a few moments as I have someone in the next room needing my assistance."

She left the room and David looked at Tony, who like him, was still very wet from the rain and they both decided to shed a few of their outer wet clothes. As they were doing so, Tony turned to the man by the radio set and said "Are we going to get supplied with fuel?" The man looked at Tony saying in very bad broken English "You will be getting food a little later" when the man said that, David looked at Tony and they both began laughing with Tony saying "Oh that's good, that will suit us, we can fly very well on that, thank you very much indeed" Having divested themselves of their outer wet clothes they sat in the two armchairs near the kerosene heater and from the warmth of the heater they both were soon asleep while the man with the bad English went into the other room.

After two hours he came back with cups of hot drinks and food and woke them up. Having that small kerosene heater in the room providing the heat, when they awoke they found that their clothes and shoes were soon dry and they began putting them on again. It was after they had eaten that the woman who had been acting as a nurse came into the room and said "We should be able to start boarding in about 30 minutes, but at the moment we are awaiting for three more people to arrive." David quickly interrupted her "We can't take off yet because we don't know whether anyone has refueled the plane." She turned immediately to the man by the radio set and began speaking to him in his own native language, both David and Tony were very impressed and knew from the manner in which she was speaking to him, that she was very fluent with his language. When she had finished talking she said to David "They will start refuelling when the rain eases, which should be in about 10 minutes time." David and Tony looked at each other and shrugged their shoulders and she smiled, knowing what the shrug of their shoulders meant, then without another word to them she turned as though to go back into the other room, but turned to face them saying "You have to remember that here on this island there is no big rush, things get done at their own pace, otherwise they don't get done at all"

However being impatient and knowing he liked the look of her, David asked her "I apologize if this appears rude to you, but please could you tell us your name and also tell us where did you learn to speak their language so fluently?" She replied "You are not being rude to ask me my name, it is Kathy Goolaburra and I sense, in fact I can tell, that both of you are looking at me being dark skinned, speaking perfect Australian as well as speaking foreign languages, and you are wondering what I'm am doing here on this island." She was smiling all the time while she was speaking, then she looked around before speaking again. "First of all I cannot tell you why I'm here, but I can tell you that I am an Aborigine and was born in Australia and I studied psychology at a university in Melbourne and I read an extra subject in languages to gain my degree. Then when I was 21 years of age I joined the RAAF, and two years ago I was transferred to another section and then I was asked to come here, and by doing so, I have been able to quickly pick up their language but not their dialect. Now does that satisfy both of you?"

Standing there listening to her lovely pleasant accent and looking at her beautiful good looks, David was saying to himself you are not what you say you are, because knowing she was well educated he thought you are something special and I would like to meet you again back in Australia. Then David quickly said "Thank you Kathy. You are a very remarkable young lady and I'm sure both Tony and I would like to meet you again when we get back to our aerodrome, so don't rush off when we get back without seeing us before you go." Kathy was laughing as she said "You flying types are all the same. I know all about you brylcream boys with that twinkle in your eyes, but I will see what I can do when we land back home." David was now looking out of the window and seeing the rain had eased considerably he said "It's not raining so heavy now, do you think they could be refueling our plane?" Kathy replied "I would think so but don't worry they will soon let us know when they have finished."

Thirty minutes later, David and Tony were getting impatient to go and were wondering what they could do to hurry things up, when suddenly in the distance they again heard sounds of small explosions, they both looked at each other and David said "Tony does that sound like gunfire to you?" Tony thought for moment before replying "Well yes it did, but why have small arms fire here on this small island?" they were about to go into the other room and ask a question when Kathy appeared with a badly injured man who could hardly walk.

Kathy said "Quick. Please help me get him on board." They both momentarily forgot about the gunfire and helped Kathy quickly take the injured person to the plane and put him on board and as she was about to return to the control building to get her belongings, she to them "The plane has been fully refuelled" David replied "Good, because Tony and I can now complete our preflight and then we can take off". Kathy went back to the building and it was then that a car quickly came into the airfield and stopped outside the building, four men got out and the men rushed forward to see Kathy coming out of the building and they all hurriedly boarded the plane.

Luckily, David and Tony had completed their preflight and had started to warm the engines when the men inside the plane shouted out "Okay we've shut the door and we are seated so let's get going" and knowing all were on board with their luggage they began to take off. After the plane took off and they were flying low over the woodland surrounding the airstrip, David suddenly felt something like small pebbles hitting against the rear fuselage of the plane and then it stopped. David shouted out to the men inside the plane "What the hell was that racket all about?" One of them came to him on the flight deck and said very quietly in a highly intellectual voice "Don't worry old chap, they just fired at us to say goodbye for leaving their island. By the way it's always nice to know how long it will take us to get back to the aerodrome you are taking us to?" David quickly looked at the individual and was attempting to assess him but was unable to do so, or come to a conclusion, then in a voice showing no emotion said "I should say in approximately six hours. Is that all right?" The man replied "Of course old boy no problem at all."

Without another word the man returned to his seat, but a few moments later as they flew over the small harbour of the island, David heard a huge explosion and looked out of the window and saw a ship on fire with big flames rising up into the air, then Tony came into the flight deck and said. "The passengers said that explosion was caused by a gas cylinder that was being unloaded from a small ship on to the quayside." David looked at Tony and quizzically said "How the hell do they know that?" David paused for a moment then he said "Tony there's something suspicious about these guys and I don't like it and I think we are being used for something I don't like. When we get back I'm going to find out and I'm going to start asking some questions" When Tony left him, David sat there for some time just flying the plane, contemplating on what these highly educated people were

38

doing on that island and then being in such a hurry to get off of it and he was also thinking about when landing at the airfield he thought he could feel someone near to him, and he was coupling this thinking with the explosion at the quayside, together with these people he was transporting back to Australia, suddenly, it was because he was worried he began thinking of a bible quotation he knew and began repeating it out loud.

*Be strong and of good courage,*
*Be not afraid, neither be dismayed;*
*For the Lord thy God is with thee,*
*Wither so ever thou goest.*

It was when Kathy appeared on the flight deck and sat beside him that he stopped reciting the bible quotation, not knowing she had heard him saying it. When he looked at her she was looking out of the side window and somehow she knew he was looking at her, because she turned her face and smiled at him saying "It has been a long time since I have sat in this position in an old plane such as this one." David paused for a moment before he said "Kathy I know you have said that you will not tell us why you were on that island and I respect your wishes and I'm certainly not going to press you why, but certain things have happened and I'm going to find out why they happened, some way or another. Now is that all right between us?" She was again smiling as she said "Of course I wouldn't want it any other way." While he was adjusting some flight instruments and checking his flight plan, he said "Kathy can I also say something and you promise that you will not be annoyed," but before he could say anything she interrupted him saying "Well I can't answer that until you ask me, can I?"

David looked at her as he said "By golly you are a smart one aren't you? Well I'm a little embarrassed because I want to say to you how much I like the look of you." She had a smile on her face as he was speaking to her and was nodding her head. David saw her smile and said "I do apologize Kathy if I am embarrassing you, but when Tony and I first saw you we were both amazed by your beauty and mannerisms, and we discussed your attributes at some length and the conclusion we came to is that although you appear to be a helping hand, you are also very efficient and something special and we both want to take you out for a meal, now please think what I have said before you give me an answer, and take your time because we will not be landing for some time yet?" Kathy sat there smiling looking out of the window and laughingly she began quoting a rhyme:-

*Twinkle, Twinkle little bat,*
*How I wonder what you're at,*
*Up above the world you fly,*
*Like an angel in the sky*

David was laughing at the ditty she had quoted and as he looked at her and noticing she was smiling, he was about to say something when suddenly Tony came on to the flight deck. She went to get up, but Tony said "No stay there Kathy, I just want to give David an update on the route but if I was you Kathy I would try and get some sleep because you look very tired." After Tony left she said to David "I think I will take Tony's advice and get some sleep, but in answer to your question I promise both of you I will give you my answer when we get back home and David, can I suggest to you that you have a private word with Group Captain Gerald Thomas concerning the other matter you have mentioned." She left her seat and went back to others leaving David perplexed and thinking very hard about the last piece of advice she gave to him.

It was while they were flying across the Pacific Ocean, that telephone calls were going back and forth from America to the Island they had left. When Gerry Giovanie heard of the loss of the ship and all its contents, he immediately telephoned Monte Carlo, and spoke to Marcus Lorenzo. When Marcus heard the ship had sunk and everything was lost, he roared into the telephone, "Gerry you do realize what the loss of that ship and its contents has cost me? Another thing I have promised Luigi Muraditori, who covers the Mediterranean and is head of the Mafia in Milano, that he will have all the guns and drugs he wants, and he wants that stuff immediately and I need his money. Now I've got to get on to him and let him know what has happened, but while I'm doing that, I want you to get some of your boys to Australia to dispose of that crowd who blew the ship up, especially that Aborigine girl and if it is possible, do it before they get much older, is that understood?" Marcus paused before saying "When you have made those arrangements, telephone me and tell me where and when it happened Ok?" When Marcus had finished talking Gerry replied "It could take up to four days to arrange everything, but my boys will certainly complete the job within a few days and I'm thinking of getting Bugsy Malone to do the job."

Marcus shouted back "I don't care who does it, as long as my orders are carried out. One more thing, I don't want any finger, or trace of the killings pointing to us. Is that understood?" Gerry was beginning to feel annoyed of being told what to do at a job he was very good at, and before he answered he sheepishly replied "Yes, Ok boss, leave everything to me." He was very annoyed when he put the telephone back to its stand, and waited to cool down, before telephoning Bugsy Malone.

Over the Pacific Ocean, the plane piloted by David was making good progress and as he hadn't much to worry over the flight journey he was thinking very seriously of the conversation he had with Kathy, together with her rhyme and he was wondering how she knew Gerald Thomas. He was also thinking why had she said he should talk to Gerald Thomas and he began thinking what could be the connection between Group Captain Thomas and the crowd they were bringing back and as he was thinking of all these things Tony came into the flight deck. He was smiling as he said "Well David, when we get back I do hope that in your post flight debriefing, you will put in a good report for the navigator, who has performed wonderful work in providing you with the correct course through that terrible weather and especially on the journey back, has given you a perfect flight plan. Before I forget, are you coming to church with me on Sunday?" David looked at Tony and with a big grin said "Buzz off you stupid idiot. But thanks mate for your navigation and a good flight and yes I'm coming with you to church but all I'm concerned about now, what am I going to say about the holes in the fuselage and how were they caused?"

Tony replied "Just tell the truth. How do you know what caused them. You only know what that chap who appears to be the leader of this group, told you and who we have brought back, then let them back at home sort it out with these chaps."

David felt very relieved and said "What a good friend you are to me, having you around me gives me great confidence because you always talk sense. I'll do exactly what you have said." When they landed they taxied to a place near the control tower and before David had switched the engines off, a car came to them and all the passengers left very quickly with the injured man and they were gone before David and Tony could complete their post flight. When they had finished their post flight details and alighted from the plane, the squadron adjutant came to them and they were expecting a rebuke from him on the state of the plane, but all he said "The Group Captain would like to see both of you tomorrow morning in his office at 9.00am with your report. You can leave the plane here because I have arranged for station flight to tow it back to the hanger and from what I've been told, both of you have done a fine job. Well done"

The following morning David was awakened at 7.30am and after he had dressed, shaved and had his breakfast it was time for him to see the Group Captain. Tony was waiting outside the office when David arrived who said "Good morning Tony I suppose now comes the rocket for getting the plane damaged and if the Groupie says that, how do I say it was not our fault? Because I don't know what happened, all I can say that we don't know what actually happened?" Tony said "David stop worrying. It will be all right because I believe while we were finishing the post flight report last night, I saw those who we brought back going into his office and it wouldn't surprise me if they haven't already explained everything to him." Tony paused for moment because they heard movement in the Group Captain's office. With nobody opening the door Tony continued speaking "Any way for your information during the flight home Kathy and I had a long talk and we are going to meet again. I have given her my telephone number and she has agreed that when she is available, she and I will be able to go out together." David was a little disappointed hearing that news but was quite amazed and thought for moment then said "You lucky old so and so. I was hoping to ask her for a date because I do honestly feel she is a beautiful girl, so all I can say to you is, all the best mate and treat her well."

Just as David had finished speaking the door opened and they were told to go in, Group Captain Gerald Thomas smiled at them telling them to be seated. He opened a file and looking at both of them he said "First of all I would like to congratulate both of you on the trip you have just completed. I do know that you are both unaware of the circumstances of the trip or why it had to be made and I know you have both made enquires. However all I can tell you, the trip was most important to the Australian national security." Gerald Thomas paused as he looked through a file he had before him and then said looking at Tony "I would like to address both of you by your Christian name, therefore Tony, I have it on good authority that since you have been in the RAAF you have performed your duties excellently and you are a credit to your squadron, but you are coming to the end of your short term agreement with the Air force and I was wondering whether you might be considering signing on for another short term, because if you are, I will certainly recommend you." Tony was amazed at the Group Captain using Christian names on such a formal occasion and was feeling slightly embarrassed.

He paused before answering "Well sir, I have been considering signing on again, however I have been offered a position teaching mathematics and navigation in a Technical college in Melbourne and I have an interview next week, and as the college is near to my family's home, I would like to be able to take the challenge of teaching to adult students."

Gerald Thomas said " Congratulations. I believe that is a very good position to take and knowing you have an interview I would be the last person to try to dissuade you, or even to try and persuade you to sign on again. Therefore I do wish you every success in your new position. Now if that is your wish, would you leave me to talk to David about a few other things and again I wish you good luck with your teaching position" After Tony had left the room Gerald Thomas looked at David and again began smiling as he said "David I believe you are wondering what the dickens is he going to say to me. Well I am going to ask you a similar question and upon your answer I will able to continue with what I would like to say. First of all I have noticed that you served with distinction during W.W.2 and after your demob, you left the RAAF, then you went to university and after obtaining your degree you signed on again for a 5 year short term agreement with RAAF that will be coming to an end very shortly, so the answer I want to know, are you going to sign on again for another short term of duty?"

David was amazed at the question and took a long time to answer before speaking "To be perfectly frank, sir, I haven't given it much thought." Gerald Thomas was quick to answer "Good, because that leads me to ask you, would you be prepared to work flying for the Australian security services on Intelligence work?" David thought very hard for a moment before he replied "Again sir, I cannot answer that question either, all I can say is, I know nothing at all about them and do not know what it might entail" Gerald Thomas face had a broad smile on it as he said "I think I had better explain to you a few things. Over the past 18 months you may not have realized that you have been selected to fly many missions without being told what they

43

were, and on every one of them you have never complained or tried to find out what those missions were, and on this last flight you never asked who, or what, your passengers were doing on that island and why you had get them off that island in a hurry." David quickly interrupted Gerald Thomas by saying "Sir it wasn't my duty to ask those passengers who they were. All I did, I spoke to Kathy Goolaburra that I was worried because I thought they may be in the drug traffic trade and I didn't want to get mixed up in that type of work."

Gerald Thomas smiled as he put his hand in the air and said "David please, it is all right. Kathy Goolaburra has explained to me what you said to her on the return flight home. Now let me explain some things to you. It has been suggested to me by people in very high places, who have been watching you and how you have performed over the past 18 months, they feel that they would like you to join the Australian Intelligence Security Services (AISS) on a full time basis. Now before you start asking questions like salary and other things, I can assure you that if you do decide to join, your original 5 year contract will be fulfilled and you will receive your rightful payments and you will immediately be fully employed on an excellent salary with the AISS which is attached to the RAAF."

# CHAPTER 3

## (Joining the-AISS)

David looked speechless and all he could say "Sir could I have a moment to think about what you have just explained to me?" He sat there for a few moments and then said "Sir would it be possible for you to explain to me what my duties would be if I were to say yes to your proposal?" Gerald Thomas had been reading David's file and he looked at David and said "It is because what I am asking is important and very confidential, I must know, what is your answer to the proposal?" David listened to the Gerald's question and gulped a few times saying out loud "Oh well, in for a penny and in for a pound" then he said "The answer Sir is, Yes, and as I'm still attached to the RAAF, I'm willing to take the chance and join the AISS." Gerald Thomas got up from his desk, walked round and locked the door to his room before resuming his seat and saying "David I'm very pleased to hear you say that, because you are just the experienced person we have been looking forward to having on our staff. Many senior people have observed you in your work over the last 18 months and the one person you impressed most of all, was the man who spoke to you when the plane was being fired on as you left the island. He was most impressed by your calm nature and you never asked him questions and when he alighted from the plane, he, being a very senior member of the security forces, spoke to me and said he wanted you to be a member of the AISS."

Gerald unlocked the door then lifted up the telephone and spoke to someone saying "I require the tea now please." David was in a slight daze over what he had been told and what he had let himself into, then the door opened and a steward brought in the tea trolley containing tea, cakes and biscuits and the steward poured out the tea and retired. After the steward had left the room, Gerald again locked the door then saying "David now that you have agreed to become a member of

45

AISS I can tell you that while you were flying home we, and many of the other security services, were listening to the telephone calls that were being made to various people around the world." It was the look of amazement on David's face that made Gerald stop speaking for a moment then he said "Those people I am talking about were talking about the loss of a ship and its contents at the island. Now before I continue with any more information. I require your signature on these two forms, one is your contract and the other is similar to the one you signed when you rejoined the RAAF, it is another document of the Secret Service Act." After David had read and signed them, Gerald continued talking "Now I can tell you why we in the security services are very worried at what is taking place throughout the world. All I am about to tell you is highly confidential and must not be repeated to anyone." David was nodding his head in agreement at the same time saying "Yes Sir" Gerald carried on speaking "The reason I am allowed to tell you this, is that during your final stay with your squadron, you are going to be entrusted with another special mission, which is a tough one because you will be sent abroad, but first I must tell you who you are going to investigate. They are a group of people who are known to us as the Triumvirate group and the three top men are known to everyone throughout the whole of their organization, by three classical mythological names."

David said "I am sorry to interrupt you Sir, but I didn't read or study mythology at university, why are they only known by mythological names?" Gerald Thomas was little annoyed at being interrupted again but said "David please be patient, I am about to tell you why, but there is something else you should know." Gerald paused to drink his tea and David thought that it would be a good point to ask a question saying "Sir I am pleased that you are telling me about the secret operations that I am about to be involved with, but surely being a new boy I will not be connected with such a big operation as the one you are about to explain?" Gerald put his cup down and very sternly said "David you must stop talking and curb your impatience, it is becoming most disturbing and if you continue with this type of behaviour, it will not matter how many people have vouched for you, I will terminate this interview with immediate effect and that will mean your future in the Air-force and with Security Service will also terminate. Now do you understand what I have said?" David was nodding his head as he replied "I do Sir and I am very sorry for my impatience." Gerald immediately smiled at David saying "I'm sorry I had to talk to you like that but what I have to tell you is very important and very complicated but when you realize how many people have recommended you for this position, you will then know how much we are looking forward for you working with us. Is everything clear now?" David never answered but just nodded his head in agreement.

Gerald stopped for another moment then said "The Israeli secret service called Mossad and the C.I.A. have had agents that have penetrated the Triumvirate group and they have found out to whom those mythological names are attached. Now I do implore you to commit to memory and remember the mythological names because these names are used and you must know immediately who they represent" David was listening intently as Gerald carried on speaking "The first name, Poseidon, is the name used by the head of the group and his true name is Marcus Lorenzo and it has been discovered why he has chosen that mythological name. It is because POSEIDON was a Greek God of the sea, whose fearsome rage could bring violent storms and earthquakes upon the world and as Marcus Lorenzo has a fearsome rage, he felt that the name suits him." Gerald laughed and he said "The name of HADES is used by Mario Lorenzo, the deputy head of the group, who is the brother of Marcus Lorenzo. It is said that he uses the name of Hades because Hades ruled the Underworld, which is the subterranean Land of the dead, and I do assure you David, that Mario shows no mercy on those he kills and according to the ancient writers of mythology, this underworld is guarded at the entrance by CEREBERUS which is a monstrous dog who ensures that all who enter the Underworld never come out of it alive. This third person who uses the name of Cereberus is not well known to us, because all that is known about him, is, we believe he is a Playboy and lives in England who is thought to be the nephew of the Duke of Chardminster. These three people are the brains behind a very big operation that deals in the buying and selling of antiques and they are the drug peddlers of all kind of drugs. The reason why they are doing this is, that by using some of the money they get from selling the antiques and drugs, they are buying Uraninite and then supplying the middle-eastern countries with the Uraninite, which is commonly known as *pitchblende*."

He paused for moment to look at his notes, and then he continued speaking "Yes I thought I was right. I am sorry because for a moment I had forgotten the name of *Pitchblende* and then I remembered what

47

it contained, that is what happens when one is getting older and is trying to think too much. I thought I had made a mistake about *Pitchblende*, but I was right because it has variable amounts of Radium, Lead, Thorium, Helium, Argon, and Nitrogen. This gang is also getting Thorium in a heavy white powder form, which is used mainly for making ceramics, but as it is also used in nuclear fuels and we know that Middle East countries are very keen to have Nuclear energy, we believe it could be a serious threat to our lives."

Gerald Thomas stopped speaking to look at David, who was busily writing this down. Gerald said "I see you are putting this in writing, but be very careful what you are writing does not fall into the wrong hands. Now I want you to listen very closely to what I am going to tell you, because now comes the most important part of the story, We are certain that the Triumvirate group also supply Uranium and Plutonium to those countries" Gerald stopped talking and was looking at David to see his reaction to that news. David's face had a look of amazement on it. Gerald again began speaking "Now to get money to buy from the countries willing to sell them those atomic fuels, the Triumvirate are in the business of obtaining antiques and drugs and selling them at exorbitant prices to the art world and to those pimps who run the big drug gangs and we are certain that they are also selling guns and ammunition to the Al-Qaeda."

Gerald again paused for moment looking at his dossiers but before speaking again, however David said "This is a much bigger operation than I could ever imagine and please forgive me but may I ask you a question Sir, because I have never heard of the name Al Qaeda and what does it represent?" For a fraction of a second Gerald looked annoyed then he realized the importance of the question David was asking and he replied "David I forgive you for this interruption and you are perfectly in order to ask that question. First of all Al Qaeda is a new name for the local tribesmen who live in the hills of the North-West frontier of British India, who owing to their warlike nature have been fighting everyone who enters their territory since before the 19th century and from that period of time when after many battles they have gained a special importance. We know that the fighting causes a constant drain of their men and money and many countries have tried to fight them and usually they end up retreating, badly mauled by the tribesmen. It is now believed by the countries in the Western world that because these tribesmen are being led by people who have an even greater ambition. They are becoming more prominent and are aiming to get more ammunition and weapons so that they can carry out their warlike behaviour. We believe that the Triumvirate is supplying them with those armed materials in return for drugs that the Triumvirate sell to further their own cause. So in effect we are dealing with two separate organizations and trying to prevent further blood shed. Now I hope that answers your question?" David didn't reply and only nodded his head.

Gerald looked again at his papers then looked up and began speaking "David I have to inform you that the countries of America, Great Britain, Israel, France and Germany have all their top secret service agencies working together to try and stop the Triumvirate group from distributing their main supply to those middle-eastern countries, who we know are in the process of making weapons of nuclear destruction and of those countries who are out to destroy our national economies. It is hard for us to trace the supply routes of the countries supplying the antiques drugs and ammunition to the Triumvirate and up to this present date, all those countries I have mentioned have lost quite a few of their secret service personnel in their attempts to find them."

David was now quite interested and was about to speak but listened as Gerald continued speaking "All those countries, including Australia, are concentrating all their efforts in finding out who is supplying the Triumvirate to obtain those antiques, drugs and ammunition which enables them to make the money so that they can the buy nuclear fuel to sell to those middle-eastern countries, and to sell ammunition to those who we also believe are connected to Al Qaeda. I need not impress upon you how dangerous this work is, and the type of people we are dealing with, because the Triumvirate will stop at nothing to get rich through this dangerous work." Gerald paused for another break then he began speaking again "You will be working immediately for AISS but during the next six months you will still be in the RAAF and you will be flying usual missions, only this time you will know that the flights are of a very secret nature and you will know whom you will be transporting, but on all occasions you must not identify yourself to any of your passengers or indicate to them that you are connected to the Intelligence security services, and I suggest that you never inform any of them what you are doing, or what organization you have joined, because at the end of six months, you will officially leave the RAAF and it is recommended that you will be sent abroad again and eventually join a Telecommunication company working in London."

When David came out of the office he went to the officers mess to have a meal when he saw Tony, and as David sat down at the table Tony said to him "That was a long chat you had with the Groupie wasn't it?" David just smiled and said "Yes it was and I thought it would never end, he kept saying to me that he wanted me to stay in the RAAF and because I love flying and the only way I can fly jet planes is in the RAAF I agreed to sign another short term in six months time."

Tony was eager to know how David's interview went and asked "Was he pleased with you because you agreed to sign again and did he want to know what type of work you wanted to do when you eventually leave the RAAF. Well I hope you parted on good terms with him when you told him you were leaving the RAAF?" David was laughing when he said "Yes and he even shook my hand when I told him I wanted to work in a telecommunication company" The look on Tony's face when he heard David's remark about working for a telecommunication company made David laugh, but David stopped laughing and looking very serious at Tony he said "Tony I know you will shortly leaving the RAAF and you are going for that interview next week" David stopped talking for moment and began looking very serious.

Then he began talking again saying "I know you are hoping to work in that top Technical college and I wish you every success but I am a little upset because I don't think I will be able to go church with you this Sunday because I'm being sent away on other duties and if I don't meet up with you again before you leave, I do want you to know that you have been a very good friend to me and we have been in some tough situations together and I feel I would like you also to know, that with all my troubles past and of all my troubles to come, I will never find a better friend than you and I wish you every success with your future job." Tony was embarrassed as he said "Don't get too sentimental now, because we will see each other again and you know that I'm hoping to meet Kathy again and then you, Kathy and me can meet and have a good lunch and a chat about things and see how each of us are doing in our respective jobs." They shook hands and Tony left.

David was sent to America where he met and became friends with Bruce Robertson, and twelve months later when he returned to Australia, he was sent on more trips, but whenever possible he went to church, and on the Sunday shortly before his next flight it was as he walked to church he began remembering the flight with Tony to that Pacific Island, then during the church service he felt as though Tony was sitting beside him. The very next day while he was making a short flight to another country, he had been thinking of all the information Gerald Thomas had given him, when suddenly he began thinking about the sensation of Tony sitting next to him in church. When he flew back and landed his plane, as he left the flight control office he could see a woman standing close to the Group Captains office and was surprised, but very pleased to see it was Kathy.

He walked towards her and as he got nearer he could see she had been crying and was wiping her eyes, when he approached her he said "Kathy what ever is the matter, why are you crying?" before he could say anything else to her, she interrupted him, "David I am very sorry I have some bad news. After talking to Group Captain Thomas I have come here to personally tell you that Tony has been killed." David was shocked hearing that news and was just about to speak again when Kathy said "Could we go somewhere quiet before I say anything else?" It was a bright sunny day and they walked solemnly away from the office, right across the aerodrome where they could be alone, but still within the confines of the aerodrome. Kathy said "David I have been with Group Captain Thomas and I have told him the bad news and after listening to me, he suggested that I speak to you and tell you everything, especially about Tony's death."

David was still in shock at hearing the news of Tony's death and sat on the grass and as Kathy was talking she sat beside him saying "David, Group Captain Thomas has had a very long chat with me, and I have been told by him that he has spoken to you and therefore I know that you have joined our organization and he has advised me that I have to tell you that Tony died and also to tell you how he died, because Tony was murdered last Thursday." David was visibly shocked and was shaken to hear her say that Tony had been murdered, when suddenly he began thinking how strange it had been in church on Sunday when he thought he could feel Tony's presence as if he was sitting beside him.

David had tears in his eyes as he asked her "You say Tony was murdered. When did he die, by whom and what for?" Kathy was looking at David as she said "Would you like a few moments to rest and go somewhere to have a drink, or would you like to go to a pub and me to tell you the full story there?" David sat there for a moment with tears in his eyes and with a dismal look on his face, he said "I

51

think I would like to hear the full story here, so carry on and tell me." Kathy held David's hand and said "Do you recall that trip you made with Tony, when you came to collect me and those other people from that island and when very shortly after we had taken off, the plane was hit by bullets and then there was a big explosion as we flew over the harbour. Well I can now tell you it was a ship that those men and I blew up and it caught fire because the ship was carrying armaments for the Triumvirate gang?" Before David could speak Kathy carried on talking "Gerald Thomas has informed me he has told you about the Triumvirate people and it appears that they lost many things over the loss of that boat and because of that explosion sinking their ship, they have also lost money and contraband, and they have put a contract out, to kill all those who were on that island who caused their boat to explode and kill a number of their people."

Kathy had tears in her eyes as she looked at David before she continued speaking "After we came home, Tony and I met on a couple of occasions, and unfortunately it must have been on one of those occasions that he was seen with me in Melbourne and it is assumed that the Triumvirate people must have thought he was one of us, because last week when he was in Geelong he had parked his car in a car park near the school and after he had been teaching at the university he went to the car park and when he started his car it blew up and he was killed instantly." Kathy paused and looked at David and said "Do you wish me to continue?" David was nodding his head, then Kathy said "The remains of Tony's car have been forensically and scientifically searched and they have found remains of the explosive that caused the car to explode, from that evidence, we are certain the Triumvirate group are responsible for his death. David I am sorry, because he was innocent and I feel responsible for his death. On one occasion when Tony and I met we were having a meal when I saw someone who I recognized was connected to the Triumvirate group, but I couldn't warn Tony without giving my cover away. I do honestly feel that I should never have met Tony in the first place and it's a pity that he was seen with me. Mike has told me to tell you we must now all be very careful."

As Kathy began to cry David put his arms around her and said "Kathy you must look at it sensibly and try to look at it from another point of view. Having listened to your story I'm sure everyone feels it wasn't your fault because whatever, or wherever Tony went on the day he died, his number came up on that day, and he could have died an ordinary death or have been killed just crossing the road." It was when Kathy stopped crying and was wiping her eyes she said "I know you and Tony were very good friends, and I really thought that you would hold me responsible for his death." Still holding on to her hands and lifting her up from the ground, David said "Kathy there is no chance of me holding you responsible for Tony's death, you have to remember it wasn't your fault. Now come on, let's go and have that drink and a bite to eat."

While they were eating the meal David said "You know I'm very pleased that Gerald Thomas has told you that I have joined the same organization as you, and I'm hoping that maybe one day you and I could be working together." Kathy was smiling as  David continued "Because in a few weeks time I'm going to England and I can tell you that I am working under the auspices of the British security network, and having been to England during W.W.2, I'm really looking forward to it, but I want you to promise me that you will keep in touch with me, so that when I come back here we can meet together again. Will you promise me that?" Kathy sat there for moment looking at David very intently as she nodding her head and replied "I will do my level best to keep that promise to you and thank you for listening to me." David then said "Kathy do you remember on that flight back from that island when you were sitting next to me in the cockpit and you suddenly repeated to me a small rhyme. At that time I thought it was lovely of you to say it to me because it meant so much. Would you like me now to repeat one to you?" Kathy was nodding her head and smiling as she said "Yes please". David said  "Well I hope you like this one because here it comes:-

*You can't enjoy smiles if you haven't cried tears*
*You can't feel good if you haven't felt bad,*
*You can't appreciate life if you haven't felt death,*
*And you can't be happy if you haven't felt love*

Kathy leaned over and kissed David and said "David that was lovely and I shall always remember it, and thank you very much for being so very sweet. You have made me feel much better" David began to enquire if she would like to leave and she agreed and he escorted her back to Gerald Thomas's office where he left her, while he continued his duties with RAAF. He was ordered to fly one more mission during his last two weeks then his period with RAAF finished, and he was told to report to Gerald Thomas where Gerald said to him "David I hope you have enjoyed your last few months with us and I'm very pleased you have joined us in the Australian Intelligence Security Services (AISS), because you have performed your duties excellently and having been to America it is hoped that you learnt a few more details and we now feel you are now ready to join our fictitious computer company in London, the one I mentioned to you when we first spoke together." Gerald asked David "Would you like a drink before you leave?" David was amazed at this generosity coming from a very senior officer and was about to answer when Gerald said "I'm having a nice cup of coffee and then I'm having a brandy. Now would you like to join me in wishing you a bon voyage?" David felt he couldn't say no and nodded his head as he said "Thank you very much Sir, I would be delighted" and he sat down while Gerald poured the coffee.

It was while they were drinking the brandy that Gerald said "I do apologize because I forgot to inform you that you will be soon joining that friend you met in America called Bruce Robertson and I believe from what I have just been informed, that you and he will be working together in England." David was amazed and very delighted to hear that Bruce Robertson was working for the American Intelligence Security Agency and he would soon be in London working with him.

David was about to speak but Gerald Thomas began talking again "That means you will be beginning your work on good terms with someone you know and trust. Now please be careful and you have to remember that you have to be very careful to whom you talk to and with whom you confide, because I hope you will soon carefully learn that the Triumvirate always have information about our staff and they have their own horrible methods of dealing with them."

Observing the look of concern on David's face Gerald paused for moment before saying "I do assure you David that the Triumvirate members are very experienced and are expert in disposing of a human body. As I have just told you, many highly qualified and experienced men of the International Security Agencies have met with unexpected and horrible deaths, which have been carried out by the Triumvirate members. There is however one thing that all the Agencies know and that is, we are all certain there is a leak in the system All the International Security Agencies (ISA's) feel sure that the Triumvirate are being supplied with information from someone who is within one of our Agencies, and all of us are looking at all the personnel in our respective agencies to discover who it is." Gerald paused again to have a drink of coffee and then he said "David I'm sorry that I am being long winded about the problems we have, but it is better that you know and understand what the Triumvirate is all about and what we are doing to combat the problem and what all our allied countries are up against and how they are trying to combat the same problem." David interrupted Gerald "I apologize for interrupting you Sir, but if the Triumvirate are as big and as powerful as you are saying they are, from the manner in which you have just described to me, it does appear that most of the countries are at war with them so why do we allow the Triumvirate to continue to operate and cause us so much worry?"

Gerald said "Thank you David for apologizing and you are right to believe that most countries are at war with them. However I can tell you that unfortunately for us, the Middle-Eastern countries trade with them and they are the Triumvirate allies and they are always ready to help when the Triumvirate get into trouble. Now you must realize that as we rely so much upon those Middle-Eastern countries for our oil, so we have to tread very softly so as not to upset them. Now I can tell you that the senior people in England believe that they have strong grounds to suspect that there is a group of people who are in England, who are conveying vital information via the organization to the Triumvirate." Gerald paused because he could see the look of astonishment on David's face and he began speaking again "Who ever they are, all the countries are working together looking for connections, knowing that the informers are supplying the Triumvirate with all of our intelligence information and therefore we feel that it could be someone in a high position within our intelligence service, possibly in England. At this present moment we have a good team working on this project, and hopefully we will soon find out who is responsible and hopefully apprehend the leader of that group because every country is looking into this problem very urgently and you will be joining that team to become one of the people helping us to find out who those informers are."

Gerald paused to look at some papers then he began speaking again "In one way I am sorry you are leaving Australia and I should advise you that it has been circulated amongst your squadron colleagues that you have signed on for another short term and have been posted to a new position within the Australian Air Ministry. I am sure there are people in your squadron who will miss you, but your sudden departure to a higher position will allay all suspicion. I am glad you have joined the AISS and I am also equally sure that you will enjoy and meet some very nice people who are in the ISA's. There is one other piece of news I should tell you. Last year, the British found one of their senior scientist, a Dr.Klaus.Fuchs had been sending atomic information to Russia and he was sentenced to 14 years in gaol. Recently the British Foreign Office have  announced that they have received from the French security services three telegrams sent by two Foreign Office officials called Guy Burgess and Donald Maclean who have been missing for some time and it is believed those two men are now in Russia. The reason for me telling you this information is that America and Great Britain are in the process of investigating the leakage of all atomic secrets during and since the end of the war and a few weeks ago in America, a man called Julius Rosenberg and his wife Ethel were sentenced to death for sending atomic secrets to Russia during the war years. It is known that the Rosenbergs had been sending their secrets to an international Soviet spy ring, to which Klaus Fuchs was connected, and we know that this is a world problem as money speaks all languages. At the moment we are not sure whether the Triumvirate are also connected to this type of work and therefore we are investigating this point as well, because we can never be too careful. Now I believe I have given you everything you ought know and I don't think I can add anything more, so it just leaves me to wish you good luck and to remind you to be very careful in what you do."

It was after David had stood up, shaken hands and had thanked Gerald for all the advice he had given him, he left the office and walked away to his room to collect his luggage, where he sat there for a few moments thinking of past times. He began remembering the unusual events that had happened to him, and he also remembered his wartime days and the dangerous flying trips he had flown. He began smiling as he remembered the day he and Jack Donoghue had visited that old church and of meeting the vicar who had explained to them the sad death of Mabel Flitch, then when they came away from the churchyard Jack had said he felt as though someone had had been standing beside them. Remembering the name of Mabel Flitch reminded him of the trip to Berlin. The plane had been badly damaged and how Jack Donoghue had managed to work out a course for home, even though he had lost most of his maps and he began remembering how Jack told him to pray for a ghost to help them. Then he remembered how had prayed earnestly and he felt that Mabel Flitch was standing beside him, and how he had landed the plane by the aid of Fido and how Fido had dispersed the fog by flames. He was still smiling as he remembered looking at the tombstone of Mabel Flitch and saying to Jack how sorry he felt about how she had died, then how Jack too had felt her presence and telling Jack of her being his guardian angel. He remembered the time when he fell near the edge of a great gully and how he felt as though someone had saved him from falling down a very steep decline.

These thoughts set his mind thinking about life after death and it particularly made him think of the time when he was in church and he felt that Tony was sitting beside him. Thinking of Tony reminded him of the trip to the island in the Pacific Ocean when he had felt someone, other than Tony, sitting beside him helping him during that very bad storm.

He was still sitting there, smiling, when an orderly came into the room to tell him the car had arrived to take him to the railway station. As the car left the main gates of the aerodrome he thought of Kathy and how she had attracted him but how disappointed he had been when she and Tony had begun courting, then he remembered Tony's death and how it had affected him and also the time when Kathy had come to him to tell him of Tony's death and he had somehow managed to say the right words to comfort her in her distress. It was then he knew he had always believed that Mabel Flitch was there to help him and he knew he felt that his feelings in life after death were stronger than ever, and he believed he would always feel that either Tony or Mabel Flitch would always be near when there was danger, guarding and watching over him.

David arrived at the headquarters of the AISS where at the reception desk they directed him to an office on the second floor where he was very surprised to see and be introduced to the man who had come onto the flight deck and spoke to him on the plane when they left the island in the Pacific Ocean where there had been a big explosion in the dock area. As this person shook hands with David he said "Good morning Mr Hogarth, my name is Jonathan Braithwaite and I am extremely pleased that you have joined our very elite force. I am given to understand that Group Captain Thomas has explained practically everything to you and therefore there is no need for me to reiterate it. I also know he has informed you that you are going to London to be working for a company under the title of Data

Telecommunication. Having been in the RAAF you are well informed of telecommunication work so when you are in London working in the shop that you will be using for your base; there will be all the telecommunication equipment and accessories for all the telecommunications that may be required, but they are there as pseudo guise.

Your main duties are to assist the British security (MI6) and you will be directed from there by a Mr. David Crossley who is in charge of the British security and this will remain so, until you have been informed or transferred to another country. Otherwise he is the person you are attached to and he will advise you of your duties. However do not be too surprised if you are instructed to meet other people who are from this southern part of the world. That is all I wish to say to you except to wish you a bon voyage and here are all your necessary papers and vouchers, now be careful and good luck.

# CHAPTER 4

## (The Triumvirate)

The three men in a large flat in Monte Carlo were Marcus Lorenzo, who is also known as Poseidon, his brother Mario Lorenzo known as Hades, and Nicholas Pitman known as Cereberus, the nephew of the Duke of Chardminster and a cousin to Susan Pitman. These are the top men of the infamous Triumvirate gang who deal in forged antiques, drugs and prostitution, besides dealing with some Middle Eastern countries with contraband.

Marcus Lorenzo is a dark handsome man, 44years old and is having a love affair with an Italian Contessa in Italy. He was born in Milan of an ordinary working class family and his brother Mario born 4years after him, lives with him. When Marcus left school he worked hard trying to earn money doing menial jobs, but he eventually found that he could earn better money looking after girls who were prostitutes. When Mario left school Marcus persuaded him to help him look after those girls and when more girls began working for them, it was through dealing, peddling drugs and looking after the prostitutes that they became very rich.

It was a chance meeting when Marcus met an ambitious man called Luigi Muraditori, who was connected to the Mafia in Milan and wanted guns and ammunition, and after many meetings with him, Marcus and Luigi became good friends. One day Luigi and Marcus were sitting in the sunshine outside a café in Italy drinking coffee and were discussing the gun situation, when a very well spoken Englishman asked if he could sit at their table. At first they were reluctant to say anything pretending not to understand, but looking at the Englishman, Marcus nodded his head to Luigi and they agreed he could sit with them. Marcus spoke to him in English and said "What are you doing here in Milan?" The Englishman replied "I am on a short holiday and I'm looking for an art studio where I could sell a few paintings." Asking him about the paintings and how much was he going to sell them for, they were amazed at the price, Marcus said "What type of paintings are they?" he replied "Antiques". Immediately they both became very interested with the thought of the money that antique paintings could be sold for, and as they continued to speak to this man they became more and more interested and began to be very friendly towards the Englishman who couldn't speak Italian. Being a cautious person Luigi became very suspicious of the Englishman, he had a feeling that the paintings could be stolen and spoke to Marcus in Italian telling him of his fears, but Marcus, also speaking in Italian told him not to worry and told Luigi to take the Englishman to Luigi's brother-in-law's shop. Luigi said in broken English to the Englishman "I know of a shop that might suit you, he sells antique paintings and I believe he might be able to help you" unbeknown to the Englishman, Luigi was talking about his brother-in law.

The Englishman's smiled and said in his very cultured voice "Thank you very much indeed I have looked everywhere around here but couldn't find any suitable shop."

Marcus immediately spoke in English "I do apologize I feel we should have introduced ourselves. Luigi and I are Italian and my name is Marcus and this is my friend Luigi and its Luigi's brother-in -law you are going to meet." The Englishman acknowledging their introductions proffered his hand and said "My name is Nicholas Pitman and I would like to thank you for helping me." After shaking hands with them, Luigi said "If we can use your car I will show you where the shop is situated." When they arrived at the shop, they parked Nicholas's car and knowing that Nicholas didn't speak Italian, Luigi spoke to Marcus in Italian "Marcus you stay here and watch this Englishman and I will talk to my brother-in –law."

When Luigi and Marcus had taken Nicholas with the paintings into the shop the shop owner when he examined the paintings he knew immediately they were not genuine. While the shop owner spoke to Luigi in Italian, Marcus occupied Nicholas's attention by speaking to him in English. Having had a quiet word with Luigi, the shop owner made an offer for the paintings that was immediately accepted by Nicholas. The shop owner said in Italian to Luigi "I do like these paintings and I would like to buy more. I know I can sell them quickly. Can he get some more for me?" Luigi translated it to Nicholas, who quickly replied "Certainly, I can obtain some for him, but it will take me time to get them. Will that be all right?" Luigi translated to the shop owner who, with a smile on his face nodded his head and shook Nicholas's hand. With all the arrangements having been made, Nicholas departed leaving Marcus and Luigi in the shop. Nicholas left the shop happy, knowing that he was now going to earn more money. Within four months Nicholas was supplying the shop with more forged antique paintings and it was because of this dealing that he became well acquainted with Marcus. One day Marcus said to Nicholas "Would you like to earn more money, because I know of someone who wants some drugs?" Nicholas was at first taken by surprise, but realizing that it would mean more money coming to him he quickly replied "Yes I know where I can get drugs at a reasonable price." With Nicholas supplying the drugs and the forged antiques and with Marcus, selling the paintings with the help of Luigi's brother-in-law and Mario distributing and selling the drugs, the Triumvirate gang was created, and Luigi became a big man in the Italian mafia world, with Marcus supplying him with drugs and the armed weapons to maintain his standing in Italy.

One day Marcus met a person who came from a Middle Eastern country and during their conversation about weapons, the Middle Eastern man who knew that Marcus was able to obtain certain weapons, asked him if he could also supply any nuclear materials to certain Middle Eastern countries, adding that a payment of a considerable amount of money would be forwarded to Marcus if he could do so. For a few moments Marcus deliberated and then thinking of the huge sums of money that was being offered, he said he would speak to his two other directors and would let the man know within 7 days. When they met again 7 days later, Marcus spoke to the Middle Eastern man and after a good deal of time spent in negotiation an agreement was made, to supply the nuclear fuels together with armed weapons.

The Middle Eastern man then told Marcus the name of the person he was to contact when they were ready for delivery and collection of payment and then he enquired where these fuels and weapons were coming from, but Marcus refused to answer him, only saying "What port do you want them delivered to?" The Middle Eastern man gave the name of the port and left very hurriedly.

It was a lovely sunny morning two weeks later, and in Marcos Lorenzo's large flat on the top floor of a large complex of expensive flats situated in Monte Carlo. Nicholas Pitman was sitting next to

Mario Lorenzo on the veranda overlooking the esplanade in Monte Carlo harbour, drinking a large scotch and soda. They were both admiring the scenery of large yachts moored there, when Mario's older brother, Marcus Lorenzo, came onto the veranda and stood there looking at them. After a few seconds he began talking "Now look here I don't want you two sitting here drinking and just admiring the view, because we have a lot to do and talk about. You both know that there is a large shipment coming from Venezuela and realize its coming through the port of Recife in Brazil." He then paused to look very sternly at them. Then when he saw he had their complete attention he said "Now I want you to know why I am directing this consignment through Recife and not Porto Alegre. I have just had a tip from one of our agents in London that the CIA, FBI, MOSSAD and MI6 know of our original routes, so I have decided to alter the route of transport. This time we are bringing some of the drugs wrapped in the copies of the artwork of the Netherlands Renaissance painter called Robert Campin, and his work has been identified as the Master of Flemalle and is highly thought of by those in the Art world. Because of this I have arranged that a large sum of money is paid to some high officials in the Custom's and that means this consignment of his paintings will not be opened by those Custom and Excise people, that is why I have arranged for some drugs to be put within the framework of the packages of the paintings." Marcus was looking at the other two men when suddenly he appeared to lose his temper and stamped around them and then as he walked around he began shouting at them. "I wish you both would stop looking down at those women in their bikini's and pay more attention to what I'm saying." Marcus hurriedly went back into the flat and then he came back to them with a piece of paper in his hand. Marcus was now very annoyed saying " I want you two to know that you must remember that Painter's name and to arrange for our people who collect the stuff to be very careful with those wooden boxes, because they not only have copies of that chap's paintings, which are very expensive, but there is also the drugs wrapped within the framework of the packages of the paintings." Nicholas Pitman said to Marcus "How much do you think this consignment is worth on the open market?"

Marcus replied "It's funny because when ever I mention money, or the word money is mentioned, you always pay great deal of attention and you don't think of women then do you? Well this consignment is worth just over £2.5 million because the paintings alone will bring us in more than £1 million and with the drugs, well I hope we should make another £2 million or more, so with luck we should clear about £3 million plus and that will help us pay for and provide the nuclear fuels for that person in the Middle East and that is where our main profit is coming from."

He paused "Now lets stop sitting here drinking my scotch and why don't you start thinking of helping me make some money to buy the scotch" Marcus could see that they were amazed at the profit they could be making and he relaxed and began smiling as he again related that figure to them, but then a frown came on his forehead and when he spoke again he pointed to Nicholas Pitman and said " and I have a special job for you to do." Before he spoke again he poured himself another drink, settled back in his chair and began to speak "Nick I don't want any hitch up this time and ..... Oh I forgot to tell you I have ordered the consignment of paintings to be sent to my place in Hamburg and then after they have been carefully repacked they are not going to Italy but going to England instead. All you two have to do in Hamburg is to arrange for the drugs to be taken away from the paintings and stored until we are ready to distribute them through our agents and we can then transfer the paintings to London." He paused as he turned towards Nicholas "I am arranging to send the bonds to you via your friend Andrew Ashley-Grove, I want you to tell him to be ready to receive them and if he asks what they are for, tell him they are payments for the antiques." He stopped talking to pour himself another drink then when he had again settled himself into a chair he said "Nick these bonds are worth a lot of money and are being sent via Gee Gee in Las Vegas to be delivered to Ashley-Grove's home in England, so make sure you are there when they arrive and take them to your uncle for deposit in the usual place of safety. When they are deposited tell your uncle to get me some more cash about £50,000 will do but not in large currency notes"

While they were enjoying sitting there on that lovely sunny day, the telephone rang and after Marcus had answered it he said to them "Pierre Bouverie who owns the motor yacht 'Pricilla', has invited us for trip and to have lunch with him on board and I have agreed that we go" but before he could saying anything else, the other two rose from their chairs and moaned asking "But what time do we get back?" Marcus replied "Don't worry about the time, it will be all right for us to complete the other arrangements I have made when we get back." Mario was a little upset having his day rearranged for him for no apparent reason and said "Marcus what have you got in mind for us today? You don't usually make your mind up quickly without first having thought every thing out before hand. What have you arranged and what about any plans of Nick's and mine that we have arranged for today?" It was only because Mario was his brother that Marcus kept his temper under control, and then with a smile on his face he said "It's a lovely day for sailing Mario, so why don't you wait until we are on board the 'Pricilla' enjoying sailing the sea and having a lovely meal on board with a few nice glasses of wine then I will tell you what I have in my mind for the evening, so stop your moaning."

Mario knew of his brother's moods and therefore he knew that Marcus had something urgent he wanted doing right now so he never answered. It was when they had sailed for a while and after they had a nice cooked meal and were relaxing in the ship's large lounge Mario noticed that they were well out of sight of the coast and going further out to sea and were going fairly fast. Mario then said to Marcus "Ok brother. We are well out to sea, where are we heading and what for?" Marcus took another sip of his wine and said "I didn't want to spoil anything today for anybody, but when Pierre told me his yacht was ready and could do the round trip without causing any trouble." He paused.

Then looked at them saying "I knew the time had come to go to Corsica and pick up a consignment of drugs that had been delivered there yesterday and I knew that Nicholas would like to have some money to spend on those beautiful girls he likes to have around him and, you Mario I'm sure would be perfectly happy having more money to spend on that lovely wife of yours." Marcus paused again for a moment because his statement caused a few comments from both Nicholas and Mario, but before they could say anything else Marcus continued talking "I knew that you two had really nothing to do today and rather than wait another day to get the drugs away from Corsica, I decided on the spur of the moment that with your help we could move them ourselves. There is about a half million pounds worth of drugs to be put on board this boat and when we get back to Monte Carlo, Pierre will eventually ensure that they are taken to a place of safety." Mario still wasn't satisfied with what he had heard and said "I know Corsica is not too far away but it is still daylight. Where do you intend to moor this yacht and get us to store the drugs on board without being seen by the local police?" Marcus just smiled at him and said "You still don't believe your big brother do you? You still think I don't plan anything

64

before I make a move. Well to put you in the picture, yesterday when I was told that the drugs had arrived in Corsica, I asked Pierre to get this yacht ready and full of fuel, so that we could sail today so that we could get there and back to Monte Carlo by the early hours of tomorrow morning." Mario was about to speak again but Nicholas spoke first saying "How do we get the consignment on board?" Marcus was beginning to get annoyed with them keep asking him questions and said rather gruffly "You both enjoy the money you get from these consignments and you both forget that up to now I've done all the arranging without any mishaps happening to any of the consignments. I haven't let anyone know of this one taking place and it is all arranged for some of Luigi Muraditori's men to be there to help us load the drugs on board when it all nice and dark. We will be met in a little bay near Ajaccio and if we are very quiet we can creep in and with their help within a short time we will be on our way back to Monte Carlo. Now are you both happy with those arrangements?" Both Nicholas and Mario were very quiet and felt very sheepish when Mario said "Well it sounds like a nice days work. Let's hope that all goes well." A few hours later with the consignment safely on board, they were soon sailing back to Monte Carlo.

While that had been going on in the Mediterranean, in America Gerry Giovanie who was 45 years old and known to his friends as Gee Gee, was with a part time actress. Gee Gee was known for his handsome good looks and his habit of gambling in Las Vegas, he was also a ruthless gangster and was also known for his love life with the movie starlets in L.A. He was well known to many organizations, including the C.I.A., and to the spy agency of Israel called Mossad, who knew that he had several connections with the Mediterranean Mafia.

It was after their boat trip and when they reached Marcus's flat with Poseidon, Hades and Cereberus sitting on the balcony in the early morning sunshine and drinking, that Gee Gee was having a sexual relationship with a part time actress in Los Angeles.

It was while he was having this relationship that Gee.Gee received a telephone call from one of his aides informing him that Mark Broadbent was flying to Las Vegas. Gee Gee was very annoyed at being interrupted, but hearing that news he immediately telephoned his home in Las Vegas and spoke to his valet, Capio. It was because he had a close relationship with his employer that Capio was not only employed as a valet, he was also a guard to Gee.Gee and was told to go to the airport and wait until Mark Broadbent had landed. He was told to watch and follow Mark, then report back to Gee.Gee and inform him who was with Mark, what hotel he was staying at, and whether Mark had spoken to anyone. When Capio replaced the telephone receiver, he knew that this assignment must be very important. He went to Gee.Gee's private room opened a special cabinet, and found a file marked Mark Broadbent, inside the file were papers and a photograph. After reading one of the papers he knew that Mark Broadbent was a very important person and looking at the photograph and committing it to his memory knowing he would be able to recognize him, he put the photograph and file back in the cabinet and left for the airport.

Mark Broadbent was a very rich contractual entrepreneur, who could organize anything from building contracts to musicals. He had flown into Las Vegas from San Francisco with his wife Melinda, together with his two lovely young daughters and they had booked into the plush Mirage hotel, which was situated in the midway of Las Vegas Boulevard (the Strip), which was not too far from the airport of Las Vegas. Mark knew that besides the trip being a holiday for his family it was also an assignment, and the reason he booked into the Mirage hotel he knew that he had a quick access onto highway 15, and if he had to leave early he would have an easy access to the airport, or be able to drive a car to Los Angeles or San Francisco. After they had landed at the airport, Mark knowing the importance of his assignment and having been taught to be a cautious individual, he kept a close eye on who was around as he collected their luggage and suitcases from the carousel. Then as he walked from the carousel with the luggage towards Melinda and his children he noticed a person standing nonchalantly by a pillar post who looked as though he was pretending to be reading a newspaper. Mark thought the person looked strange and very suspicious, but not knowing Capio, therefore not recognizing him, he thought he had better be on his guard. He began to hurry towards Melinda, and then he hurried her and the children into the waiting car, but because of his assignment he was unable to inform her of his unusual behaviour or his concern.

The reason for making them hurry was that, he was concerned about the suspicious nature of the person he had seen at the airport, standing close by the pillars, and it was later that evening while he was having a meal in the hotel restaurant, Mark told his wife that he would like to have a walk around the Casino, but Mark's wife,

Melinda, knew he would probably play one of the slot machines, he asked her if she and the girls would mind finding their own enjoyment by going to the hotel floor show and seeing some of the beautiful Las Vegas and famous showgirls. Feeling that Mark's request and behaviour was due to his connections with the C.I.A. and that he must be worried, Melinda was not surprised by his request so she agreed and after finishing their meal, she and the girls went to the floor-show while Mark went into the Casino.

Mark immediately began looking around at the people playing the slot machines, and as he walked around very slowly just looking at them playing, he thought he recognized one of them, but for a moment he couldn't think where he had seen him before. Remembering the incident of the unusual appearance and attitude of the person he had seen at the airport, he continued to walk cautiously around but all the time he was critically gazing at everyone, and when ever possible he occasionally played one of the slot machines. He wandered around the slot machines still trying to look casual, but at the same time he was interested in all those around him, surreptitiously looking at that same person he had just seen who was busy playing a slot machine. Mark stopped walking looking hard at that person, as he put a lot of money into the slot machine, when suddenly he could see the face and knew it was the person he wanted to meet. Mark stood there and was contemplating his next move, while at the same time he was recollecting and remembering his flying days in the Army service and remembering how he had first met Bruce Robertson and how they had become good friends while they were training and flying in Utah. Mark was remembering their service life together, and when they were both being discharged from the air force, that they found they had both applied for a job that required ex-servicemen with flying experience and afterwards they had joined the same company in Washington D.C.

Unobserved by Bruce, Mark stood close by watching him playing the slot machine, when suddenly the lights on the machine began to glow and flash, and a bell started to sound very loudly. While the bell was ringing and the lights were flashing the slot machine was shedding out coins and Bruce was doing his best trying to catch them in plastic containers before they fell onto the floor. He was doing his best to avoid attracting attention but within a few moments many staff came running quickly to the flashing slot machine and began talking and questioning Bruce, and then he was taken away by the staff to the office of the senior Games Manager, who questioned him again before paying out the winnings marked on the slot machine.

When Bruce came away from the senior games manager's office with his winnings and a big grin on his face he suddenly saw Mark, but before Mark could say anything, Bruce was looking at him saying "Excuse me, do you know me, haven't we met somewhere before?" Mark smiled as he replied "Yes we have. It was in Utah when we were in the Army Air Force together and I used to call you Bru Bru the big bear. Do you remember me now Bruce?" Hearing Mark speak his pet name, Bruce couldn't believe what he had just heard, because besides being embarrassed at being seen gambling and winning, he had just recognized the person who had spoken to him, and he replied "Why blow me down it's Mark Broadbent, I knew I recognized the voice but I couldn't for moment recognize your face because something has changed, now wait a minute I know what it is, it's your moustache that fooled me and besides that you have put on a little weight, but I recognize you now, and without that moustache you could still look as young and handsome as you did when I last saw you." Bruce was standing there, still looking amazed and holding a lot of paper money in his hands when he said "What in blazes are you standing here in Vegas for watching me waste my money but win a fortune".

Mark was grinning at him as he countered the question by saying "Bru Bru, by the look at that money you are holding you didn't lose, so how much did you win?" Bruce replied "Well only three thousand dollars. You see I was putting one dollar in at a time, then two, then three, then one dollar again. The winning line came up when I had put one dollar in. Mind you if it had come up when I put the three dollars in, the winnings would have been a much larger amount." Bruce was laughing as he said "I would have won ten thousand, but look here, don't let us stand here wondering how much I could have won, Let's go and have a drink with the money I have just won. What about a quiet place over there, where we can talk about old times and be open to each other" Bruce was standing there with a smile on his face looking at Mark because he somehow felt that the meeting with Mark Broadbent was not as accidental as it looked. He suddenly remembered that he had read that Mark was now regarded as an entrepreneur and his brain was working very fast as he said "Well now that I have won a few dollars, are we going stand here chatting or are you going to have that drink with me?" Mark quickly replied "That would be a darn good idea if we have that drink. I was going to play a few slot machines myself but seeing you had just won a jackpot, I would say the other machines are probably empty and I would most likely lose, so to save me losing my money, with you buying me a drink will be a good idea". As they walked away Bruce burst out laughing at Mark's remark, because he said "With what you own I know you don't need to win any money because I also know you are well loaded." Mark ignored that remark and thought Bruce might not know what he was doing in Las Vegas. It was after getting their drinks and when they were sitting at a table, that Bruce said to Mark "Ok what's the deal? What are you doing here in Las Vegas or are you going to ask me to work for you on one of your building contracts?" Before Mark could answer that question, Bruce carried on speaking "The last time you and I really worked together was after we left the air force and we both worked for that telecommunication firm in Chicago with a funny sounding name that was selling telecommunication equipment, but that was 15 years ago. I do realize and I know that a lot of things have happened to both of us since then, and things have probably changed, whether for they were for the good I don't know, but what I want to know is, what is this is meeting all about? I hope you won't mind me saying to you, that I have read in the papers that you are a entrepreneur and a very complex person and knowing and remembering what you were like when we were together in the forces, I somehow feel that this is not a fortuitous accidental meeting with you and also knowing that you are a successful business man, you had better start briefing me and we'll see if I can be of any help to you."

Mark could see that Bruce looked annoyed so he smiled as he looked at him, but the look on Bruce's face was enough to warn him that Bruce didn't know what to make of this casual meeting. Suddenly Mark remembered how quickly Bruce could lose his temper and he didn't want him to cause a scene. It was after noticing Bruce's bewilderment and possible annoyance that Mark put his hand in his pocket and drew out his wallet and as he did so, an address card fell on to the table facing Bruce. Looking at the card Bruce saw that it had the address of a telecommunication company in Washington D.C. but it was the look of amazement on Bruce face that brought a smile to Mark's face.

At first Bruce was confused knowing that the telecommunication firm at that address was run by the White House and was the pseudo name for a branch of the C.I.A., Bruce suddenly went silent and began to look all around the bar, just to see if he could recognize anyone, or if anyone else was close enough to hear what was going to be said. Mark could see Bruce was confused and could be ready to listen to what he had to say and smiling he offered him a cigarette. Then speaking very quietly and distinctly he said "Bruce what I am about to tell you is top secret. First of all I know you are surprised that I'm here, but I think you ought to know that both you and me are working for the same organization, and before you ask me how I know that you are not only a telecommunication salesman, but a member of another organization, I can tell you I do know why you are here in Las Vegas because I organized it."

Bruce looked at Mark incredulously and quietly said "I don't believe it, you can't be working for the same organization as me. How can you be, because you left the Data Telecommunication Company and you are now the Chairman and Chief executive of that Multi-building complex called the Charleston Development Company "Mark quickly interrupted Bruce saying, "That's correct but I am still connected to the Data Telecommunication Company and I am on the board of directors of the Chicago section and secondly I have come to tell you that I also feel you should know that I know something about Hades, Poseidon and Cereberus, those three mighty, or almighty Gods of Roman mythology. Now does that help you?" Bruce was amazed hearing Mark mention the names of those three Roman Gods, and realizing Mark was on the board of directors he felt he must be telling him the truth. Bruce quietly said "Okay Mark I understand what you what have said could be true, but first of all how are you in the same type of business as me and what am I suppose to know about your visit here today?" Before he began speaking Mark ordered another round of drinks and was smiling again as he spoke "Well the first thing I must say to you is well done on being very cautious and checking that I am a bone fide person working with the same telecommunication company as you, and I also feel that congratulations are in order on you winning 3,000 dollars and buying me a drink, and I feel sure that after telling you what position I have in the company, you will be aware that I am also in the position to know what is happening within it. I feel the most important part I should tell you, that when I arrived yesterday at the airport with my family I noticed someone who looked suspicious. I was followed by that person and I've had a good look round here but I can't see him around, so please be careful because I feel that Gee.Gee has put one of his boys on tailing me, but before I say anything else, what I really want to know from you, have you heard about the demise of Harry Barterloni?" Bruce was shaking his head and hearing Mark speaking of Harry's death, he was shaken and again began shaking his head and immediately asked "How did Harry die, was it an illness, or was it an accident?" It was while Bruce was asking the question that Mark looked around before replying "Well it happened two weeks ago. Harry had just flown into Los Angeles from Chicago on a business trip and was staying at the Hilton hotel at the airport and he telephoned the firm in Washington to say he had arrived in Los Angeles safely, and he also told them the name of the hotel where he was staying and he said that he felt that Gee Gee knew he was being followed by him."

Mark paused then began "When the Chief Executive heard Harry say that about Gee Gee, he told Harry to lay low and not to do anything, but to keep hidden and just watch Gee Gee and his lads from a distance." Bruce interrupted Mark "You know I can't believe that Harry is dead. We worked together on many assignments over the past few years and he was so careful and we solved many problems together and we also had a great time and became close friends". Mark began talking very softly "Bruce, we in the office know all about your friendship and connections with Harry, and that is one of the many reasons why I am here." then seeing that Bruce was upset by Harry's death Mark paused to light a cigarette then said "Would you like another drink and wait until you have recovered from the news I have just given you?" With Bruce nodding his head Mark waited a few more seconds before he ordered the drinks. While waiting for the drinks to arrive, he was looking at Bruce and he could see the news of Harry's death had upset him, but he carried on speaking "We know that Harry had arranged for the maid to give him an early call the next morning so that he could telephone you what he knew of Gee Gee movements and also the day that Gee Gee could be leaving L.A. for England, but unfortunately for us the next day, when the maid when into the bedroom to wake him, she found Harry dead." Bruce was still upset about Harry's death but Mark continued "At first his death caused a slight problem with the Hilton hotel staff together with the local police, but we soon sorted that one out with the Los Angeles. D.A and also with the hotel management. We arranged for Harry's body to be taken away to the mortuary and then we had it transferred to one of our private places where we were able to carry out an autopsy, where it was confirmed that his death was not an accident, he had in fact been poisoned."

Mark was again looking at Bruce before he began speaking and being satisfied with the look of surprise on Bruce's face, he continued speaking "Our autopsy found that Harry had been sprayed with a chemical called Fentanyl, which is a poison that is sprayed onto the bare skin and absorbed through the skin. Lucky for us the spray also went onto Harry's clothes and it was only from Harry's clothes that the C.I.S. researchers found it. It is a very potent chemical" he paused again before he carried on talking "Through our investigation we have also found that in Harry's hotel room the telephone had a micro-chip which recorded all his calls and one of those calls was to you and therefore Gee Gee knows all about your presence here and that spells trouble. Knowing that you and Harry were working together to follow Gee Gee and with Harry being dead we had to move fast to contact you and warn you to be careful. That is one reason why I couldn't telephone you, just in case the telephone in your room has been tampered with. Now my visit to you is not only to inform you of Harry's death and to warn you to be careful, but also it has been arranged for you fly to England and contact a fellow friend of yours, called David Hogarth, who we know is also working for an Australian firm in England, which has the same type of dual telecommunication company as us." Mark stopped speaking, because Bruce was still shocked not only by the news of Harry's death, but what had just been told to him about Mark being chief and he said "You know it is a very strange world we live in, because the first thing I find is you standing close to me while I'm winning a few dollars, then I learn that you and I are connected in the same kind of work."

Bruce paused before he said "And now you inform me that a very good friend of mine died recently in peculiar circumstances and then you tell me that an old flying buddy of mine called David Hogarth, whom I last saw when he was in the Australian air force, also works for a similar company as me." As he spoke Bruce could see a smile on Mark's face and he waited a few moments. Then he said "This is really strange and it must mean that we are all interested in telecommunication, Roman mythology and the writings of Shakespeare, but what bugs me most of all what is your position in all of this?" Hearing Bruce's remarks Mark began nodding his head "Yes and I'm sure you are right." then as he lit a cigarette he said. "As to

72

your last question on my position, I have just told you that I am on the committee of the company and I have some very important news for you and for you only."

Mark paused to light another cigarette and to look at some papers, then he laid a couple of them on the table with the heading of the papers towards Bruce who was smiling as Mark said "As you can see from the heading on those papers, I am the C.E of the Chicago branch and I, and my committee members, want to know certain things. Now this is very important because we must know who is connected to Gee Gee. What we do know is that Gee Gee is a crook and well connected to the Mafia but what we want to know, did you see anything of Gee Gee, or where he went before you came here to Las Vegas or do know anyone who is connected to him?" before Mark could say anything else, Bruce quickly replied "No Harry said he would telephone me if he found out anything" Mark spoke again "Oh damn, that's a pity because we must find him. We have had word from Mossad, that Gee Gee has sent something to London and we believe he could soon be flying abroad very shortly and from what we have been informed we also believe he is going to England." but before Mark could carry on talking, Bruce again interrupted him by saying "Mossad, what does that stand for?" Mark smilingly replied "Oh! Damn, haven't you been informed of anything? Mossad is an intelligence firm in Israel who we are working in close contact with. It is an old company that looks after all sorts of strange antiques and is interested in such things as Roman mythology, together with old sayings and Shakespearean writings, in fact they are doing the same work as us. But remember being Jewish they could come up with something new very quickly"

Hearing Mark's reply to his question and from the way Mark's eyes were smiling while he was talking about the firm called Mossad, he knew straight away that it must be another agency similar to the C.I.A, Bruce said "Ok I get it, You have come here to inform me that I am being moved to another place. Is that right and if it is, what is the place that I'm being sent to and when do I have to leave?" For a brief moment Mark felt sorry for Bruce and paused before he replied "I'm sorry Bruce you must leave tomorrow and please remember that it is most important that you catch that early plane flying to England tomorrow morning. All the flying arrangements have been made and you are flying on an America Airlines flight to Heathrow and everything is paid for. All you have to do is get to the airport very early and pick up your tickets from the booking desk" Bruce thought for a moment and said "You don't leave me much time to arrange things do you?"

With a huge smile on his face, Mark replied "Yes that's right because everything has been arranged for you. One thing we haven't taken care of is how you can spend some of your winnings treating those lovely air stewards on the plane. By the way I had better give you the new address of David Hogarth and don't lose it as it is the only one I have with me here". Mark withdrew from his wallet a card and gave it to Bruce, and began saying. "Bruce I am sorry that it is such a long time since we last met and this is such a brief meeting, but I am sure you will realize, especially with the death of Harry Barterloni, how serious and dangerous things are. I do assure you that you will be kept informed through David Hogarth before it gets too big and we cannot control it and hopefully we would have sorted out our other contact problems in London"

Mark then withdrew from his pocket a rather long slim brown envelope and was looking very hard at Bruce as he said "This will help you understand the reason why it is so important for you to go to London." Mark handed Bruce the envelope saying "It is important for us to have one of our top agents negotiating the work for us abroad, especially in London and therefore I do suggest that you read the contents of this letter as soon possible, because I know it will help you to understand the problem we face, but always remember please be very alert and careful" It was at that moment Mark saw on the television screens that were on the walls around them, that there had been an earthquake tremor in San Francisco. Mark stopped talking and said hurriedly to Bruce "Oh look at that" pointing to the television "There's been another big earthquake tremor in California." Both were now watching the television screen and listening to the announcer when he said "The epicenter of the earthquake is on the San Andreas Fault......" but while the announcer was saying something else, Mark spoke to Bruce saying "Bruce I'm sorry I have to leave you now because that earthquake tremor is on the San Andreas Fault and our home is quite near that fault.. I must telephone home to find out if it is as bad as the one we had before, because that was something like a 7.1 quake and that time we lost a lot things and money. I'm beginning to think that I must have had a premonition that this was going to happen because just recently I have been reading some papers that belong to our daughter who is at university and she had some homework to do on earthquakes from a Professor, called

L.W.Braille of Purdue University and his paper was about the San Andreas fault. Now I must go Bruce good luck." Bruce interrupted him saying "I'm sorry to hear about the earthquake would you like me to cancel my flight and come and help you at home clear up some of the mess?"

Mark immediately replied "Thanks Bruce for your offer but until we get home we will not know what the damage is and by the way, your flight is of more importance." Mark stopped and thought for a moment then said "I was telling you that it was on the flight here when I was reading those papers of Professor Braille about earthquakes and I read all about the faults in that area. In fact Melanie and I have discussed moving to another area, but as I'm worried I must hurry now, because if Melanie has seen or heard of the earthquake, she will be worrying and wanting me to be with her and the children and to take her home as quickly as possible. Bruce I promise, I will arrange to meet you again when you come back to America and then we can have a longer chat."

# CHAPTER 5

## (London)

It was during Bruce's flight to England and unbeknown to him, that David Hogarth had landed in England and was booking into a flat near Green Park. When Bruce's flight reached Heathrow, he hired a taxi to take him to his hotel in London and he made contact with a Mr Richard Crossley who had been to Eton College and finished his education at Trinity College, Cambridge University. The following day, in Richard Crossley's office he met with his friend, David Hogarth, and after being told that they were going to work together, they were given their instructions and were pleased to know that they were both working for the security services of the own respective countries, but under the auspices of the British Security agencies (MI6). They were instructed that their first assignment was looking for people in England associated with the American Gerry Giovanie and at the same time they were told to keep a strict surveillance on Nicholas Pitman.

They had a small office that was quite near to Victoria railway station, under the title of Data Telecommunication Co, and one morning they received a letter asking them to meet some reporters from a National newspaper. David immediately contacted Richard Crossley and asked for advice and he was told that he and Bruce must speak to the reporters, but to be very cautious. David telephoned the newspaper that had sent the letter and spoke to a Miss Nancy Oldfield and made arrangements for her to meet him and Bruce in Simpsons restaurant in the Strand. When David and Bruce arrived at Simpsons for the meeting they were surprised when Nancy introduced them to Wendy Willerby and Susan Pitman and she told them that they were all reporters, but she omitted to tell them that she was the daughter of Lord Oldfield, the owner of the Newspaper "Daily Tribune" where they all worked and Wendy was the daughter of Lord Willerbey and

Susan was the daughter of the Duke of Chardminster. After all the introductions had been exchanged the girls immediately began asking many questions, especially about the finances of the Data Telecommunication Company, but both Bruce and David managed to evade the many embarrassing questions, and Bruce even managed to answer, evading the questions of the company's finances, by eventually asking the girls to have lunch with them and it was during the lunch period, that David who was sitting next to Susan became friendly with her, and Bruce who sitting between Nancy and Wendy became friendly with Nancy Oldfield. It was after the girls had left to go back to work that Bruce said to David "Well I wonder what all that was about. Did you notice when that girl called Susan Pitman was questioning me on the company's finances how I managed to evade the question?" David was smiling as he cautiously said "Bruce you handled the situation beautifully but that lovely looking girl called Susan Pitman appears to be a cagey young woman so we must be very careful."

During the next few months, Bruce was occasionally seeing Nancy Oldfield and David had met Susan Pitman on another occasion, but it was a few months later that David telephoned Bruce to say that he had made an appointment with Susan Pitman to fly her to France for the day from Biggin Hill airport where he had hired a small twin engined aeroplane, called a Piper Navajo and was flying to an airfield near Lesquin which was just outside of Lille.

In acknowledging the call and knowing that Nicholas Pitman was Susan's cousin, Bruce said to David "Oh good because I've just made another date with Nancy Oldfield but where Susan is concerned, you ought to be careful and remember that Susan's cousin is Nicholas Pitman and he is also a very dubious character so you will have to be very cautious what you say to her, but all same buddy, have a nice trip"

When they reached Biggin Hill aerodrome Susan said "David this must be costing you a lot of money if you have hired a plane and a pilot to fly it" David was smiling as he replied "Don't worry, when I booked the plane I showed them my flying log book and they knew I that I had to have a licence to fly a plane, so there is no problem." When everything thing was settled they took off and Susan could see that David was a very competent pilot After landing at the airfield near Lesquin, which was near a small town called Douai, situated between Arras and Lille they were having a nice quiet walk round the shops, then they went into a small restaurant in one of the old streets flanking one of the quays of Douai, David was looking intently into the blue-green eyes of Susan and thinking how beautiful she looked with her dusky hair, which was nicely curling just above her eyes, and he was thinking of her and was trying very hard to make it a proper arrangement between them. It was whilst he was looking at her that he sensed she was somehow playing a part and was worrying over something, then suddenly he remembered Bruce's warning and he thought of her beauty and all the things she had said to him and he began to think his thoughts could be a fantasy of his imagination. It was while thinking of those thoughts it reminded him of a poem he had just read of William Wordsworth called the 'Phantom of delight' and as Susan was sitting there looking beautiful, he began to recite the poem out loud

> *Strange fits of Passion I have known*
> *And I will not dare to tell*
> *But in my lover's ear's alone*
> *When once to me befell…….*

Susan interrupted him saying "That is a nice piece of poem you are saying, who wrote it?" he replied "It's supposed to be one of William Wordsworth, but I feel I have not quite repeated or finished it correctly", she immediately asked "That doesn't matter, but what made you recite it now?" for a brief moment David thought of his answer then he said "Well with the sun shining through the window on to your hair and making you look so lovely, it reminded me of how mysterious you can be and that poem came to my mind" He knew that ever since they had first met 18 months ago, he felt she was a lovely girl and he would like to be serious with her. He knew that she was a newspaper reporter, but he somehow couldn't quite understand the reason why he sensed that whenever she was alone with him, she always appeared nervous as well as being very cautious with her words. For some time he had tried to fathom why she was so nervous with him and one occasion he had spoken to Bruce who had informed him that she was the daughter of the Duke of Chardminster, therefore he knew he would never try to be anything but himself and should always treat her with respect.

Somehow he sensed it was her family, together with her cousin who were influencing her thoughts about him. He knew he had to find the reason why she was always nervous and fearful whenever she was alone with him and today was no different. He therefore decided that he must act positively and not be over confident, then again he remembered Bruce's advice to be careful. He also felt if he wasn't careful, there would be a dispute between them and it would probably spoil the lovely day he had planned to spend with her.

Having eaten their meal, Susan could feel David looking intently at her, and she rather tentatively said "Why are you looking at me like that? Is there something I should know or is there something you are worried over and would like to tell me? he continued to look into her eyes and stretched his hand across the table to hold her hand and he was looking at her as he answered "No there is nothing wrong. I told you a short while ago, everything has been taken care of and the only thing left is to get the flight clearance papers signed over here before we fly back to England. Now drink your coffee and then we can have a stroll around the town, or would you like me to show you something of Lille before we fly back home?" Susan smiled and asked him "Do you think we will have enough time for you to show me a few more places around here at Douai and also in Lille?" he replied "I'm sure we can have a good try to do that" Leaving the restaurant they walked leisurely along, holding hands and looking at the fine facades and terraces in the old streets. Soon they reached the large main square dominated by the town hall. David was pointing to the belfry of the town hall, when its carillon of bells began playing a tune. As soon as the bells had stopped playing Susan said "David that was lovely how........", but before she could say anything else, he replied "Every quarter of the hour" Susan was astounded by his very quick answer, and asked "How on earth did you know I was going to ask you that question?" He looked at her and his eyes were smiling when he replied "That's easy to answer, but I don't want to disillusion you, because that is the first question everyone asks who has never been here before, and before you ask me another question, I can tell you that the bells were badly damaged during World War 2 and were repaired only a short time ago."

Susan was listening very intently with inexplicable awe while he was speaking about the old town, yet at the same time she was also very impressed with his knowledge of the wartime damage to the buildings around the place and this reminded her of what her family had told her about David so she said "Were you a pilot during the war?" David didn't answer her and pointed to the Town Hall, this made her look at the lovely structure of the Town Hall, but before she could say anything, he suddenly had a strange feeling that Mabel Flitch was beside him and was warning him of danger. Susan turned to look at him but she could see that a change had happened to him, because he was looking over his shoulder when suddenly he said "Right! Let's get a move on otherwise it will be too late and we will not be able to see the lovely sights of Lille" Susan began to think he looks a little agitated and very worried, but as he hadn't said anything to her, she kept quiet. When they were in the car they had hired, and were on their way to Lille, Susan noticed that he kept looking into the car rear mirror.

He could see a red saloon car following them and he knew it had been parked near them in the car park at Douai. He began driving a little faster and soon they were speeding past the airport of Lesquin, where they had landed earlier that morning. While all this was happening Susan was sitting in the car watching and wondering why they were speeding so fast. She could see David was concentrating very hard on his driving, then he quickly looked at her, looked again into the rear mirror and seeing the red car was still following them, he said rather meditatively "It's a pity we will not have enough time for me to show you the contemporary art museum in Lille, it really is a lovely place to see." Then he rather thoughtfully said "And I am also sorry that we will not be able to visit, what is supposed to be the largest bookshop in France." They kept going at high speed along the road and when they were nearly in Lille, he noticed that the red car was now behind a lorry and they were hidden, he quickly decided that he would drive into a car park where he knew he could park and hide the car. On reaching the car park he parked the car and he urged Susan to begin walking quickly away, but didn't say anything to her because he didn't want to upset her, but somehow he had a feeling that the red car was around somewhere and danger was near and he also had a strange feeling of Mabel Flitch being beside and guarding him. While all these feelings and thoughts were going through his mind he tried nonchalantly to point out various places of interest to Susan. She seemed to know that David was somehow acting strangely and had suppressed his agitation and she was surprised that he kept it under control while he was pointing out places of interest to her, It surprised her that she became very impressed by his knowledge of the area, but somehow she was still a little mystified by him hurrying along. Soon she was thinking and mentally saying to herself "How does he know so much about this area and why is he in such a hurry?

80

It was a short walk from the car park, and soon they were in the centre of Lille. She was looking at the exciting ancient buildings when suddenly he appeared his old self again and began pointing in the direction of the opera house and was exuberantly saying "Can you see that comic figure on the side of the wall of that building near the opera house?" Susan turned to look at the figure and said "Yes" what is it?" David replied "Well it is there because it has been entrusted with a very important role, but I think that it would be better if you and I were to come over here again in early September." He stopped talking because he could see a look of disappointment on her face when he didn't continue talking about the figure on the wall, then he continued "I know that there will be a huge fair that comes here at that time of every year and takes over the old quarter of the town, and then you with me I can explain to you what that figure really means." Susan was disappointed and said "Oh that's not being fair because I would love to know why it is there" he was now broadly smiling as he replied "Well it will give me another excuse to invite you to come over here again with me, doesn't it?" Unbeknown to Susan, he had noticed for sometime that two men had been following them and one of the men was looking very disheveled. David knew they had been following them around at a short distance behind them ever since they had left the car park and he was slightly concerned. At that moment just as Susan was about to say something he very hurriedly said to her "Come on, its time for us to go home."

His abruptness shook her and made her feel annoyed, but she never showed her feelings and rather petulantly walked quickly beside him, at the same time thinking that David was a peculiar person. Suddenly she remembered that just as she was leaving home this morning her cousin had said to her "Be very careful of David Hogarth because I have been told that he is not to be trusted" and she remembered her father saying "That is quite correct what Nicholas has said, because I have heard the same things said about him"

It was when they reached the car park, just as Susan was about to get into the car she was remembering what her father and cousin had told her and she again began to lose her composure and began to think of how David had behaved today by always walking very quickly and looking over his shoulder and appearing uneasy. It was at that moment that an idiosyncratic feeling came upon her, because she suddenly realized that she knew so little about him. All she knew about him was that he worked for a company called Data Telecommunication, which she had been told specialized in telecommunication software, and sometimes he would have to travel abroad. It was then that as he was about to put the car key in the car door, he saw standing on the other side of the car park, that rather unkempt man who had been following them. However before he could open the door of the car, or even say anything to Susan, she suddenly shouted to him in a rather agitated tone of voice "David this time I don't want to be told to wait until September, I want the truth. You know that I like you and I enjoy being in your company, but I feel you should know that my father, and some of my family resent you and at breakfast this morning when they heard that I was coming here with you today, they said I was a fool and that I should be very careful and after the way you behaved today I am beginning to believe they were right. Today you have been driving very fast and hurrying me along all day as though there wasn't a moment to lose, and I have noticed you keep looking over your shoulder as if you are expecting something was about to happen, or that someone is following you. Now tell me, are you expecting any trouble?"

Not getting a reply from him because he was looking over his shoulder at something in the distance, she paused for a moment to look at him and then behind him and then she carried on speaking, "Well are we being followed? Because I think you know I like being with you, but I hardly know anything about you, except that you appear to be a highly paid salesman working for an American company called Data Telecommunication." She paused because of the look on his face, then began speaking again "Now when I told Daddy this morning the name of that company you are with, Nicholas replied that when he had made some enquires about that company, he could find no record of it anywhere in the financial newspapers." David was shaken by her remarks, but he soon recovered his composure and began laughing. Susan didn't like him laughing and to stop him she began speaking with an unpleasant sounding voice "David! I don't want any double talk from you, all I want are some straight answers. I know you live in a very expensive flat in London and you keep going abroad for long periods. Then you never seem to want to tell me anything, or even discuss with me where you have been, or any of the people you may have met. All I know about you is the position you hold in your job and that you can fly an aeroplane, but that is not enough for me."

Susan paused again for a moment then said "Secondly I would like

82

to know more about you, your parents and your family, and where you went to school. Then I would like to know what you did before you became a salesman, and when you have told me that, I will know if my family is wrong in their thoughts about you and whether I am right to believe you are the person I believe you are." David was looking at her with a passive expression on his face he was also thinking that after having spent a nice day together with her, he would have thought she would have been in a more tractable mood and he was shaken by this unexpected outburst, but he began remembering the advice Bruce had given to him of being careful and he quickly gathered his thoughts and began thinking of the unkempt individual who was looking and watching them from the other side of the car park and he turned to face her saying "We have exactly 30 minutes before we are due to take off and fly back to England. Therefore in order for me to answer the questions you have put to me, I suggest that we retire to that small café over there, where we can sit in comfort and have a drink." He was pointing towards it, but before she could answer him, he was holding her arm and began to walk her quickly towards the café, and as they hurriedly made their way she was walking quickly beside him.

When they were inside the cafe and seated he ordered coffee and a couple of cream cakes, then facing her he said "You mentioned few moments ago that you had a problem because I go abroad quite a lot and when I come back I never discuss, or tell you where I have been, or even whom I have seen. My answer to that question is why should I tell you? What is it to do with you? Your next question was, you would like to know about my family, where I went to school and what I did before I became a salesman. Why do you want that information?" He was looking straight at her and his eyes were smiling when he said "Why should I tell you those things. Is it because your family doesn't feel that I am good enough for you or the right person to be associating with or even better still, is it that you feel that I could be seeing another girl? However I think I am right in believing that you are curious and concerned about me, because you said your family told you something about me this morning?" As he said that he had a smile on his face and she began to wonder why he had smiled, but she could feel herself blushing and was about to speak when he said "However before you answer those questions, I am going to leave you with a question and one I would like you to answer truthfully. Do you remember the day you and I first met and can you also tell me where it was?"

Susan looked at him quizzically, because his question suddenly reminded her of her school friend called Nancy Oldfield and she remembered that Nancy had previously said that Nancy's father wanted her, Susan and Wendy to interview two men and she began to remember the day very well, because it was approximately 12 months ago, when she had been told to have a newspaper interview with two men concerning a firm called Data Telecommunication which she had been previously informed was trading suspiciously. She was also remembering it was the same day when she, Nancy and Wendy Willowbey had arranged to meet at Simpsons in the Strand. She also remembered when she entered Simpson's she was surprised to see Nancy and Wendy were talking very animatedly to two men and when Susan went up to them, Nancy introduced Susan to them and she began remembering these were the two men she was to interview.

She was also remembering how handsome David had looked and she also recalled his firm handshake. She now knew he was 32 years of age and looking at him she felt that even 12 months later, that disregarding his bad habits of not telling her anything, he hadn't altered in appearance or lost any of his mannerisms. She thought she felt the same about him now as she did when they first met, but she also knew she was worried, because her father, family and cousin had warned her that he was on a different social level and was not the right person for her and he shouldn't be trusted, and also his firm's dealings was suspicious. She felt her family was wrong and she didn't understand why they had told her he was bad. However she began thinking that there could be some substance in what they had said because she was suspicious of the way David acted on occasions when they had been together and this made her feel uneasy. While she was thinking on what to say, David was also thinking she was taking a long time to answer and thought it must be because she is a daughter of a Duke, then suddenly she said "Well I have told you that some of my family, as well as my father, resent you. However I like to make my own opinions and for once I would like to feel that I am right in my viewpoint of you, and, Yes, I do remember where we first met, it was in Simpsons in the Strand and you had a friend with you, who was called Bruce Robertson."

David interrupted her "That's right, but can you recall why Bruce and I were there?" Susan's face reddened as she lied "No! Why?" David noticed that her face had reddened as she began to answer him, but he didn't say anything because just as he was about to speak, a rather scruffy looking individual walked into the café and sat at a table, on the far side of the room. Susan had also noticed that when that individual had entered the café David's expression appeared to stiffen, and she also noticed that David's eyes ceased to have laughter in them and he was giving that scruffy looking individual sidelong glances. After a few moments David looked at her and she noticed his eyes were now brighter and his expression had changed to a more happier one, then in a very quiet tone of voice that she found she had difficulty in hearing, he said, "The reason Bruce and I went to Simpsons was because we were to be interviewed by a reporter from the "Daily Tribune", which is, as you are well aware the paper owned by Lord Oldfield, but when we arrived there were two ladies who when we got talking to them introduced themselves as Nancy Oldfield and Wendy Willerbey but Bruce and I were amazed when you came in and both Nancy and Wendy said they were your friends. Then Nancy told us you were the reporter from the "Daily Tribune" who was to interview us and it was from the questions you put to us, that both Bruce and I realized that all three of you were trying to obtain some information on why our company, which is an American Company called 'Data Telecommunication', was so successful in its field of work. We told you then and I will reiterate it now, that it was a question that Bruce and I could not answer as we are not experts in business accountancy because we left the financial part of the company to our accountants. However we did answer your question about the company's thriving expertise, and we told you, rather cheekily, that we were always willing and able to travel abroad at a moments notice, because it brought the company success and we brought in good business." Susan interrupted him by saying "When are you going to let me ask you some questions?"

David ignored her question and interruption and carried on talking "Then Bruce and I decided to buy another round of drinks and invited you, Nancy and Wendy to join with us in a meal. All three of you agreed and we sat at a table in the corner and you and Nancy continued to ask us questions. Now from the way you have just spoken and addressed the situation and from what you appear to be thinking, it does appear to me that you are still uneasy with me. Am I correct in saying that? "

Looking at David's rather stern features, Susan's face again reddened and said "No it's not that at all" and she began blushing again as she said "It is because just before I left home this morning, and when my father and cousin appeared, they told me that you were not to be trusted and said that the company you work for was a bogus one and they also said you were up to something suspicious and underhanded and I wanted to find out the truth." She was now getting very agitated, because she had noticed that while she was talking, that even though David appeared to be listening to her, he kept turning his head and looking at that unkempt individual who was sitting at the table on the other side of the room. After she had finished speaking, David waited a few moments and began talking to her, but she could hardly hear him because he was speaking very quietly "You said you want to know about my parents, well they are both English. My mother was born in London and my father was born in Yorkshire and after he had served in the army for 5years, he retired and he met my mother and soon afterwards they were married and they emigrated to Australia." It was at that point she interrupted him saying "Can you speak a little louder, I'm having trouble hearing you because you are speaking very softly."

David nodded his head and in a louder voice said "They first lived in Geelong which is near Melbourne and now they live just outside of Sydney in a place called Penrith, which is not far from the Ku-Ring-Gai Chase National Park and that is a really lovely place especially in the summer time. My sister Penny married a civil engineer called Guy Williams and they have two daughters called Rachel and Nicola and they live in a lovely bungalow near the Blue Mountain National Park. Which is another lovely place to see" At that moment Susan again interrupted him saying "How old are your sister's children?" David replied "I believe Rachel is 8years and Nicola 6years of age" he frowned for moment before he carried on speaking "I think that's right, because it is some time since I have seen them and time flies so quickly." Then as though he remembered something he said with a big smile "Oh yes, what else was it you wanted to know?" Before Susan could answer him, she noticed that he again gave that unkempt individual another glance before speaking quietly again "Oh yes I remember. I believe you think that there is something mysterious about me, and you would like to know more about me. I don't know why I am going to tell you, but I will. For my schooling, I went to a state school in Sydney where I played plenty of sports, especially cricket, and even obtained a scholarship in Science, Maths and Physics. It was because I have always been interested in aeroplanes and flying, when W.W.2 was declared and Australia became involved in it, I eventually volunteered for the RAAF and was trained as a pilot and was sent to England where I flew Lancaster bombers. After the war I was demobbed and went to university and received a degree in Physics.

David paused to get his breath and then began speaking again "After W.W.2 I volunteered again for a 5 year short term for the RAAF." he paused again and looked at Susan saying "Am I boring you with all this, because you look bored stiff?" She was little taken back by that remark and became rather flustered as she replied "No No, of course not. I am finding it very interesting."

"In that case" said David "as we do have a few more minutes to spare, I forgot to tell you that when I was in the RAAF for the second time I flew jet planes, and I was posted to a couple of squadrons, before eventually joining the Australian renown Blue Streak No.151 squadron, where I met two people who were to have a great influence in my life. One was my Group commander, who was a superb person called Group Captain Gerald Thomas and the other person was my flight commander called Squadron Leader Mike Taggert."

David paused and at that moment Susan noticed that he gave that unkempt individual another quick look and glared at him, then he quietly carried on speaking, "Some time later after I had joined the squadron, Squadron Leader Mike Taggert was promoted and posted away, but sometime later I received letter informing me to report to Brisbane" looking again at the unkempt person, he carried on speaking quietly saying "You know it was amazing because the person who I had to see in Brisbane was none other than Group Captain Gerald Thomas. The outcome of that visit was, I was ordered to fly to many    places I had never even heard of before, and at that time I was enjoying that free and easy service life, but suddenly I realized that my period of service had nearly reached its termination whereby I could either sign on again and remain in the RAAF. until I had completed 25 years service, or I could resign." he paused and asked Susan "Are you bored yet and would you like me to stop?" She smiled as she replied "No I am not bored, in fact I am finding all this extremely interesting. Please continue."

He looked at his watch then said "Well to close this little story I can tell you that I chose to resign. Then much to my surprise I was told again to report to Gerald Thomas, who at the end of the interview, said that he knew of a vacancy with an American Company called Data Telecommunication, who were looking for a salesman with flying experience who had knowledge of Physics and telecommunication, and was offering a good salary, I jumped at the chance of the job, I went for the interview in America and there I was lucky, because I met Bruce Robertson, who was someone I had met when he was on an exchange from the U.S. Air Force with the RAAF and it is strangely coincident because I found out that he was working for the Data Communication company and was being posted to London. I was amazed at being told that we would work together as a team and we would be based at the company's London office. I arrived in London before Bruce, and I had managed to rent a flat near Green Park in London, then it was sometime after starting work with Bruce that we met you, Nancy Oldfield and that girl called Wendy, at Simpsons in the Strand" he paused for a moment before saying "I know that there may not be much truth in what I am about to say and it may also seem trivial to you, but I know that Bruce is keen on dating Nancy and I believe he has been seeing her, whilst you and I have been seeing each other occasionally ever since that meeting at Simpsons, whether that means much to you I don't know."

Susan again began blushing, but he continued speaking "You now have the full picture of me and as we have a few more minutes to spare, how about you telling me some of your little secrets, or of the family skeletons that are in the wardrobe?" All the time Susan was sitting there listening to David telling the story of his life and family, it was because of the free lighthearted manner in which he spoke, she was wondering whether to believe him because it made her instincts as a newspaper reporter feel, that he was relating a fictitious story of his life to her and she became doubtful of it because he had made it sound like a novel that always has a happy ending. Somehow she knew that those instincts made her realize, that though she wanted to believe him, there was something about the whole story he had related she felt was incomplete, because it didn't appear to be the truth.

She realized that while they had been going out together, his feelings towards her appeared to be getting a little stronger every time they met. Then she remembered what her family had said to her that morning and she also remembered that when she had been out with him, there had been many occasions when something unusual always happened and it was because of those incidents, she felt there was something about him that made her hesitant to reveal to him the full details of her family. While she deliberated on her reply, she noticed he kept giving the unkempt man sitting near them, quick glances, and then he noticed she was looking at him and he very quickly turned his attention towards her, and became impatient and in a rather impetuous manner said "Oh, come on. Surely you can remember your family. Or don't you want to tell me about them?"

Susan rather querulously replied "No its nothing like that at all, I was trying to formulate the correct sequence of when and how we met and to enlighten you with details that you may not know. That is of course, unless Nancy has told Bruce and he has told you, though I don't think you know that Nancy Oldfield is also a reporter for the 'Daily Tribune' and she is the youngest daughter of Lord Oldfield who owns a large newspaper company that prints the 'Daily Tribune and Wendy is the daughter of Lord Willowbey who was the Chief Executive of a Life Insurance Company." David interjected saying "Susan I am sorry to interrupt you, but Bruce hasn't told me anything at all about Nancy or Wendy and he tells me even less of what he and Nancy get up to when they go out together and he doesn't even say where they may have been, or who they may have met, and I am certain he wouldn't want me to tell him what we have been up to when we go out together." Susan quickly replied "Oh do shut up! So today you have learnt something from me haven't you? Well you may as well know, Nancy and I went to the same school of St.Margarets Boarding school for Girls, which is near Eastbourne and despite the different social levels of our families Nancy and I made a perfect couple and have been staunch friends ever since, and then we met and I got to know Wendy through her father's connection with Lord Oldfield."

All the time Susan was talking she was also getting very annoyed because she could see that David kept looking at the unkempt man who was sitting close by, and appeared to be not listening to her, but then he quickly turned to face her making it look as if he was paying attention to her while she was speaking.

Even though he was occasionally looking at that person, he was listening intently to her and was saying to himself "You are not telling me the truth about yourself, because I know you are the daughter of the Duke of Chardminster and that you are also a reporter for the "Daily Tribune" and you have a naughty cousin called Nicholas Pittman and I wonder why you are trying to hide that information from me and I also wonder what are the other things you are hiding from me?"

She had paused for a moment before she said "Have I got time to tell you a few more things?" David was nodding his head and was about to speak but before he could say anything she shook her head to stop him and continued, "My father and stepmother live in a small village called Flimwell, which is situated in the West of England. It is a lovely village with a beautiful village green and pond and it is very picturesque, especially in the summertime when the village green is aglow with all the colours of the flowers and the pond is alive with bird life – I have an older cousin who helps Nancy's brother run a small antiques business. Since that meeting in Simpsons, you know that I work for a newspaper company. I am 28 years of age and you also know that I am single and I have a flat in Burleigh Mansions near Hyde Park. Now you know all about me and as you can see, although my life has not been as exciting as yours, there are no skeletons left in my cupboard." Looking at David whose eyes appeared to be smiling, she said to him "Are you happy now that I have told you all about myself?" David had a big smile on his face and was tapping his forefinger to his lips as he said, knowing full well he wasn't speaking the truth, "Yes. If that was the truth I must believe it and now that we have opened our hearts and told each other about ourselves, perhaps we can now be nice and amicable to each other and make our way to the airport and fly home."

While they had been in the café having their talk, back in England Bruce had been out with Nancy and they met the Hon. Andrew Ashley-Grove who immediately on meeting them, showed Bruce great disrespect by ignoring him and inviting Nancy to a Gala Ball, which seemed to embarrass her, then to Andrew's amazement she looked at Bruce saying "I am very pleased to accept Andrew's invitation and you won't mind will you Bruce?" Bruce found it very hard to hide his annoyance but vowed to himself he would seek more information concerning the Hon. Ashley-Grove

In the café in France, just as David had just finished speaking he noticed that the unkempt man had risen and was leaving the café. David quickly looked around and said to Susan "Come on let's get going". When they were outside, as they were walking to their car David saw the unkempt man in a telephone kiosk speaking rather heatedly into the telephone to someone, David held on to her arm and made her walk quickly to the car. When they had reached the car, she was breathing heavily and breathlessly asked "David why the rush?" he rather impassively replied, "Quick get into the car and don't argue about it." His abrupt manner annoyed her and on their way to the airport she remained quiet. At Lesquin, David was driving very fast, and didn't even say a word to her, she was still wondering why he was in such a hurry and she also noticed that he kept looking into the rear window mirror, which made her turn her head and she could see a red car not far behind them, also going fast.

When they reached the airport, and had parked the car, she impatiently said "David is something wrong? I suppose you know you were speeding very fast along that road just now and it is a good thing the French police were not around, but why all the rush? Is it something I have said or have done, that has upset you?" Remembering the red car she had seen traveling very fast behind them she somehow knew from the tone in his voice it had altered, and he was lying when he replied "No. It wasn't anything you said. It is just that I have suddenly realized and I forgot to tell you that I have to be in the office in London early in the morning for an important meeting. So wait here, while I go to the flight control office to get clearance for our flight back to Biggin Hill." She sat in the car watching David hurrying across to the flight office, then he started to run and within a few moments later he came out and was running towards her and when he was at the car he breathlessly said "Come on get out of the car and get into the plane we are okay to take off right now." Just as their plane began to gather speed going down the runway, they saw a red car come speeding into the airport and park in the car park. However they didn't see the driver, who was called Paddy Foulds, hurriedly getting out of the car and run into the flight office, where he began asking if it was an English man and woman who had just taken off and asked if they were flying to England.

It was gradually getting dark as they flew across the French coast and Susan said "Look at the sun being shaded by those clouds" David said to her "That horizon is not looking too good because that is a Nimbostratus sky and that means rain is imminent." Susan was soon listening to David talking to flight control as they flew into the darkness of the night, and never said a word to him, because she knew he was concentrating flying the aeroplane by the instruments, however she was still very anxious to find out why David had been hurrying her around most of their time and driving very fast to the car park in Lille, then driving very fast back to the airport. Somehow she felt that it was something more nefarious and then thinking of that red car that had speeded into the airport, she was sure that the car had something to do with their hurrying, rather than David hurrying home for a meeting. Having found out that it was David and Susan who had just taken off, Paddy Foulds was soon in a telephone kiosk telephoning someone in Paris. When the phone was answered, Paddy said in English "Can I speak to Poseidon please?" A voice at the other end of the phone replied in English "I am sorry sir he is unavailable at this moment." but then another voice interrupted and said " Who is that?"

Paddy replied "There I will make a bed of roses, with a thousand posies." Hearing that phrase, the voice in Paris answered "A cap of flowers and a kirtle, embroider'd all with leaves of myrtle .Who is that?"

Paddy Foulds replied "It's Paddy Foulds here sir, I just wanted to make sure I was speaking to the right person. I am sorry to trouble you, but I missed them and though I tried I couldn't delay them and they have just taken off, flying back to Biggin Hill"

Cereberus replied "Damn and blast. This is Cereberus here. Was that young girl called Miss Pitman with him?"

"I'm not quite sure sir, but I believe so" replied Paddy Foulds.

Cereberus replied "Right. I will have to ensure that he doesn't get very far in England, so you can leave that part to me and I will see to it. I don't want Miss Pitman hurt  Now did you hear that? I don't want her hurt.  Be careful. You are to go back to England as soon as possible. Goodbye."

While that telephone conversation was taking place between Cereberus and Paddy Foulds, David and Susan who had been flying for about 20 minutes were in thick cloud and the plane was beginning to vibrate and go up and down, with rain lashing on to the fuselage, making Susan feel very scared. David quickly turned to look at her saying "Don't be frightened. They wouldn't have let us take off if it was going to be a bad storm. It's only heavy rain and being in this thick cloud it is causing atmospheric disturbance which is causing the buffeting and making the plane go up and down, but it wont be long before we are out of this cloud and then we will be flying over the English coast. Unfortunately I have been told, it will still be raining fairly heavily when we reach Biggin Hill airport"

While David and Susan were flying across the Channel, it was in a luxury flat situated in Paris, that two men, one called Mario Lorenzo who was known as Hades to his gang members, and the other, his older brother Marcus Lorenzo who was known as Poseidon, were talking to each other with three beautiful girls seated with them. A third man was standing at a cocktail bar pouring cocktails drinks into glasses. One of the girls said "Nicholas why don't you come and sit down here beside me and relax for a few moments? Nicholas Pitman who was known as Cereberus to the other two men, walked over with the drinks and as he sat down, Marcus Lorenzo who was seated nearby, and knowing of the recent telephone call Cereberus had taken, quietly said "Would you like me to arrange for someone to meet the plane at Biggin Hill?" Nicholas also replied quietly "Yes I think that would be a good idea, but I don't want my cousin hurt in any way." Marcus Lorenzo was sitting next to a girl and was holding her rather tightly but when he heard Nicholas Pitman's answer "Yes" to his question he dropped the girl rather heavily onto the couch and went into another room and telephoned England and spoke to Sandy Foulds, who is the brother of Paddy Foulds. When Marcus came back into the room he said to Nicholas "It's all been arranged for Bruno Giovanie and Charley Jaques to meet the plane at Biggin Hill airport and I have told Sandy to tell Bruno not to harm the girl and I know Bruno will follow those instructions, so let's now drink that he and Charley Jacques will ensure that David Hogarth is well and truly dealt with."

While all that telephoning had been going on, David and Susan were in the aeroplane being shaken about by the storm they had flown into, and even though she was feeling quite unwell and thinking it was a scary and frightening flight, she was very grateful listening to David calmly talking to the flight control at Biggin Hill asking them for permission to land. Soon after landing and parking the plane, they went to the flight control office and after David had cleared the formal paper work and Susan had gone to the toilet to clean herself after her air sickness, they passed through customs and walked outside to the car park.

It was as they were walking to their car that David noticed parked near their car, was a black Mercedes car with two men sitting in it watching them. As they walked towards their car, David again had that unusual feeling of Mabel Flitch being beside him. It was raining very heavily as they drove out of the airfield car park and Susan was concerned because she thought that David must be tired after flying that aeroplane and thought that she should offer to drive the car, so she said "David are you quite sure you want to drive, or would you like me to drive the car? The reason I ask you is because you flown that plane all the way from France in this awful weather and you must now be feeling very tired?" David was concentrating on his driving because the wind and driving rain was making driving very hazardous and he didn't answer her straight away before he very quietly replied " No, don't worry, I'm all right thank you. I will feel much better when I get home and have a drink of whisky and a good nights sleep" It was as they were passing a small hamlet called Leaves Green, that David was momentarily blinded by the glaring head lights reflecting from his rear mirror, coming from a car close behind them, causing him to swerve slightly. Having obtained re-control of his car he took a closer look into his rear mirror and saw that the lights were coming from a black Mercedes car and he was sure it was the same car with the two men he had seen at the airport car park.

David now had a feeling of Mabel Flitch being around him and his body began to have shivers going through it, then suddenly he had a feeling of danger that all was not well and began increasing the speed of his car, then he noticed that the black Mercedes car was also keeping close behind him, because it had also increased its speed. With both cars going fairly fast in the wet conditions, David knew that the wind and heavy rain and especially the way he was driving, was causing the spray from his car to add to the difficulty for the Mercedes car driver to see properly through his windscreen. Just before the next road junction David quickly glanced into his rear mirror and he slowed down the speed of his car and turned the car lights off, then at the junction he made a sudden left turn and began to increase the speed of his car. The sudden movement of David's car took the Mercedes driver completely by surprise and he tried to stop his car to follow him. Unfortunately, because of the windy, rainy conditions and the speed of the Mercedes car, it couldn't stop on the wet road surface and it aqua-planed sideways, hitting the curb causing the Mercedes to roll over and over on to its side, where it began sliding over the wet grassy ground, and smashed into some sturdy trees which caused it to explode and burst into flames. The crashing and the noise of the Mercedes car exploding made Susan to look back through the rear window of their car, where between the strokes of the rear window wiper, she could see by the light of the flames, that a vehicle was burning. Thinking that David had not seen, or heard the explosion, she shouted to him "My God David there's been a terrible car accident behind us. Quick we must stop and go back and to try and offer our help."

David was again driving very fast in the wet conditions, still keeping his eyes and face focused on the road in front of them, then without turning his face to look at Susan he replied "I'm sorry, I can't stop here" it was hearing her gasp that he quickly glanced at her and before saying anything he saw the look of horror on her face.

Then he said "because if I do stop I will be causing a hazard and an obstruction because the road is too narrow, and also there was no room for me to turn the car round, which is another good reason why we shouldn't stop, and remember I do have a very important works meeting, that I have to attend tomorrow morning." It was because she couldn't believe what she had just heard, it made her instincts suddenly come alive and she shouted rather venomously at him "David you are the most despicable person I have ever had the misfortune to meet and I think you are a bastard for not turning back to try and offer our help. You do realize that could have been us having an accident like that and I'm sure you would have been pleased if someone came along to help us. But no, luckily it is not us, but someone else who has met with an accident whose vehicle has caught fire and burning furiously, and all you can sodden well think of is that you have that bloody meeting you have in the morning. Good Lord you are showing me another side of your complex character and I can assure you it has not shown you in good light and I also think it's bloody wicked of you not to stop and go back."

David was fuming at her remarks and was about to answer her, but thought better of it because Susan was still shouting out at him "If we go back now, the occupants in the car may have been thrown out of the vehicle when it crashed and in need of help, and although the vehicle has burst into flames, they may be still alive." At that point he suddenly saw a small lay-by ahead and drove into it and after performing a very tight three-point turn, he managed to reverse the car and continued the journey back and all the time he was driving back towards the accident, he never uttered a word to her. A few moments later, when they were nearer to the scene and they could see the flames of the burning vehicle, he rather somberly said "You do realize don't you, it will not be a pretty sight when we get to the accident because those occupants of the car could be dead and could be unrecognizable, or they could also be very seriously injured and badly burnt and look ghastly." She was nodding her head and was not looking at him as she said "By the way how do you know it's a car?"

He didn't answer her but when they arrived at the scene of the accident, the flames from the burning car made the darkness appear bright, he noticed that Susan had put her hands to her face, so he parked his car well away from the burning vehicle at the same time advising her to stay in his car. It was still raining and he took an umbrella with him and walked to the far side of the burning car, and when he looked around he was thankful that where he had parked his car. Susan could not see him, walking further on, then he found the occupants had been thrown clear from the burning vehicle, one was lying beside a tree and the other body was in a condition of being very badly burnt and disfigured. Looking at the marks on the ground and the scorched crumbled grass, David assessed that when the car skidded on the wet surface of the road, the vehicle must have overturned and burst into flames. Approaching one of the bodies by the tree, he could see the body was not burnt and he could see a face, but it was unrecognizable and thought that it looked as though the body had been thrown clear when the car had exploded, and from the light of the flames he could see that the car had crashed into another tree and from the state of that tree the car must have exploded into flames.

Looking up and across to his car, David could see that Susan could not see him, so he quickly went through the dead man's pockets and removed some calling cards, but put a couple of them back inside the dead mans pocket. He then removed an American passport and looking at the passport photograph he saw the name of Bruno Giovanie, he knew he had seen that person somewhere before, but for the moment he couldn't remember where, then he remembered the name of Gerry Giovanie and immediately knew it was Gerry's brother.

He quickly put the passport in his own pocket, he removed the dead mans wallet and without touching the money he took a few personal papers from it. From the light of the flames of the fire he could see from among the personal papers, that they were Bearer Bonds of great value. He quickly put those in his pocket and then put the wallet and other personal papers back in the dead mans pocket. It was at that moment that Susan began frantically to call out "David I can't see you, are you all right? Are any of the occupants alive?" he called back to her, "Stay where you are. It's not a pretty sight. I'm on my way back. There's nothing more anyone can do here, they are both dead." As he was quickly walking away from the burning vehicle, he was thinking that at any moment another motorist might come along, or someone who was passing may have called the Police. Knowing he had to get away from the scene of the accident very quickly before the authorities came, he again called out very loudly "Susan stay in the car I'm on my way back now." Swiftly getting into his car, David was soon driving very quickly away from the accident. Susan was still annoyed and very curious on why he was in such a hurry, and said "Why didn't you stop and see if the Police, or the other authorities arrive?" He very hastily replied "No. I had to get away because I did mention it to you earlier, and I know you get very upset when I said that I do have that very important meeting tomorrow morning that I must go to and there is no time to waste."

Sitting beside him as they drove speedily away, Susan said "David I know this may sound awful to you, but in a way I am pleased that this accident happened this evening........." then before she could say anything else and without looking at her David sardonically said "So am I." That remark shook her and she continued to speak in a sarcastic manner "That is not a very nice thing to say is it? I certainly don't know what you mean by that remark of yours, but I can say that I have now seen another side of your character and it is one that I didn't really think existed in you. First of all, if I hadn't shouted at you and called you a beast, I doubt whether you would have stopped and turned back." He interjected "Oh yes I would and I did turn back when I had room to manoeuvre the car. I think you ought to know that I have known for some time that you didn't have many nice thoughts about me and I really hoped that today's trip might have altered your mind. Unfortunately certain events have happened to make it look bad for me." She was not put out by his interjection, and began speaking again "Then at the scene of the accident you appeared so cold and calculating, as if you have been to many types of accidents, and then when you came across one of the bodies you sounded so matter of fact. I just didn't understand your attitude, because there was no sign of remorse or sadness in your voice, in fact I thought you were just a cold hearted beast"

David again interposed and sarcastically said "Now look here. Are you accusing me of not caring? What did you want me to do give them the kiss of life?" he paused for a moment and said "Oh I know what you wanted me to say to you. You wanted me to ask you to come and have a look at a mutilated dead people, so you could take some photos and have a good photograph and a story for your paper. Didn't you?" She was shaken by the tone of his voice and the remark he made, and she quietly replied "No that is not right and it is not a nice thing to say. I didn't want to look at those people. It was because I felt so upset and saddened by those two people being killed, and you appearing as if you didn't care or showing any sign of remorse." David shrugged his shoulders and saying "One day Susan, you will realize that life is not a bed of honey and roses. Sometimes just being alive can be very hard and cruel." Immediately she cried out very loudly "There you are! I am right. Not once have you said that you feel sorry for those people who died and now you saying that life is not a bed of honey and roses and being alive can be very cruel." She paused for a brief moment before saying "Yes I agree with you when you say that living can be cruel, especially with cold-hearted people like you around and with that said I feel that we have nothing more to say to each other and I will be very glad when we reach my home." Because both of them were occupied with their own thoughts and nothing was being said between them, it was as they drove along the roads David began to recite a poem out loud.

*'Oh those Stately Homes of England*
*How beautiful they stand*
*To prove the upper classes*
*Have still the upper hand'*

Hearing him reciting that poem she remarked rather sourly "After the way you have acted today that's an unusual rhyme to say and I and I think I know what you are implying by it" David replied "Oh you do well it's by Noel Coward the British actor and songwriter and I know exactly what I am implying and it also fits the mood I am in, because I know where my society place is as well". From that moment both of them never said another word to each other and he continued driving her home in silence. When they reached her flat at Burleigh Mansions he stopped the car, Susan immediately opened the door and standing on the pavement she turned and with a hard look in her eyes rather raucously said "Goodnight and Goodbye". Then without saying anything else, or even turning to look at him, she ran up the steps leading to her door and went inside. David drove away in a bad mood, and he was deliberating about the accident and whether he could have helped in anyway. He began thinking about those men who died and what they might have done to him and he became conscious of the bearer bonds he had taken. Thinking of the crash, he knew that he had been very lucky that evening to have escaped any harm and he tried to visualize what those men had been aiming to do to him and he began to get worried, then he began to think of Tony Wright and how he had been killed. Realizing that he was not concentrating on his driving, he suddenly he found himself thinking of Mabel Flitch and a feeling she was sitting besides him, and he again began thinking of danger and looked in his rear mirror thinking he was being followed again.

At that moment however, at the scene of the accident, another car had pulled up and a man and a woman were looking at the wreck of the car, which was still burning, when suddenly they saw the bodies of the dead people. On closer examination of the bodies the man said to the woman" Don't come any nearer cos one of 'em is not a pretty sight". Not realizing that the dead man was Charley Jacques, he began going through the pockets of the other dead man and removed a calling card, then the man said to the woman "Oh my Gawd, ther'e missing, un I know darn well he 'ad some Bearer Bonds on 'im, cos I was there when they was given to 'im". Pointing to the victim's whose pockets he had been searching, the man explained in a rather despondent manner "Oh my Gawd this is Gerry Giovanie's bruver and now that's buggered everything, cos all 'ell will be let loose when 'is bruver knows." The woman who was in a rather dazed and bewildered state answered, "Why, who is he and why should all 'ell be let loose?" The man looked at her so forlornly replying, "It means that Gerry Giovanie, who is a very big man in America, will be 'opping mad when he is told of 'is bruvers dea'f, an' that there's no money to pay Gerry cos there's no Bearer Bonds to give 'im. That means he'll most likely catch the first plane from Vegas to London and that will mess up all the Triumvirate plans, un things will open up and start to 'appen in a big way." The woman replied "I don't understand. How do you know all about this and why will that dead man's bruvver be hopping mad and wannur come over here and start something big and upset the Triumvirate plans?" and then shouting out loud she added "And who the hell are the Triumvirate people anyway" The man became irritated by the woman's queries and said "Oh! shut up will yer. You've 'eard and know all about the 'Nick-Nick' gang 'ere in England? I've told yer that's the gang that specializes in bank robberies and are the big traders in antiques and drugs?" The woman was nodding her head and the man continued speaking "Well, those dead men were members of a gang that we called the 'Nick-Nick' and Bruno Giovanie was the head man of the gang and both of 'em were part of a big syndicate 'eaded by a group called the Triumvirate. Bruno was the one who was supposed to be carrying some Bearer Bonds and was, as I 'ave already told yer, the bruver of Gerry Giovanie and Gerry is one the top men of a top gang in Las Vegas, 'an they are also part of the Triumvirate group. Naw looksie I keep on telling yer, that the group is a mighty big un, an I don't wunner upset 'em any 'ow" The woman gasped and then said "Just a minute, slow down. I know you know of the 'Nick-Nick' gang, because you told me about 'em when I come to visit yer in jail. But yer also promised and swore to me that yer are not connected wiv 'em, so what's that got to do wiv' us?" The man replied "You naw all about it and 'ave heard of that big bank raid last month in Birming'am?"

Hearing him say Birmingham, the woman looked at him with a crestfallen look on her face fearing the worse and muttering "Oh Gawd. Not that million pound job?" the man replied "Yer. It was when I was in the 'Nick' I 'eard that some of 'em inside wiv ' me were planning to do somefing big. Then only yesterday I 'eard that the job was done by that gang and that some of that money had bought a load of drugs, which 'ad been flown from Las Vegas and that another load only arrived yesterdia in Essex. I was asked to 'elp 'em out by collecting from Bruno some Bearer Bonds." The man paused and pulled a handkerchief from his pocket to mop his brow.

The man waited a few seconds then began talking again "Now when 'ades, Poseidon, or Cereberus 'ear's of the death of Bruno and that there were no Bearer Bonds on 'im, they're goin' to be very upset. They will also be very worried cos they will 'ave no money to pay for that load of goods that arrived yesterday. They will also know that Gerry will be 'opping mad, not only over his bruver's death, but cos they will not 'ave the money to pay him for those goods. So I'm certain he will come over 'ere and it will most likely upset all their plans. Now do you git the set up?"

While the man was speaking, an ambulance and police arrived. Seeing the two of them standing there talking, one of the policemen approached them and said "Excuse me sir, did you witness this accident, or see what happened to the car?" The man replied "No we was just passing an' we saw the crashed car, so we stopped to see if we could 'elp." The Policeman asked "What time would that be and how long have you been here and have you touched anything?" The man replied "We got 'ere about three or four minutes ago and we 'avn't touched any 'fing." The Policeman then asked "Could I have your name and address? It's just for the record and you realize that you may be called as witnesses even though you saw nothing." The man quickly replied "Er! Yer! Yer" he was shaking his head as he looked at the woman and he began moaning and swearing at her The woman was anxiously trying to calm him down said to him "Paddy calm down the policeman is only doing his duty and wants our address. Give him our address Paddy, it won't 'urt us will it?"

Looking at his wife and then going to the policeman, the man replied "This is what you git for trying to do someone a good deed. My name is Paddy Harman and this is my wife, Maire and we live at 'The Hollies' Pickhurst Lane, Hayes. Now if you want to know why we are out so late in this bloody awful wet wever, it's cos me bruver insisted we play anuver game of cards and I lost a few bob." The policeman smiled as he said "I hope you didn't lose too much Mr.Harman. Well that's all I require from you for now. You may hear from us again later on, in order that we may wish to clear up a few details. I don't think there is anything else I can ask you, so you are free to go. Goodnight sir" When they had left the scene of the accident and were well on their way home, Maire was thinking of the scene and the questions the policeman had asked them and she naively said "Paddy I don't understand yer. Why did yer tell that policeman that our names were Harman and that we lived at that address yer gave him. Where is it anyway and why didn't yer give 'im our proper names and address? We've done nuvving wrong" Paddy looked at his wife and with a derisively grimace on his face and said "Yer a silly old faggot. What cher want me to tell 'im? That I've just flown in from France and that I'm Paddy Foulds, who has just been released from jail. If they knew I'd been in jail and it was me they were talking to, they would 'ave nicked me right away and they wouldn't be looking through those pockets and trying to find out who those two deadens were, they would 'ave been going frew my pockets. You ought to know that all copper's are bastards and rotten all the way frew." Maire replied in a feeble querulous tone of voice "I'm sorry Paddy, You are clever, I didn't fink proper like, did I?"

Paddy began to calm down a little by saying "It's all right Maire. You must remember never to trust a copper. The're all right looking after their own and yer must know by now, that all they ever fink abaat is for their frigging 'selves. Ok? Naw let's git well away before the coppers fink of something else to ask us" Maire spoke very quickly "How can you say things like that. You have a good policeman in that one who's called Roger and he is an Inspector and…….." Paddy interrupted her and disdainfully looked at her shouting "You must be stone bonkers, an bloody mad. That copper is as bent as a butcher's 'ook. Do yer know what he does for extra money. He gits 'is junior officers to nicks us for 'andling drugs and then he nicks the drugs that they take off the like's of us, an then he flogs 'em to the pimps in the street who we know are looking after the easy peasy girls"

Over in another part of London, David had reached his home and after he had parked his car he went straight into his lounge, went to a cupboard and withdrew a glass and a bottle and poured himself a large whisky. He seated himself in a comfortable chair and sat drinking and thinking, then shortly afterwards he telephoned a number and began speaking on the telephone to a person called Mr.Crossley "It's David Hogarth here Sir. I'm so sorry having to telephone you at this hour of the night, but I thought you ought to know that after I had flown to France with Susan Pitman, we were followed most of the time in France and after we had landed at Biggin Hill aerodrome we were again followed by two men in a car, but they had a serious car accident. Luckily their car, was behind and following us, then it skidded on the wet road and crashed into some trees, exploded and caught fire...er.. yes we are both alright and er,.... yes those people in the other car were both killed"

The voice at the other end of the telephone said something else, to which David replied "Okay sir I'll report to you later on in the morning Goodbye Sir", he remained for a few moments, sitting and thinking and then remembering that at the time of the accident he had felt Tony's presence about him and as he was thinking about that feeling, he felt as though Tony was standing near him. He looked around and saying out loud "Fancy thinking Tony is around me. I'm beginning to think I'm going mad." Then he thought he heard a voice say "You told me once that you believed in life after death, now what has made you change your mind." For a moment David was fully convinced he was going mentally ill and kept looking around then he thought he heard the voice say "The trouble with you mate, you have forgotten to believe in yourself and also forgotten what you said to your friend, Tony Wright, 'That with all my troubles past and with all my troubles to come I will never find a better friend' Why don't you believe that statement and believe that there is life after death and I do assure you I will look after you, So look after Kathy for me mate."

David sat there for a long time thinking of Tony and he was also seriously thinking about the state of his mend, then he went to bed and went to sleep. When he awoke in the morning he remembered hearing what he thought was Tony's voice and he laid in bed giving it plenty of thought, then realizing that it was his belief in life after death, and after giving it some more thought, he began to feel much better.

# CHAPTER 6

## (M.I.6)

David was seated in a room of a house in Duke Street Street in London, opposite him was seated Richard Crossley, the head of MI6, who was examining the Bearer Bonds and looking at the papers, passport and documents that David had just given him. While Richard was examining the Bonds and passport, David had been given some papers concerning the stealing of a Goya painting that had been stolen from the National Gallery in 1958. When Richard looked at him David said "Why do you want me to look at these papers concerning the Goya painting that was stolen in 1958?"

Richard replied "That painting was stolen a couple of years before you came to this country, and just recently it has been confirmed by one of our agents who have found the evidence of who was responsible for the theft, and what country it was eventually taken to. We also know that the painting was sold for a considerable amount of money, which went towards the work for the Triumvirate. We also know that Nicholas Pitman deals in the buying and selling of antiques and paintings, and we are certain it was he who arranged for the theft and for the painting to be sold to an American who was in Italy." As he paused speaking, Richard could see that David was becoming upset and paused again for a moment longer before he said "The team who found that the evidence are an excellent group comprising of two British, one Australian and one American. Now we in the security service also know of your relationship with Susan Pitman and it was suggested that I be the person to inform you of her family's dealings. David I know it must be hard for you hearing this news and I apologize about it. However it is the truth and we also do know that her cousin, Nicholas Pitman, is also connected to that Group called the Triumvirate." David sat there astounded with disbelieve, then Richard said "My first school was Eton College then I went Trinity College

Cambridge which was founded by Henry VIII and Trinity College has a motto *Virtus Vera Nobilitas* which means *Virtue is True Nobility* I think that you should remember that motto". David was thinking how he could reply to Richard when suddenly his thoughts were distracted by Richard saying "David I want you to explain to me exactly who you were with yesterday. Who you saw, where you went and what actually happened to cause the other car to crash last night." At that moment the telephone rang, Richard picked up the telephone and began speaking quietly then he said "Oh good! Yes. Show him up to my office will you" Within a few moments the door of the office opened and without looking at David, Richard rose from his chair and went to greet the person. When the person entered the room Richard held out his hand as he said "Welcome Sir. Good Morning. It is so nice to meet you again Wing Commander." Because he was seated facing the heavily curtain window, David could not see who had come into the room. Richard and the stranger faced each other while they shook hands. Then Richard smiled as he said "Wing Commander I think it would be nice if I were to introduce you to David Hogarth." Richard was still smiling as he said "I am led to believe that you have met him before." David rose from his chair and his face registered a great surprise as he turned to meet the person who had just entered the room.

Standing before him was Wing Commander Mike Taggert, David's old squadron leader. Offering his hand to greet him, David's face broke into a great smile as he said "Well. Well. Well. This is a small world. What on earth brings you here?" It was while they were shaking hands that Mike Taggert replied "David I think that Mr.Crossley will, in the next few minutes, be in a better position than me to explain to you everything and why I am here." While David thoughts were working on various theories and reasons why Mike Taggert was in the same room, Richard Crossley withdrew some papers from his drawer and began spreading them out and putting them on his desk, and he said to Mike Taggert "Before you say anything to David I would like to hear of your comments concerning Jim Laker's phenomenal bowling performance yesterday in the Forth Test match at Headingley. To take 9 wickets for 37 runs in the first innings then to take all 10 wickets for 53 runs making a total 19 wickets for 90 runs in a single test match is remarkable." Mike stood still for a moment before saying "Yes it was a remarkable piece of bowling by a truly remarkable spin bowler and my excuse for the

Australian cricket side is that they were certainly off colour and they didn't like the pitch which suited the English bowlers. Now that England have retained the Ashes, you wait and see what happens in two years time when they travel to Australia"

After Mike had finished talking Richard said to David "I apologize for talking about cricket but I had to show to Mike how pleased I am over England retaining the Ashes. Now to get back to our formal business, David a few moments ago I asked you to explain to me exactly what happened last night. I also want you to tell me, who was also present with you and it is all right for you to speak in front of the Wing Commander" At that point Richard held some papers, then handed them to David saying "and I want you to explain to both Wing Commander Taggert and me how this passport and these Bearer Bonds came into your possession." David was amazed at the tone of Richard voice and felt a little aggrieved of being asked to speak in front of Mike Taggert and explain how he obtained those Bearer Bonds and the passport photograph, so he petulantly replied "I did telephone you last night and gave you an explanation concerning what happened at Leaves Green, which is near Biggin Hill Secondly I feel embarrassed today, and I would also like to know why Wing Commander Taggert is here, because I know him"

Richard was looking at Mike as he answered David querulous reply. "First of all David, I think that I should inform you that Wing Commander Taggert is quite trustworthy. In fact I think you can be told that he is a very senior security person in Australia, as well as being a recruitment officer for the Australian security service, the AISS, and he also recruits potential English agents as well, and it is through Mike that you became a member and recommended for duties to this department as an agent for the British security." David turned to look at Mike and saw that Mike was smiling and nodding his head. At that point Mike turned towards Richard saying "Richard would you mind if I say something to David and ask him a question or two?" Richard replied "Be my guest and say what you like and ask as many questions as you seem fit" Mike said "First of all David, do you remember when you approached me and asked me if you could stay on in the RAAF?" David was nodding his head in agreement.

Mike continued "I told you at that time that you could only stay in the air force if you signed on for another 12 years or until you had completed 25 years service when, you heard that news you nearly resigned your commission. Now that part is true isn't it?" David was

106

nodding head as Mike continued speaking "Well I have a confession to make to you, because on the day you approached me and because of your conduct I had already pencilled you in as a potential officer in the Australian secret security organization, and that is why it was arranged for a certain young lady to suggest to you on your flight back from that island, for you to speak to Group Captain Thomas and after the interview with him, you were asked to join the AISS and you were told to apply for a position in the computer company called Data Telecommunication Company."

Mike took a deep breath before speaking again, "The reason I pencilled in your name was, because not once did you ever moan, or even speak to anyone where you had been, or of what you had been doing, nor did you ever enquire why you had been sent to those remote places you were told to fly to, and even when you had been sent to that airfield in Borneo, where we knew of the trouble that was taking place and shooting going on, especially near where you were to land. We also knew of the landing strip you were asked to fly to was in a great need of repair, yet you safely brought back your passengers, including one Kathy Goolaburra without any complaint."

Remembering Kathy, David looked at Mike in complete amazement and said "Oh yes I remember her and I also well remember that day and the flight to that airstrip in Borneo very well. The day had started very badly because I was not on flight duty that day, and I had arranged a date with a lovely girl, then when you called me and told me that Toby Clarke had gone sick, you cancelled my two days leave because you needed a pilot and I was choked. To say I was in a foul mood is no understatement, because the flight turned out to be a miserable one and the weather when I arrived near that landing strip was awful."

David saw a slight smile appear on Mike face as he said "When I saw the state of the weather, if it hadn't been for Tony Wright I would flown off to somewhere more decent. Do you mean to tell me that you knew before I left to fly, that the airstrip was as bad as it was and also that you knew all about that shooting that was going on there, yet you cancelled my leave with that lovely RAAF Officer and still asked me to fly there?" Seeing Mike was nodding his head, David continued speaking "Did you know that the weather was bad with very heavy cloud and it was raining very hard when I reached that area?" Mike again was nodding his head and smiling as David again began speaking "I looked hard where I thought the airfield could be and I

107

eventually found flare lights that I took to be a landing strip and thought it could be FIDO. When I asked their flight control for permission to land, a very weak crackling radio message across to me, as well as a faintly audible Eurasian sounding male voice, telling me that I could land. All I wanted to do was to get out of that murky darkness of cloud and stormy weather, I very quickly brought the plane round on to the right approach and landed." David stopped talking, laughed and looked at Mike before speaking again. "Luckily for me they had filled in a couple of the big holes in the runway, so I only did a couple of 'kangaroo' hops." At that moment Mike laughed and said "Only a couple of kangaroo hops?"

David had a smile on his face as he replied "Yes only a couple, but when I got out of the plane, it was shortly afterwards that Tony Wright and I could hear some sounds of gunfire going on in the distance, then I very nearly fainted through shock when I went into that badly built building and I found out it was their flight control. Then I began to doubt whether I was in the right place." Because he could see both Mike and Richard were smiling, David stopped talking, but seeing them smiling annoyed him and he decided to curb his annoyance, and carried on speaking "After introducing Tony and myself to the Eurasian person sitting at a desk in that flight office, we were told to wait and I can assure you at that moment in time, that after that long flight I was not in a very good mood. Then a few moments later a beautiful dark skinned woman appeared and spoke to us in an Australian tone of voice, saying that our passengers wouldn't be ready to leave because they hadn't arrived. I began to fume inwardly with rage because Tony and I were wet and anxious to get dry and fly away."

David again observed a smile on Mike face and said with a little more venom in his voice "We were wet because it had been raining very hard. All types of sickening thoughts began to go through my head, and I thought of the smuggling trade of people, then of drugs and of the stolen diamond trade and I said to Tony Wright that I'm not flying those people back with us, but sobering thoughts of that beautiful young girl flying back with us and with Tony's wise words going through my ......" he suddenly stopped speaking because he heard both Mike and Richard were now laughing out loud, and looking at them he lost his temper saying "All right so you both think I'm a bloody fool do you and that I'm a easily led individual as well as being an idiot?" Turning to Richard he began to swear saying "Well the pair of you can sod off" then turning to Mike with his voice changing and losing its harshness he said "Let me tell you Mike, even though I wanted to remain in the RAAF, I refused to sign on again because I was already very uneasy with a couple of the trips I had flown, and what with that bloody awful trip to that air strip in Borneo, that I found out had been built by the Japanese during the war, I began to realize that something unusual was taking place with the trips I was doing, and I did some really serious thinking as I didn't want to become embroiled in what I thought could be an illicit operation, or of becoming a embroiled in a conflict to which I had no control, it was only after Group Captain Thomas had explained a few things to me and gently persuaded me to join the AISS after my career with RAAF had finished, that I signed on and now you appear to be think that I'm a young useless individual, well okay I've heard enough and I'm leaving and I'm sorry to have been a disappointment to you." David was so annoyed that he rose from his chair and was about to depart whereupon Richard and Mike both quickly stood up in front of him and they held him by his shoulders and very strongly tried to sit him back in his chair, David was still being held by them, as Richard began saying in a very quiet but strong authoritarian voice "David calm yourself down and stop being a bloody fool, sit down and behave. We were not laughing at you, and we are not disappointed with you, we were laughing because we were imagining the weather conditions, together with the terrible predicament you were in of not knowing that everything you were doing was legal, lawful and above board."

Richard very strongly said "Now please sit there and perhaps we can explain a few things to you and to inform you of what is going to be expected of you, especially in this part of the world." David sat there and Mike turned towards him and said "David has Richard explained to you what you had been involved in whilst we were in the RAAF together, and also the type of work you have been doing since being employed by Data Telecommunication........?" Richard immediately interrupted saying "No I haven't. I'm sorry Mike, and come to think of it, I haven't even mentioned to him about his work with you in Australia. I know it is very remiss of me and I feel annoyed with myself that I haven't told David anything. However, I think you should know that I have mentioned to him that he is working for a government security agency, which is to trying to help combat the drug problem we are experiencing in this country and he and Bruce Robertson have done remarkable work tracing various outlets of those who could be supplying the drug." Mike replied in a very disconsolate manner "Oh dear. I suppose I must start at the very beginning. Well David, after you had joined 151 Squadron, I was told by Group Captain Gerald Thomas who is a very senior member of the AISS to watch and give him my opinion of you and it was he who brought you to my attention."

Mike paused for a moment because he could see that David was still upset, then Mike said "David perhaps this piece of information may cheer you up a little because Group Captain Thomas had been told of your demeanour and he asked to see your personal file that I obtained from the personnel department. At first I began to think that something was amiss and that you were in trouble. However after he had looked through your file and having seen your flying ability, he asked me to keep an eye on you. I was curious, but just before he was to leave the airfield to go to Brisbane, he took me to one side and informed me he was going around the squadrons looking for likely candidates for the AISS. I knew immediately what he meant because I was already a junior committed member." After another short pause he carried on speaking "He then advised me to test you on some special missions and to send him a report on your behavior afterwards. It was after I sent him my reports that within 12 months I received a notification from him saying that my reports on you had been confirmed by other members of the other secret services, who had also verified that you were the type of person the AISS were looking for, and that I was to prepare you for intake into this Service." David immediately interrupted saying "But I was already in the Services" Mike replied "Yes I know but that was the RAAF, and I am referring to the AISS as the Security service, because every country has its own abbreviations for it and I don't want to confuse you by referring to England's M.I.6, and the American C.I.A. and France's DGSE or their DST, or any of the other countries abbreviations, because the countries of England, America and Australia and Israel all work in close cooperation. At the moment France is outside our control, but on many occasions France has cooperated with us, and we hope they will continue to do so with the adventure we are now exploring. Have I made myself clear on those points?"

David was a little perplexed by that statement and replied "Well you haven't told me anything important yet that I hadn't all ready been told of, but I don't know if I understand the adventure you say you are now exploring."

Mike nodded his head at Richard who smiled and looked at David, then Richard began to speak in a meticulous manner saying "Just in case you are not aware, let me explain to you that the security services of every country is employed in keeping their respective country safe from all types of espionage. You might recall the recent counter-espionage trial in this country that happened not so long ago when after an eight-day trial, 5 people were found guilty of conspiring to commit breaches of the Official Secrets Act, by passing information to a potential enemy, about the Underwater Weapons Establishment work at Portland.. The Lord Chief Justice (Lord Parker) sentenced Gordon Lonsdale to 25 years in jail, and Peter Kroger and his wife Helen were each sentenced to 20 years and Harry Houghton and his fiancée Ethel Gee each sentenced to 15 years. We, who were in the Security Service in England at that time, were extremely pleased that we managed to catch those people and it was because of the disclosures during the trial, that the Heads of the Western and Commonwealth security forces met and agreed a combined operation plan on counter-espionage, this is one of the many reasons why you, and others like you, are seconded to countries to combat that espionage, and on such work as the Triumvirate gang are doing. I think that is all I want to tell you at the moment because I am sure Mike would like to continue talking to you and enlighten you with a few more details." Mike said in a very in a very stern manner "What I am about to reveal to you is of a very highly confidential matter. Remember this, because nobody must know of this adventure, except those of us in our respective Security service. The three Security Services, of the British, Australian and American have each established and confirmed that there is at this moment in time, a very big illicit operation going on by a group called the 'Triumvirate'. What nationality they are we have yet to confirm, because we are not entirely sure from what country they come from. We do know that there are three people who are at the head of that group who are known as Poseidon, Hades and Cereberus and are the leaders of that group called the Triumvirate"

Mike again paused to look at Richard who was nodding his head then he continued speaking "The reason you are being told this, is because you are associating with a young lady, whose family we have strong reasons to believe is somehow involved with, or connected to, the Triumvirate gang and the incident that occurred last night with the two deaths of those two men, in that burnt out car and of you finding and bringing to us the Bearer Bonds and the passport you found on one of those dead men who you have explained was Bruno Giovanie, highlighted our suspicions and we were….."

David really burst forth his temper on Mike as he said "Now look here Susan Pitman is a beautiful lady and yes, she is the one that I have been associating with recently and I have unofficially been informed that her cousin is supposed be involved with dubious antique dealings, and I doubt if she is involved with that. If these so called Security Services are as good as you say they are, you must already know that Susan is the youngest daughter of the Duke of Chardminster and I can hardly believe she is involved with, or even connected in such a 'cock and bull' story that you are telling me." Mike said "David will you please shut up and listen to me and let me explain a few more details." Mike was getting irritable with David interrupting him and paused for a moment.

Then he began speaking "First of all when you telephoned Richard last evening, he knew I was in France staying at the Ritz hotel near Paris on a covert mission that was connected to last night's incident, so he immediately telephoned and informed me of your telephone call and he gave me some details of the accident to the car and of the deaths of those men, hence me being here this morning. Now the one thing certain we do know, is that there is a big leak in the Special Branch of the Metropolitan Police and we have a good idea where that leak is coming from……" David again interrupted saying " Well if you do know who is doing the leaking, why don't you go in 'nab' the person who is doing it and that will stop the leak?" Mike lost his patience and said "David why is it that a sensible person like you will not obey instructions and keep quiet? I do advise you to listen and keep to memory an old adage:-

*A wise old bird lived in an oak*
*The more he saw the less he spoke*
*The less he spoke the more he heard*
*People should copy that wise old bird*

If you did listen, you would learn and hear a lot more, especially what I would like you to hear, that is if you want to continue working with us in the Security Service. Well do you?" Richard could see that both Mike and David were annoyed with each other, so he immediately rose from his chair and stood in front of David saying

"David. Please calm down and listen. I am certain that you will understand when you hear everything that we in the Security know of what is going on." Richard then turned towards Mike and said "Mike I think the time has come for us to open out to David and give him the full facts of the details we have so far."

Mike looked a little apprehensive before he spoke "David what we are going to relate to you is of a very sensitive matter and one that we feel that you can be trusted with, and I will quote you a Latin saying, ne obliviscaris, so that whatever happens, no-one must know about this. Do you understand? With a slight smile on his face David replied " I believe I have understood everything you have said so far, except for the Latin expression. You see I didn't study Latin at college, or university, so I don't know what it means." Mike replied "I used that Latin expression to bring home to you the importance of what we are going to communicate to you and by the way, 'ne obliviscaris' means 'do not forget', because unbeknown to you, when you were in the RAAF and you were selected to work for us in the Security Services, your social behaviour and personal credentials all underwent a very careful and critical examination, which I am very pleased to inform you, proved to be in your favour. Unbeknown to you the work you have done over the years for the Security Services is well appreciated. However we can now get to the present time and to your present Security work. At the moment things are getting imperative and one has to be very careful, all I ask you to do is to remember that Latin expression I used just a few moments ago, 'ne obliviscaris'. I don't want to frighten you, and we don't want to lose you, especially if it was through your own negligence by letting your heart rule your common sense. It now appears that things are beginning to warm up. We feel that last night's little episode is going to cause us a lot trouble and therefore everyone has got to be on their guard against all emergencies."

Richard interrupted by looking at Mike and saying "Mike, I think we should have a short break for a few moments, because I'm sure that David would appreciate a short break and a nice cup of coffee, as much as we would." Everyone agreed and as Richard telephoned for the coffee, David asked to be excused to go to the toilet. Immediately he had left the room Richard said "Mike I know you are in a much senior position than I am in this world of Security setup, and as David is one of your men I feel you should know that in our setup in Britain, even though he has been seconded to us from your country, he is still highly regarded and well thought off and we would not like to lose him, so I plead with you, please be careful and be a little gentle when you explain to him about Lady Susan, because it is going to be a big shock to him when he hears the facts."

Mike offered Richard a cigarette and was nodding his head then David walked back into the room. "Ah" said Mike "Would you like to drink your coffee first, or drink it while I carry on talking?" David answered "As time is getting short and it seems as though this is going to be a long session, I think I would prefer to drink my coffee while you are talking." Mike said "Just a few moments ago, when I mentioned the name of Susan Pitman, you sent out a lot of steam and became upset. Now before I mention her name again, I am going to ask you to remember that small Latin expression I used of 'ab obliviscaris', because I don't want you to forget anything I am about to impart to you. Now we have heard from our colleagues in France, called the DGSE and if you have never heard of them before, DGSE is short for Direction Generale de la Securite. They are the French top foreign intelligence service, and they have informed us that the Hon. Nicholas Pitman has been under their surveillance for some considerable time, together with another person who is connected to the English security services" David again lost his patience and interrupted Mike saying "Look I don't know what you are trying to imply, because I have only met Susan a few times and I am hoping that it will lead to better things, and I don't know whether you, or the British intelligence know that I was first introduced to her through Nancy Oldfield."

Mike looked very sternly at Richard then he slowly turned and said to David "I am going to use another Latin expression because I think the time has come for hard straight talking. Now don't interrupt me again because we don't want to come to 'a verbis ad verbera' which when translated means *from words to blows*" Mike stopped for moment to drink his coffee then looking at David said in a very tough sounding voice "You appear to have altered since we were last together and from the manner in which you are conducting yourself I am getting a little concerned over your attitude and I want a reassurance from you that before I carry on, you will stop being high handed and let me finish." Without waiting for an answer Mike carried on speaking "I want you to know what is troubling us, and by us, I mean both the Australian and British Security Services, and Richard also wants to know do you wish to resign or stay with us?"

David could see from the expression on Mike face, as well from the tone of his voice that Mike meant what he had said. Looking at Richard, David began to be very embarrassed as he said "To both of you I apologize for my outbursts. I do want to stay with you and I didn't mean what I said. You see the trouble is that I do believe Susan is a respectable person, but being influenced by her family"

Mike was nodding his head as he began to speak again "Yes she probably is and both Richard and I already know about your relationship with her and we accept your apology, but as you have now brought Susan's name into the picture I am going to tell you something that will most likely make you want to rant and rave, so be prepared for some unfortunate information. Let me explain what we, in the Security Services, have found out." Mike was looking intently at David as he said " Now is it all right for me to begin?" David nodding his head in agreement so Mike carried on speaking "Well the first thing to begin with is, can you remember that story of a few months ago, where a senior German minister went missing whilst on holiday in Corsica?" David was looking apprehensively as he replied "No. I don't remember that incident very well. All I can recall of it is what I read in the newspaper about a German diplomat who had left his wife suddenly and gone away with his girl secretary and had disappeared. At that time I didn't connect it with us, or with our work. I just thought it was a sexy diplomat who had gone off with his secretary" Mike said "Yesterday we have received news from the DGSE that the German diplomat has been staying at an hotel in Ajaccio and he had informed the hotel manager he was going sailing. The DGSE have also established that the Diplomat was last seen in Ajaccio talking to none other than, Marcus Lorenzo and the Hon Nicholas Pitman, who is as you are well aware, the cousin of Susan Pitman, who is also a great friend of Nancy Oldfield."

Mike paused to drink his coffee then said "Now before you start thinking of interrupting me again, let me inform you that we do know that both of those men buy and sell antiques, and they are also very heavily involved in the buying of drugs and drug peddling throughout the world. We know that the German diplomat is also very heavily involved in a drug peddling operation and also getting his drugs from those two individuals, however because of his matrimonial problems, we know his girl secretary is demanding from him a large a sum of money otherwise she will expose their relationship to his wife and also his illicit activities. Now before you start jumping to conclusions,

115

let me inform you that we are certain the girl secretary will be got rid of, possibly murdered, not by him but by the Triumvirate, and if possible we don't want that to happen." David interrupted at that point to say "May I ask a question? If she was murdered, why should her death have anything to do with our operations?" Mark quickly replied "It would upset us, because her death would upset our operations because she is the daughter of Lord Leslie Willerbey," David gasped when he heard that news, but Mike was still talking "who was the Chief Financial Officer with a very big Life Insurance company, who just before the company was taken over by a big foreign consortium he was made redundant, but he had made sure that his daughter was very heavily insured for life and being a close friend of Nancy Oldfield, we cannot have the international media probing into her death because it will upset all of our future programs and operations."

David gasped when he heard that Wendy Willowbey was the girl secretary, he was also amazed because he could not connect the possible death of her with his type of work.

Mike was looking, and could see by the look on David's face, that he was shocked by the news he had just heard.

Mike continued "By the look on your face David, I believe you are shaken and still a little mystified by my last remarks concerning Wendy Willerbey. Well, the Security forces suspect she is trying to blackmail the German diplomat, because she doesn't trust him and knows of his dubious connections with the Triumvirate, and as Nicholas Pitman is the leader of the London part of the Triumvirate group and is also romantically involved with her, it is because of that connection, that we feel it could lead to a big split between the three big men who we know are in charge of that group." David interrupted Mark saying "Mark, I'm very sorry but up to a few moments ago I thought I was beginning to understand what you were leading up to, but now I am confused and I feel I need a little more information on how last nights incident has anything to do with what you are saying." Mark could see the logic in what David was asking and said "I think it would be better if Richard should now brief you on last nights incidents and its connections to what I am have been saying." All the time that Mark had been talking Richard Crossley had been looking through a mass of files relating to the Triumvirate and hearing Mark mention his name he looked up and said "Sorry Mark I was busy looking at the files and I do apologize to you David because up to now you have been told that we are only interested in the drug traffic that is going on in this country, and I again apologize, because it is more complicated than that. It has come to the knowledge of the three major security forces involved in this operation, that the money from the drugs trade is going towards a much bigger and more terrifying trade of buying nuclear weapons for foreign countries." David was stunned hearing that statement and was about to ask a question when Richard began talking again "David I am sure that you have many questions you would like to ask, but I do feel that Mike, being a senior member of the Australian security, should enlighten you on the details, of what both the British and Australian securities have learnt of the Triumvirate operation"

Mike was sitting there just looking at Richard and David when suddenly he heard his mobile telephone ringing. Mike apologized to Richard and said "I know this call is urgent so will you excuse me if I take it here now". Withdrawing the mobile from his pocket he began talking and listening, then he said "Right leave it with me. What airport is he leaving from and what time does that plane leave. Right. I've got the info, and many thanks for the news and for being in touch with us. Be careful and mind how you go." Mike switched the mobile off then he looked at Richard and said "That was one of our men in America who have been tailing Gerry Giovanie." Richard could see from the way Mike had spoken that all was not well and said "Is everything all right with our observations of covering Gerry Giovanie." Mike nodded his head as he said "Yes. Our agent said that Gee Gee is leaving Las Vegas on the 10pm flight today for Heathrow London and he also said that the C.I.A. know that Gee Gee has killed one of their C.I.A. agents who was tailing him, but because they didn't have enough proof that he actually did it, they couldn't arrest him so they followed him from Los Angeles to Las Vegas. It now appears that the C.I.A. have made a bit of a mess up over that killing of their man, because our agents over there said, they have heard that Gee Gee is very upset over the death of his brother and the C.I.A. have warned our agents that Gee Gee knows he is being followed."

Richard went to a large filing cabinet and withdrew some papers and a revolver and handed them to Mike then turning to David, Mike said " I'm afraid that the rest of what I was going to tell you will have to wait until you have a further meeting with us." Then turning towards Richard who was lighting a cigarette, Mike said "It takes approximately 6 hours to fly from Las Vegas to Heathrow direct, so if Gee Gee leaves at 10pm, that is 4pm over here and it is a 6 hours flight that is if the flight doesn't encounter bad weather conditions, it will mean that somewhere between 10 and 11pm tonight, the plane should be landing at Heathrow. David we want you to be there to watch where he goes and whom he talks to. Do not let him see you so be very careful and I think it would be a good idea if you have someone else with you. I think it would be ideal if that someone is one of our top agents and who has worked for us for some time and knows how to perform her duties." Mike paused to look at a photograph then said "Now here is the latest photograph we have of Gee Gee," handing the photograph to David, then he said "take it with you and be careful. He is very dangerous, and I have been told he is very upset and a very tough nut to crack." As David looked at the photograph Mike handed him the gun and remarked "Yes he does look a tough nut but at the same time he also looks a handsome person and I can see that we might have some trouble from him, so we will have to be wary." Before David could say anything else Richard said "David. You have a gun but we don't want any shooting or trouble at all at the airport. What we want to know who meets GeeGee, and for you to tail him and inform us where he is staying and if possible who he has with him." Mark spoke "Richard I think it would be a good idea if David could now meet the person who we feel should be with him. David I do believe you know and have seen this young lady before who is in the next room." Richard went to a door to the next room. David was astounded to see Kathy Goolaburra walk into their room and was even more amazed when Richard said "David I would like you to meet your partner for this evening. Kathy this is David Hogarth, meet your companion for tonight's work." David was still shaken by the beautiful person standing before him, who was holding out her hand and smiling as she shook his hand. Feeling the strength of her handshake, he somehow knew that tonight's work was going to be one of great joy. With a big smile on his face and turning to Mike and Richard he said "At first I wasn't looking forward to the work tonight but I can say that with Kathy's appearance and what we have to do, I am going to enjoy working with her and I hope she will enjoy working with me." She looked at him and with a lovely smile said "By the looks of it and when I know what the work will be, I might be able to say that I too will enjoy working with you, but I feel you ought to know that I'm not an easy person to work with and I'm no pushover" Richard and Mike were both nodding their heads and laughing at her remark and as they looked at each other they knew immediately they had made a good match for Kathy and David to work together. Mike said "Right I think first all we should brief Kathy what her duties are, and what the dangers could be, and then I feel that we should all go to lunch to discuss details and to ensure that we have studied all the angles so that we will be ready for any emergency, and Kathy I am sure you will probably have realized that David already knows that if there is an emergency you both have our permission to ring us direct on our private phone number if there is any danger to either of you."

After the lunch break and going back to the office, where they were further briefed, it was later on that night when they were driving along the M4 towards Heathrow, that Kathy said "I think it would be a good idea if we told each other what has happened since we last met and if we have any love partners." At first David was amazed at her openness and of the way she had phrased the question, after giving it a little thought he said "Well I suppose I might as well start by saying that I have been meeting a young lady, but we are not engaged, just going out together. Her name is Susan Pitman and she is the youngest daughter of the Duke of Charminster. By telling you about her I don't want you to start getting ideas that I'm a social climber, because I'm not. I met her by what I believed was a chance meeting about 18 months ago, but since then I have found out it wasn't a chance meeting" He stopped talking, looked briefly at her then began talking again "My pal Bruce Robertson and I had just arrived in Britain and after a couple of months we received a letter asking us to meet some reporters and after Richard had given us the clearance to proceed, Bruce and I had a meeting in Simpsons to meet Nancy Oldfield, a reporter who is the daughter of the owner of the 'Daily Tribune, and her friend Wendy Willowbey to discuss why the firm we work for, called Data Telecommunications, had such good profits but didn't show in their company reports how the profits were made. After being introduced to those two girls we were also introduced to Susan Pitman and I have since found out that she is also a part time reporter with the 'Daily Tribune' and her cousin Nicholas Pitman is also involved in the illegal operation that you and I are combating against. Last week I arranged to meet Susan and I hired a plane and took her to France for a day out and when we arrived back in England at Biggin Hill, we were on our way home and the car behind us crashed and because I couldn't turn our car around or stop immediately to offer any help, she became very upset and we had words and when we arrived at her home she said goodnight and goodbye and I haven't heard, or seen her since".

While David paused for breath, Kathy was very quick to say "David please forgive me, I'm not prying, I'm grateful for you telling me of the relationship between you and Susan and having seen her, I do understand how you feel about her. Perhaps I am being too critical and I don't want you misunderstanding what I am about to say, however I can understand why she hasn't spoken or contacted you again, because I believe it is her breeding and she feels she is on a higher social standing than you, and has possibly been told by her family that she must not associate with a person below their standard. There is also the fact that because she doesn't understand the type of work you do, she might also feel that you are being dishonest, but what I cannot understand why her cousin's illegal work has anything to do with her. Surely she cannot be held responsible for any of his bad doings." David understood Kathy's logical thinking and said "I agree with you, however unfortunately the trouble is bigger than what I have told you, but there again I don't know what you have been told about our whole operation or how long you have been over here." Kathy replied "I have been with M.I.6 for some time. I came over to England shortly after informing you of Tony Wright's death and I have been working with M.I.6 ever since, and Richard Crossley is my boss as well as yours, but I think I should first tell you that I am still unmarried and I have no boyfriend."

Kathy was smiling "David I think you should also know that after Tony had left the RAAF, when ever it was possible he and I were seeing each other, and his death disturbed me very much. However since I have been in England I have, for the past three years, been investigating the Police in this country because I have been informed there is someone in their organization, who informs the Triumvirate of all of our moves. Up to now I, and several others of our staff have been unable to trace the leak, but just recently we now think we have a good lead, in so far that we are certain it is lower down the chain of command within the police force. When I reported to Richard Crossley today to tell him of our good news. I arrived at the office early, because I knew you were waiting outside to go in and see him. It was after my conversation with Richard that I was told to wait in the other room to his office, that is why I was there this morning, and being there I suppose knowing that you and I knew each other very well I was the first person Mike Taggert thought of, who could be your partner tonight."

They both laughed at her suggestion and suddenly they realized they were approaching Heathrow and began to speak about their tactics and where they should stand. After much discussion Kathy suggested that they act as a loving couple so that he could watch over her shoulder while she could watch over his. With this form strategy they positioned themselves to view the passengers coming from customs exit. Watching the passengers going home from their holidays, with some of the couples coming off the aeroplanes looking very rich and happy David said "Kathy wouldn't you like to be like one of those rich people just jetting around the world with no worries?" but before she could answer he began to hum a tune. When Kathy heard him humming the tune she said "David are there any words to that tune you are humming," he replied "Yes I have forgot most of them, so I only know a few. Would you like to hear them?" Kathy replied "Yes it will take some of the boredom of this job away" David again began to hum and then quietly sing:-

*It's the same the whole world over*
*It's the poor wot gets the blame*
*It's the rich wot gets the pleasure*
*Ain't it all a blinking shame?*

"Oh David" cried out Kathy "That's not very nice is it? It reminds me of when I was very young and we were poor. Can't you think of something much happier to sing?" Just as David was going to answer her he pulled her towards him and cuddled her and then he couldn't resist the temptation of kissing her and that kiss certainly took her by surprise and she began to respond. Kathy whispered "David I know we are supposed to be acting as lovers but there's no need for you to go any further than acting, by which I mean not performing." While Kathy was speaking, David was still cuddling her and whispered "Watch out he's just coming out of the Nothing to Declare exit". As David spoke he was watching Gerry Giovanie (Gee Gee) and two other men walking beside him, then suddenly David stiffened, because he saw Gee Gee go up to three women who were waiting at the end of the exit, then he recognized Nancy Oldfield who went up to Gee Gee and kissed him.

Then he saw Gee Gee, who was now smiling, introduce the other men and he gasped when he saw and recognized Jeannette Pitman go up to Gerry Giovanie and kiss him and Susan Pitman went to one of the other men and kissed him, all this happened while Nancy Oldfield

121

was kissing the other man. David mind was in such a state and he kept whispering to Kathy "I don't believe it. I don't believe it." She interrupted him saying "What is the matter, what is it you don't believe. If you let go of me perhaps I can have look and probably tell you the answer to your query." It was at that moment that Susan Pitman turned her head and looked in their direction and saw David and Kathy with their arms around each other then seeing Kathy disengaging her embrace from David and looking in her direction, Susan hurriedly walked away. Kathy looked at David and said "So much for that then. We know who those three women are and we know they are with Gee Gee and two other men, now all we have to do is to follow them and see what they are up to and where they are heading and try and find out who the other two men are."

As they walked to their car Kathy could tell by David's dejected walk and by the tone in his voice he was not happy with what he had seen, and it was when they were in the car and following Gee Gee and his two friends with the three women, that she said "David earlier I did tell you that I was not married. What I didn't tell you I was engaged once and one evening after I had a hectic day tailing a suspect and losing sight of him I went to his house and having the key to his front door I went in., then I went into his bedroom there was my boyfriend naked in bed with a woman. I can tell you from that moment I lost all faith and trust in men." It was because of the look on David's face that she paused for a moment then said "David don't look so shocked, the reason for me telling you this is because I was told of your relationship with Susan Pitman and I am telling you that you must not lose faith in yourself, or lose your trust in everyone, because everyone is not like that and Susan must have had a good reason for kissing Gerry Giovanie's friend. You must know her better than any of us and have a good idea why she did that?" David immediately replied "No I have no idea at all, I wish I did, because the only thing I can think of and remember is what she finally said to me the other evening so it must be her social upbringing"

Listening to Kathy speaking, David began to realize that she was a very wise woman who possessed sense and logic and he began to let his emotions calm down, He then began to concentrate on his driving and follow behind the big car that had Gee Gee, his friends and the three ladies inside. They eventually came into Trafalgar Square, David made sure that he and Kathy stayed a short distance behind the car, before it turned into the small turning leading to the Savoy Hotel.

David drove past the Savoy Hotel and parked the car a little further on and they waited approximately 15 minutes before going into the hotel. On approaching the desk they asked the desk porter if a Miss Susan Pitman had booked a room, the desk porter looked at them suspiciously and asked who they were, Very quickly David replied pointing to Kathy "I'm her brother-in-law and my wife here is her sister and all we wanted to know that she has booked safely into this hotel." The desk porter smiled at them and showed them the signature book and they saw that the two men had booked one room.

Then they had a surprise, because they saw that Jeannette and GeeGee had booked a double room and Susan and Nancy had booked another double room, and then Kathy looked at the signatures of the other two men. On the way out of the hotel David asked Kathy if she had noticed the names of the signatures of the other men she said "I did look at signatures and I think one began with a letter M for his Christian name and his surname began with the letter L, but I'm sorry I couldn't distinguish the rest of it and I couldn't distinguish the names of the other men" David began to look worried and said "I know it is late but I think it would be a good idea if we telephoned Richard or Mark." Kathy said "David it is very late and I think we should wait until the morning to inform them of the other men." They stopped near their car before David answered and said "I've made my mind up and I'm telephoning Richard to inform him of the other men, because he might know from our description of them who they are." After telephoning and speaking to Richard, David stood still for a few moments and said "Kathy, it appears you were right by saying we should wait until morning, because Richard says that we have to wait until he has spoken to Mark Taggert."

However very shortly afterwards David's mobile began to ring and when he answered it he said "Kathy that was Richard, it appears that one of those men could be Mario Lorenzo who is known to the Security Services as Hades, and Richard said that Mark now believes that with those two men being together things are going to get hotter and we have got to be here at dawn and try to follow them." David began to look at his wristwatch and saw the time and then noticing that it was foggy he said "It's getting very foggy. What part of London is your flat or house?" she replied "I have a flat at Welling in South London". David looked at her and said "As it's very late and foggy I will take you home in the car" she tried protesting, but due to the thick fog he wouldn't listen to her protestations. Most of the way she was protesting to him to drive slowly because of the fogging conditions otherwise he might have a crash and then he would be in trouble with Mike Taggert and she was also telling him that it was a long way to her house. Although David was driving faster than Kathy liked, he was driving very carefully and he said "Mike will probably moan at me again if I crash and I don't want to crash. Talking of crashing, reminds me of the time I had a nice rich girl in my car and someone was chasing me, and after the car behind had crashed, all she did was moan at me for not stopping to help the people chasing me and I did go an try and help them but it was too late. Any way don't let us talk about us crashing, let us talk about the rich people in this world and say what a rotten lot they are. Oh by the way I have remembered a few more words to that little song I sang to you the other evening." While he drove along the road he began to sing

*"She was poor but she was honest, victim of a rich man's game,*
*First he loved her then he left her, and she lost her maiden name.*
*It's the same the whole world over, it's the poor wot gets the blame,*
*It's the rich wot gets the pleasure, ain't it all a blinking shame"*

Kathy said "I still don't like it because as I said the other evening, it reminds me of my childhood when we were very poor and that part of the song that says the poor always gets the blame, reminded me of the white girls trying to take advantage of me at the school I went to before I graduated to university." She stopped talking because she was beginning to be very worried about David and his singing and the manner by which he was driving the car. Then she thought it might be a good idea when they arrive at her house that she invites him inside for a rest and a cup of tea. Outside her house Kathy surprised David by saying "David it is now 1.30am and I do know where you live and it is a long way to go in these foggy conditions and you will not be able to be at your place before 3.00am and we have to be back at the hotel by at least 6.30am before they get up, so I think it would be better if you came into my home and slept here. But before you get any ideas, you are sleeping on the bed couch I have and I will sleep by myself in my bedroom." Knowing the fog was very thick David realized he had a long way to go home and that due to the state of the weather it was a good suggestion. Kathy woke him at 5.00am with a cup of tea. At first he forgot where he was, but as he was drinking the tea he looked at his watch and said to her "You couldn't have had much sleep last night" she replied "Yes I did. You have forgotten that despite your singing, I did fall asleep on the way home from the hotel." He didn't disagree with her but as he looked at her he was thinking what a beautiful and very unusual woman she was and he began comparing her with Susan. It was while he was washing and shaving he was thinking of Kathy and thought she had a strong willed character and he began to see her in a different light. He knew she was good looking and she had a nice trim figure and he thought that when she met the right man she would make that person a very good wife.

He was very quiet in the car on the way to the Savoy hotel, and as they went along, every now and again he looked at Kathy and noticed the nice dark skinned features of her face, and the way her hair was combed in a very neat way, then as he looked at her he began to see the difference between her and Susan. The more he thought about it, he realized that it was due to Susan's family social position, that she had a different personality and mannerism than Kathy. While thinking of Susan he remembered how badly she had behaved on the evening of the crash, and he began to visualize Kathy being with him on that occasion and he couldn't imagine her acting the way Susan did. With those thoughts going through his mind he began losing his bad mood and then he began remembering the way Kathy had acted when they had been together in Australia. Turning to her he said nicely " Thanks for letting me stay at your place last night I'm sure it was the right thing to do, because I would have been very tired if I had gone home to my place." At first she thought he was being sarcastic, but as he continued talking she could tell by the tone in his voice that he meant what he was saying, and so laughingly she replied "That's all right David I thought it was only right to help you, but I didn't want you to think that I had any other motive". He was laughing with her when they reached the hotel and they had discreetly parked the car, it was then that they both felt that a much better relationship had begun between them. David immediately said "I think it would better if one of us was at the Strand main entrance of the Hotel and the other one near the rear entrance which leads to the Embankment."

Kathy readily said "If you like I will go to the rear entrance, I have a mobile and we can keep in contact if anything transpires." It was after waiting nearly an hour when David's mobile rang and Kathy was talking to him saying "I haven't seen them come out yet, have you seen anyone?" She could tell by the tone of David's voice that he was unhappy with the situation.

Earlier that morning, a telephone rang in a flat in the Savoy hotel and Mario Lorenzo awakened and very moodily answered the phone, "Yes who is it" on hearing it was his brother he jumped out of bed, and began walking up and down while Marcus discussed details of what had happened at the crash at Leaves Green and telling Mario how the Bonds were lost. Mario was looking through the window across the river Thames and began shouting to his brother "I don't care what happened to those two men I want those bonds and we have to find them and I have a good idea how we can find them. Last night I met the mother and daughter of that duke. I know they are related to that playboy you call Hades. Well I don't trust him cos' he's heavily in debt." He paused for a moment, then watching a small tug towing some barges down the river he said "and you and I know that he is playing along with us to get out of debt by selling those antiques and drugs. I'll have to talk you later about him when I think of who can help us deal with him" Putting the telephone down he spoke to Gee Gee who had telephoned someone in Stepney on his mobile phone. 10minutes later Mario left the hotel in a car driven by one of the members of the gang who Gee Gee had telephoned. When Mario left the hotel he left a note for Nancy telling her he had to go to a meeting but would be telephoning her later that day and stated that he would like to meet her and would she bring Susan with her because someone else liked her very much. At the breakfast table Jeannette, Nancy and Susan were surprised that Mario had not arrived at their table, but when Gee Gee arrived, he looked very handsome and sat next to Jeannette. While they were eating their breakfast Nancy noticed that Gee Gee was being very friendly towards Jeannette and she could see that Jeannette was enjoying the attention he was paying to her. It was during the meal that Gee Gee gave Nancy the note Mario had left. After reading it, Nancy looked at Susan and said "It's from Mario and he has said he had to go to an early meeting with someone. He says he would like us to meet him and Gerry sometime later today at the "Daily Tribune" office and he would be telephoning my father to tell him we were going to be there." Gee Gee turned to Jeanette and said "I have to go to the cemetery now and after I have attended my brother's funeral I will be pleased to accept your invitation to visit your home in the country." Knowing that Jeanette and GeeGee had shared the same room, neither Susan or Nancy was surprised to hear GeeGee speaking on intimate to Jeanette.

After leaving Jeanette and GeeGee in the hotel where he was still arranging to meet her at her home in the village of Flimwell, Susan and Nancy shortly afterwards booked out and ordered a taxi and left for Fleet Street and the 'Daily Tribune' office. It was as David was speaking to Kathy on the mobile that he saw a vehicle leaving and thought he recognized Susan in a taxi. David immediately interrupted her saying "Hell I think I have just see Nancy and Susan leaving the hotel in a taxi.

He stopped talking and thought for a moment then said "Blast we are going to miss them, but wait a minute I believe they appear as though they are going in the direction of Fleet Street, now I wonder if they are going to the 'Daily Tribune' to see Nancy's Father?" Within a very few minutes David had collected his car and was meeting Kathy behind the Savoy hotel on the Embankment. They telephoned Richard Crossley who told them not to go to Fleet Street but to report back to his office. When they arrived, they were immediately told to go into his office and on entering the room they found Mike Taggert already there, but it was the tension within the room that surprised both Kathy and David. The first to speak was Richard saying "First of all thank you for getting here so quickly. Mike has had a message from Abraham Filligoti that has altered all of our plans." Richard turning to Mike said "Mike I hope you don't mind but I think it would be better if you told them the news," but before Mike could say anything David said "Richard I think better if we know who is this chap called Abraham Filligoti? I've never heard of him before and where does he fit in to our organization?" Richard replied "Mike will tell you all you want know. Now don't start an get impatient again, just sit down and listen." Mike light a cigarette and began smoking and waited a few moments.

He sat there just thinking then he said "So you want to know who Abraham Fillgoti is, well he is the head of Mossad which is the secret service in Israel and while I am telling you about that one, I think you should also be aware of the DGSE (Generale de la Securite Exterieure), which is the French foreign intelligence service and they have a very good agent called Henri Fouchard who could be contacting you at any time, because he has your telephone number, however he may also contact you through the DST (Direction de la Surveillance du Territoire) which is the French counter intelligence agency. I think it would be a good idea if both of you have all their telephone numbers in your possession." Then looking at Richard he said "Richard will you prepare those telephone numbers for them."

Mike paused again as he also gave David some papers who started to look at them, then when Mike began speaking to him he said "David I think it would be better for all of us here, if you and Kathy looked at those papers when Richard and I have finished talking to you. We have a very busy schedule today and both Richard and I want to get through it without too much delay. Now as you have just heard, you heard me mention the name of Abraham Filligoti I had a message from him with the news that he has definite proof that Nicholas Pitman and Gerry Giovanie are flying very shortly to South America to hasten some drug exports. We believe this is because the Triumvirate group is very short of money. Filligoti says the reason Nicholas Pitman is going because he is in charge of that part of the trade and Mossad has heard that Poseidon, who is as you know Marcus Lorenzo, has ordered that Nicholas Pitman must be there to ensure that everything goes smoothly with the drug supply and the reason Gerry Giovannie is going, is to incorporate more of the local men to assist in the packing of the drugs and also to help in the eventual transport of them to Europe and if there are any holdups he will have the man power and weapons to deal with it and also, Mario Lorenzo is going to Mexico City, why he is going there, Filligoti is not sure, but we feel it must be to do with the transportation of the goods"

Mike stopped talking for a few moments while Richard said to David and Kathy "What you have heard from Mike means that a dangerous event is going to take place and we have spoken with all the people of the National securities concerned, and they are willing to assist us over there in South America, to try to prevent the supply of drugs. We know that each security is sending at least four people, and with a secret American back-up, our manpower should be sufficient. What we also want you to know is, as you are both really part of the Australian security who have been seconded and attached to the British security, I wish to add, and I am allowed to tell you, that you are both considered two of our top agents. Now having told you that small piece of information, are you both prepared to go with two other British agents, or would you prefer to remain here?" Kathy looked at David and with a brief smile upon their faces Kathy said "I believe I'm right in thinking that David would like to go and so would I." Mike and Richard were both laughing as one of them said "I lost. I owe you a fiver"

Richard then turned to Kathy and said "Kathy before everything is arranged for you to leave, we must know. Have you found out who that person is in the police force who is giving the information to the Triumvirate group?"

Kathy said "Yes Richard we have, and we believe the information to be true and the evidence in my report will prove to be Harold Phillips a police Chief Superintendent. We know that he is heavily in debt due to his expensive living and we also know he is in the pay of the drug barons here in London. We have also discovered and also know that Nicholas Pitman is a close friend of his and he is connected." Hearing that news pleased Richard who said "Well done Kathy we seem to be making some further progress and let's hope the progress continues in South America." Mike said to David and Kathy "Well done Kathy but I think that you two should meet the two agents who are going with you and I feel that tomorrow would be a good time for you to meet them. Therefore you can have tomorrow as a day off duty, but report here at around ten in the morning."

The following day David had arranged to meet Kathy early that morning and over a cup of coffee they related to each other about the times they had in Australia and by the time they reached Richard Crossley's office they were on very intimate terms with each other. When they were in the office and just before the other two agents arrived, Richard said to Kathy "Would you like to hear what we have found relating to your verbal report to us yesterday on the police." she very seriously and nervously said "Yes I think I would like to know ......" but before she could carry on speaking, Richard interrupted her by saying "Kathy you have performed a wonderful job, and because of your report we have apprehended a member of our own M.I.6 staff. The Honorable Andrew Ashley-Grove who has been a member and one we trusted for many years, but it looks that through his excessive drinking and life style he is now facing serious charges of relaying official secrets that could be useful to an enemy of our country. Kathy, we have also arrested and charged Harold Phillips early this morning. All Mike and I can say to you is, we offer you our sincere thanks to you and say well done and we hope you do well in South America, and by the way we have asked Bruce Robertson to carry on with your type of work while you are away."

Mike then said "Richard having mentioned South America, it reminded me that we have their air tickets." Then speaking to David and Kathy he said "You will leave for Brazil from Heathrow, two days from now at 10am and arrive at Rio de Janeiro at 4pm their time, now that means it's a 10 hour flight. There is a flight to Porto Alegre two hours after you land, but I think it would be advisable for Richard to pre-book a hotel for you in Rio and then the following day you can catch the 10am flight from Rio to Porto Alegre where you arrive there at 12am fresh and ready to proceed. You can then collect the car, which has been pre-booked for you in Porto Alegre, and proceed to Tupancireta,which is the area where we know the drugs are being prepared to be dispatched to Porto Alegre, where a ship will be waiting to bring them to Europe." After listening to Mike giving them the details of their expected journey Kathy asked "You mentioned Tupancireta. Where is that in Brazil and how far is it from Porto Alegre, and if it is a long journey by car where are we expected to sleep when we get to Tupancireta?" Mike replied "That is a very good question Kathy and I can tell you it is approximately 100 miles. So you should be able to do that journey in approximately 5 hours allowing for the road conditions. We will not pre-book your hotel in Tupancireta but we do know that there are a number small hotels, which I am sure will suit all of you."

Richard then spoke "Mike I think we should now explain to them that their main role is to apprehend all the drug smugglers and let the Brazilian authorities take control of the drugs." Mike said "Yes that is right I should have informed you that it is arranged that the members of the gang who are Brazilians will be turned over to the Brazilian police and all the other countries in this big operation will apprehend their own people of the gang then taken take into custody. Now are there any other questions you wish to ask." David asked "Who are the other two members who are coming with us and have they been briefed on this operation? Richard quickly replied "They are coming here at 12.00 today to get their orders and they will be briefed and they will meet you here in two days time and you will all be transported by our staff to Heathrow in time to catch your plane. They are two very good agents who having worked with Kathy on the police operation and are well known to her, they are Bob Statham and Kevin Mitchell." Kathy was smiling and nodding her head at David when she heard their names and said "Richard may I ask you to accept my thanks, because having worked with those two for a some time, I do know that they are both excellent people to work with and I feel a lot better knowing that they are coming with David and me." Richard replied "Excellent. Lets hope that you succeed and come home safe after an excellent operation"

Two days later in Richard Crossley's office Richard said to David "David I would like to introduce Bob Statham and Kevin Mitchell to you and you have already been told by Kathy that they are two good people to have on your team so I will leave you to inform them of what is expected of your team" then looking at Kathy he said "I'm sorry Kathy I should have introduced you to them but I knew you knew them and therefore I wish you all well on your trip to Brazil"

While Richard had been talking to Kathy, David had been given a file of papers to read and amongst them was a copy of the days "*Daily Telegraph*".

Glancing at some of the news he read that there was a communist threat in the Formosa Strait that was getting progressively more serious and he said to Richard "Will the Communist uprising in this area of Manilla have anything to do with our operation?" Richard quickly looked at him and answered "No not all, it is an all Chinese affair and we have only been informed of it because the Americans are concerned that an attack against Formosa would be extremely dangerous." David was only partially listening because he was reading about the first flight of a new supersonic research jet plane that had taken place in England and he was thinking what it would be like to fly through the sound barrier, but he was soon brought back to the present day by the voice of Richard saying to him "David have you been listening to me or reading those papers in the file I gave to you?" David gulped quickly saying "Yes I was listening and I was just about to read the papers when you spoke to me. Would you mind if I read them while you brief the others?" Richard nodded his head and he began to brief Bob and Kevin on their duties and what was expected of them and he also informed them that as David was the person who had been put in charge of this operation he was the person from whom they must take their orders.

While David was reading the papers in the file and knowing from what he had read that it was going to be a dangerous operation, he began to feel worried about Kathy being with him and then he felt very pleased that Bob and Kevin were coming with them.

It was when they were on the transport to going towards Heathrow and they were all talking and feeling very pleased with themselves and saying to each other that they were looking forward to their 10 hour flight to Rio de Janeiro, when David said "I hope it is a good flight, because I have been thinking of this trip and what we are expected to achieve and I'm sure it will be a stiff test of character for all of us and because of those thoughts I am reminded of a piece of Shakespeare that perhaps fits the mood I am in and I thought you might like to hear it"

David laughed as he said that and was still laughing as he said "Well I suppose having said I was going to say it, I must say it to you

> *We Few, We happy band of brothers,*
> *For he today that sheds his blood with me,*
> *Shall be my Brother"*

and I hope that after listening to that piece of Shakespeare you will realize that we are a small band of brothers and we all work together as a team."

They were looking at each other and David could see that they had all fallen into a solemn mood, he said "Well I don't know about you lot but I'm looking forward to a nice cool drink." suddenly all four of them laughed and joked about who was going to buy the round of drinks when they arrived at the airport.

# CHAPTER 7

## (Brazil)

On their outward journey they discussed with each other the tactics they were going to employ when they had located where Gee Gee and Nicholas Pitman were situated. It was due to some strong head winds they encountered on their journey, that their flight took a little longer and they landed at 5.30pm feeling jaded, tired, but pleased that they were staying a night at the hotel in Rio before leaving for Porto Alegre. As they were getting into their transport to leave the airport and to go to their hotel, Kathy said to them "Don't start saying anything out loud but if you look slowly over to your right, can you see those two men, with one wearing a cap, standing by that taxi rank? Well I'm certain they were on our plane that has just landed and I'm sure that the one with the cap is Alan Carson......" Kathy was about to speak again, when Bob Statham softly exclaimed "You are right Kathy, that is Alan Carson I would recognize him anywhere. Now I wonder if he and his mate are following us. David would you mind if we all did a little detour to our hotel just to see if they do follow us?" David was feeling very impressed with his fellow travellers and said "By all means Bob. We have a little time before we need to get to the hotel, so we can start to have some fun driving around. Well done everybody."

All the time they were driving through the streets of Rio de Janeiro, they were seeing the lovely sights, while at the same time they were watching the car with Alan Carson and his mate, suddenly Kevin Mitchell, who was driving their vehicle, turned very quickly down a side road and then stopped in parking bay and they noticed that Alan Carson had not noticed what they had done. Very quickly Kevin Mitchell drove them down some side roads and back on to their original road and within another ten minutes they drove up to their hotel and when they went into the hotel they found that only two small rooms had been booked for them. After a quick consultation between them, it was agreed that Bob and Kevin would have one room and David and Kathy would share the other room. It was when they were in their room David, who was very embarrassed, said to Kathy "I'm very sorry about this arrangement, but as you know they haven't any more rooms and we didn't want to try looking for another hotel for two of us to go to, so I'm promising you that I will sleep in that comfortable looking chair and you can have the small bed." Kathy began laughing and said "David you are such a gentleman. Don't you know that I know you wouldn't try anything and even so, haven't you realized that I wouldn't let you." She was still laughing as he looked at her before going up to her and saying "Thank you Kathy" and he surprised her by he kissing her gently on the lips.

In the mean time, while both couples were settling in their rooms, just along the road in another small hotel were Alan Carson and his mate, who were wondering where they had lost David and his companions. They knew that Gerry Giovanie and Nicholas Pitman were in Santa Maria waiting to supervise the transportation of the drugs to Porto Alegre and he would be very annoyed if they could not find David's group. After a long discussion Alan and his mate decided that later that evening, they would have a walk round to the hotels that were all around the area and look at their registers and see if they could trace David and his companions.

It was a thankless task and having found not a trace of David and his team, Alan and his mate went back to their hotel but didn't look in any of the very small hotels nearby and as it was at 11.30pm, they were very tired, they retired to their hotel room and were soon fast asleep.

The next morning David had a quick wash and shower, he awoke Kathy and they packed their cases and were having breakfast when Bob Statham and Kevin Mitchell appeared at their table and began eating their breakfast. Immediately they had finished eating, it was while Bob and Kevin went for their cases, that Kathy and David went to the receptionist and paid for both their rooms but as they were putting their luggage cases in their car, it was unfortunate because Alan Carson and his mate were coming out of their hotel that was situated about four buildings away. Looking up the road Alan became excited because he saw them and he was soon on his mobile phone telephoning Gerry Giovanie. Being early in the morning Gerry was in bed with a young Brazilian girl and was not happy at being disturbed and he began shouting to Alan to get rid of David and his group at the earliest possible moment and ended his talk by stating that he did not want David and his group to be in Santa Maria within the next two days, or any of them left alive and if they didn't carry out his orders it would be to their disadvantage.

Kevin Mitchell, was coming out of his hotel, when saw Alan getting into a car, he shouted out to Bob Statham "Bob quick look, that was Alan Carson. Isn't that the car that was following us yesterday?" Bob quickly looked in the direction that Kevin was pointing and seeing a car was about to pull away from the hotel shouted "Yes we had better get a move on." Luckily both David and Kathy were already seated in their car as Kevin and Bob hurriedly seated themselves and quickly drove away. Fortunately for Bob as he drove away from their hotel, a big articulated lorry came along the road and blocked Alan's car from moving away from his hotel and following them.

Both David and Kathy were looking back to see if Alan was following, but when they saw that he had been blocked by that big lorry, they both excitedly exclaimed "Bob drive carefully. Alan has been blocked, now we can make a detour as soon as possible without him knowing." They were soon leaving Porto Alegre and driving along a small road that led to Santa Maria. As they went along they kept looking to see if Alan was following, but they couldn't see any sign of his car and they all felt fairly happy.

However because Alan Carson had telephoned Gerry Giovanie on his mobile phone and was explaining to Gerry how they had lost sight of David, it was at the end of their heated conversation that Gerry told Alan that he had better locate them and carry out his instruction on David and his group, otherwise things would be very bad for him. Alan was very upset and told his mate what Gerry had said would happen to them if they didn't find David and he said to his mate they had better do a more thorough search for David's group, even if it meant that they would have to be looking for them during the night. While Bob Statham was slowly driving along that narrow road, Gerry Giovanie and Nicholas Pitman had left Santa Maria at midday to go to the plant which was just beyond Tupancireta where the drugs were bearing prepared for transportation.

It because they had taken an unmade road through the very heavy woodland to avoid being detected, it took David and his group nearly 5 hours to reach Santa Maria. When David's group arrived there they looked around and found no sign of Gerry Giovanie and Nicholas Pitman or of Alan Carson and his mate, then having found a small place to sleep, they hid their car, and all four of them were sitting inside a small café looking out of the window casually drinking coffee and they were surprised when they saw Alan's car go slowly past, luckily they were not seen. Knowing they were near to a cross road where there was a signpost Kevin went up to it and read the sign of the road that Alan's car had taken. Prior to leaving London, both Bob and Kevin had been informed by Richard Crossley that David had full control and they must take their orders from him in this operation. When Kevin arrived back to where they were all sitting, he said "The road Alan and his mate have just taken, leads to Tupancireta. Now before you all jump in to say something should we leave and try and follow them, or should we wait a few moments before going?" David then said to them "I know that we must be on the alert at all times and I have now asked for your opinions" then without waiting to hear what their answers would be, he looked at Kathy and then the other two men and said "However I feel that it would be better if we sit here and all four of us put our own ideas forward to discuss how best to tackle the next part of the operation and afterwards I will telephone Mike Taggert to see if there has been any alterations to the raid. Do you agree?" They all looked at him and were smiling as they said "Yes"

Speaking to Mike Taggert on his mobile David was told that Gerry and Nicholas were in their vicinity and if David and his party were to look around they might be able to discern other members of the security services seated around them, who were there on the same operation. He was also told that there had been no news of Mario Lorenzo being around, David quickly looked around and thought he could recognize some people who looked suspiciously like security people, he knew he had a code word he could communicate with them if he wanted to. However he decided to sit there discussing tactics and drinking a few alcoholic drinks with Kathy, Bob and Kevin until they were satisfied which was their best tactic. After quite a long discussion they found they were satisfied that the idea of put forward by Kevin was the best approach and they would put it into force in the morning. Then David said to them "Sit here for few more moments because I want to talk to those four chaps at the table in the café opposite." He walked across the road while Kathy and the others watched him speak to the men and shortly they saw everyone was laughing then they all shook hands and David came away smiling as he crossed the road back to his team. When he reached his table he said to Bob, Kathy and Kevin "That was a bit of luck. When I spoke to Mike Taggert a short while ago he told me that the American's had some men around us and I had to look for them and Mike also said that the operation was on a big scale and it would be better to let some of the other groups know we were around." Pointing to the men across the road he said "They are Americans over there and I told them what we were aiming to do tomorrow morning and they said they had a similar plan and they had also met with the Israeli's, who also had a similar plan. So before anything else is said, I think we must congratulate Kevin on his idea because it appears the other groups have had the same similar idea and plan as his."

While they sat there drinking Bob and Kevin went across the road to talk to the Americans leaving David and Kathy alone. Kathy said "David it is lovely warm summer's evening and having had a Tequila at home, I was wondering if it tastes the same over here, therefore would you mind if I order one?" David looked at her saying "Are you sure you want one of those from here, because they can be pretty potent?" Kathy was laughing as she said "Oh yes please" He went into the small hotel and ordered a Tequila, and because the beer was warm he ordered a double whisky with ice and soda water for himself and they sat there for ages just drinking and talking. Their talk was about their feelings for each other and as David said it must be time to go to bed, Bob and Kevin came back and said goodnight to them.. Kathy who was a little drunk had tears in her eyes as she said "David you know I did love Tony and I hoped he loved me." David held her arm as he said "It's all right Kathy. We all knew that. Now don't you start crying or worrying, because shortly we have to separate, but I'll see you to your room and you go and have a lovely night's sleep and then we'll talk some more tomorrow morning." After he had finished speaking he took her to her room kissed her on her forehead, then he went to his room and when inside it, he was thinking of Tony, suddenly he thought he had heard Tony's voice and he could feel as though Tony was in the room with him. Then he thought he heard Tony say "Thank you for being so kind to her. She'll be alright in the morning." He kept looking around and said out loud "I must be going crazy because I thought I could hear Tony's voice and feel him around me." As he undressed and got into bed he felt very disturbed and hoping that he would feel better in the morning. When he awoke in the morning, he remembered the unusual experience that had happened

137

before he got into bed and he said to himself "That whiskey must have been strong and I must have been very drunk last night." then as he got washed and dressed he thought he could hear Tony's laughter.

Kathy and David were at the breakfast table before Bob and Kevin came down and she said to David "Thank you very much for a lovely evening and seeing me safely to my room. I'm sorry if I spoilt it by my behaviour by being a little inebriated." David smiled at her saying "It's alright Kathy you were not too bad and nothing happened, you were just fine, but something unusual happened to me when I reached my room and I must have been drunk as well, because I felt as though Tony was near me and I could hear his voice." Suddenly this reminded her that she had been told she could have ESP and she stopped drinking her coffee saying "That's funny, and I mean peculiar, funny, because I felt the same thing and I felt that Tony was beside me last night." David said "I feel better now you have said that, but I do think that it would be a good idea when we get back to England we both go and see somebody about that peculiar feeling we had." She nodded her head in agreement. After Bob and Kevin had eaten their breakfast and David had settled the bill at the hotel and they were all in the car, with Bob still driving it was at the corner signpost when Bob pointed to the sign post saying to David "That was road Alan's car went along yesterday, do you wish us to take it and go to Tupancireta?" David quickly answered "Yes, but go easy." then as Bob turned into the road and increased the speed of the car David immediately said "Bob don't go fast, just go slowly so that we may look and see where this place might be."

They all began speaking, but David interrupted them saying "I think it would be a good idea if we all look for a place where they could be packing the drugs ready for transportation. All I have been told it is just past Tupancireta. When I spoke to the Americans yesterday they said they had been told it was along this road, and they had been along here and seen a big brick building just beyond Tupancireta and they said it is in a farmstead with large buildings and they think that is the place." It was while they were going along the road looking at every building, Kevin suddenly said to Kathy "I know you came from Australia a few years ago and since then you have been with our British security unit for a few years, because I can remember you starting with us, however please forgive me if you think I am being rude, but having worked with you and knowing you are not only a compassionate person but also a very good security agent, you must be getting on in years and I have often wondered how old you are Kathy?" Before she could answer that question David interrupted and laughingly said "One should never trust a woman who tells you her real age. A woman who would tell you her age, will tell you anything" Kathy looked at David with gratefulness in her eyes and said "Thank you David for saying that, because I am still at a relatively young age and I can still do my job and shoot with a gun as good as any one." Knowing he had made a big mistake Kevin immediately apologized saying "Kathy I didn't mean anything by my remarks. I was thinking of the job ahead and as I said I realized that you had been with us for a long time and it's a joy to be with you" but it was because of his embarrassment that Kevin paused before saying "Anyway Bob and I know you are an excellent shot with a gun, because we have been with you when you had to deal with a person who was armed, and he was about to shoot Bob and you shot him before he could fire his gun, thereby saving Bob's life."

David could see that Kathy was beginning to blush with embarrassment and said "Ok people let's concentrate on what we are about to do. I can tell you that besides the Americans who are with us, there are other units of four Israeli agents, plus some of the Brazilian army personnel, so between all three units we have twelve security agents and hopefully a couple of helicopters of the Brazilian air force and with the Brazilian element, it could amount to a sizeable force. The trouble is however, we don't know how many men Gerry has at that farmstead." Sensing that everyone was getting nervous David thought for a moment before he said "Now let us all think very carefully, how many men do you think could be in that building waiting for us to attack them, because besides the people who are packing the drugs in the cases, there could be quite a few more of them to carry the packages to the waiting transports." After a few moments Bob said "I think there could be about 20 to 30", Kevin replied "I think about 15 to 25," Kathy said "I think it could be a larger number of people, roughly 50" David thought for a moment and said "I was thinking around the same figure as Kathy and soon we will find out whose right." then he said "What ever the number of men there are against us, with the Americans four men, the Israeli's four men and us that's twelve and then there are the Brazilians who have a large number of soldiers, and therefore I think we can hold our own. against whatever number there is in there." The others were looking at him when he paused as he sat there with a frown on his forehead.

They thought he must be thinking of the raid, because he said "Now you all know this could be a very dicey operation and we are all hoping that it will be a success, so let's look on the positive side, because thinking positively reminds me of a quotation by Charles Reade who wrote

> *Sow and act and you reap a habit,*
> *Sow a habit and you reap a Character,*
> *Sow a character and you reap a destiny,*

Now having said that to you, I know that you are all good actors and you have sowed your habits and have harvested your characters, but now you are about to reap your destiny, and I am sure it will be a good one because with a lot of good luck we will all be on the road to a healthy success. Good luck everyone."

Driving past the farmstead they saw the big buildings and when they were well past them they stopped their car and walked back to find the other units. Kathy was the first to come across the Israeli unit and then the Americans came along. When they were all together the Brazilian army chief came to them and told them that he was acting under the supreme orders of his President, who had explained to him that the Brazilian army must only apprehend the Brazilian people taking part in this operation. The Army chief said that his orders state, that the rest of the people who are involved, they must identify the people of their of their own country and then they will be allowed to take them away from Brazil, without any interference from the Brazilian authorities. Having listened to him, all the agents then agreed on a plan of operation with him, which he said would start within one hour. When they were all in position they were awaiting for the signal from the Brazilian army chief to start the affray, David was standing next to Kathy, with Bob and Kevin a short distance away. Then Kathy saw David shiver and he looked around and said to her "Kathy I doubt if you will believe me, but I've had that peculiar feeling again that Tony is standing beside us and I thought I could hear him saying "Don't worry I'm with both of you and Kathy will both be alright." Kathy nodded her head and smilingly said "Thanks for that little talk you gave to us as we were coming here David. I did hear Bob say to Kevin that he was pleased you said that little poem and it's nice to feel that Tony is still around us."

David looked at his watch and saw that it was time to move

forward. Within a few minutes of moving forward they heard gunfire with many people shouting and then people came rushing out of the big buildings firing wildly. David had previously told Kathy, Bob and Kevin to stay on the outside of the buildings to watch and see if they could catch Gerry Giovanie, Nicholas Pitman and Alan Carson and his mate if they come out. It was now mayhem with a cacophony of noise with the Brazilian army personnel going into the buildings, shouting and firing their guns, and then people began jumping out of windows and also coming out of the rear doors firing their guns and running fast into the woods nearby. Standing with David were some Brazilian soldiers who had been watching the building, suddenly a car came out of the second building driving very fast and as went past them it was firing guns from the open windows of the car, then it sped down the road towards Tupancireta.

David saw two people in the car and thought they looked like Gee Gee and Nicholas Pitman. Kathy looked around but then saw a Brazilian soldier lying on the ground badly injured, so she immediately went to him and began to tender to his injuries, but just at that moment, Bob and David who were in a different position to Kevin when Bob shouted out "Quick. Alan Carson has just jumped out the rear window of the first building and I believe that could be his mate and some others who are following him out, and they are running towards the woods with the others following them." David knowing that Nicholas Pitman and Gerry had a head start in their car, knew he wouldn't be able to catch up with them, so he shouted out "Come on we have to catch Alan and his mate before they get away." then he to shouted to Kathy "Leave that injured chap, the Brazilians will soon tend to him". Kathy shouted back "I cannot leave him at the moment he is alone. You go on, I'll catch up with you later" Hearing her reply David and the other two ran after Alan Carson, his mate and the others. They followed them for quite a long way through the woodland, suddenly they came to a river and knowing that Alan Carson was a good shot and the others could be well armed, David told very one to be very cautious and to be quiet as they went forward through the heavy woods. In the meantime Kathy, who had been looking after the injured soldier when along came some more Brazilian soldiers and seeing Kathy helping their comrade they called for an army ambulance. that soon came and took the soldier away to hospital. Kathy told the officer in charge that she had to go in the direction that David's group had gone, so he ordered six of his soldiers to accompany her and act as guides to locate David.

The six soldiers knowing the landscape, covered a lot of ground very quickly therefore they and Kathy were proceeding at a very fast pace. It was about twenty minutes later they could hear gunfire coming from the woods in front of them. It was at that moment that David, Bob and Kevin were going through very thick foliage, and David looked around because he was worried about Kathy and he also thought he could feel Mabel Flitch's presence around him, when suddenly a fusillade of shots were sprayed all around them, luckily none of the bullets hit any of them, but they stopped where they were and waited. They were still there when they heard some Brazilian soldiers coming from behind them who were talking rather loudly to Kathy and then David could see them. He was overjoyed to see her and when they were near to him he cautiously told the soldiers about the gunfire that had come from the trees in front of them. The Brazilian corporal said that about one mile further on there was a big river and he suggested that he and his men go to the north and then come towards David and his group, thereby the men they were chasing would be trapped, David agreed and the soldiers departed while David's group slowly made their forward. After waiting about ten minutes David and his Group went towards the river suddenly, and when they were close to the riverside they came under fire with the bullets passing very close to Kevin where he was standing,. Knowing this, David said in a loud whisper "Everybody keep low and try and see where those shots came from." Suddenly more shots were fired at them then Bob said "I saw where those shots came from, and who ever fired them must be close to the river." Proceeding forward very carefully, all four of them spread out and approached the river quietly from different angles.

When they were near to the spot where the shots came from, David whispered to Kathy "We need to take our people alive and back to England with us if we can." Then they heard a fusillade of gunfire from the north going towards the riverside, they saw a figure firing a gun who was in the opposite direction to them and the firing increased from all sides, David and his group knew that the Brazilians soldiers with their sub machine guns were now coming towards them and decided to move. Suddenly figures rose from the ground and began firing wildly in all directions one of them fell into the river, seeing that happen the rest of the gunmen then dropped their guns and held their hands up in surrender. Looking at those men surrendering to the soldiers, David and his group went to where Alan and his mate had fallen and then making sure they were dead, they rushed to riverside to see if they could recover the body that had fallen into the river, but looking down into the waters they could hear the person crying out in pain and seeing the blood pouring from him, they could also see the Piranha fish eating away at his legs and body, they realized there was nothing they could do to save him, Kathy immediately fired her gun and killed him. After she had shot the man she was crying as she said "I really didn't want to kill him but I couldn't let him suffer like that could I," Kevin went up to her put his arms around her and said "Kathy I was just going to do the same thing, but you were quicker and a better shot than me and there is no way for you to feel sorry for yourself, because what you did was a humane act" hearing Kevin say that to her made her feel better. Very shortly the Brazilian soldiers came to them and said they had dealt with the others and the only ones left were Brazilians and they had taken them into custody. After thanking the soldiers for their help, they said their goodbyes, then made their way to a bridge where there was a sign in English saying it was the river Jacui they were crossing over, then after many hours of walking through trees and heavy foliage, they eventually came to place called Cachoeira do Sul where they stayed at a small hotel and had a few hours sleep. The next day they managed to hire a car and drove to Porto Alegre and managed to catch a plane going to Rio de Janeiro. When they reached Rio they booked into the same hotel where they had stayed when they arrived from England. It was because they were still feeling very exhausted and tired that David told them he was telephoning England. Richard Crossley answered the call and David told him very briefly what had occurred and also told him that they were very tired and wanted to stay in Rio for two days, Richard agreed, telling him that after the two days they were to book the earliest flight back to England.

When David told Bob and Kevin that they were staying in Rio for two nights they were pleased and went to their room to wash and clean up. With Bob and Kevin gone, Kathy looked at David and said "Are we sharing the same room again?" David looked at her and with a sheepish grin said "Yes I am sorry, I believe Richard or Mark must have forgotten you were coming with us, because only two rooms had been booked for our return journey, I have enquired but they haven't any vacant single rooms left." That night David and Kathy slept together and when David awoke in the morning he could feel Kathy sleeping besides him, he leaned over and gently kissed her. As he was getting out of bed she awoke and said to him "Thank you David again for being a thorough gentleman and by the way I did enjoy you kissing me."

Just before David and Kathy had retired to their room, in another hotel room near the airport Nicholas Pitman was telephoning Poseidon (Marcus Lorenzo) in Paris and said "There I will make a bed of roses with a thousand posies" A voice answered "A cap of flowers and a kirtle embroider'd all with leaves of myrtle." Nicholas Pitman spoke again "Poseidon this is Cereberus. We have been hit very badly. We have lost most of the drugs and antiques and we have lost many men. Gee Gee is very angry. I feel that we must calm him down otherwise the Brazilian authorities will be on to the pair of us very quickly. Yes. The Brazilian army surrounded us and they either killed, or took many of the local people prisoners, some of the others managed to get away. I have no idea how they were on to us. It came as a complete surprise. Ok .I will pass you on to Gerry." Nicholas passed the telephone to Gerry Giovanie. Gerry listening to the person speaking on the telephone said "Hello yes. This is Gee Gee. Of course I'm bloody angry. You should have been here, it was bloody mayhem and quite a number of our people were killed and we've lost most of the goods. Look here, I know a few of the local people and I want to get the local mafia on to those that hit us, but Cereberus is saying no. He wants to get back to you and for you to give us the next move." There was a big pause before Gerry began angrily speaking again "Okay if that's what you want, we'll fly back to Paris, but you make sure that we hit them back very hard. Goodbye." Gee Gee gave the telephone back to Nicholas saying "Poseidon said we have to fly back to Paris, and he is going to fix the next plan on how to deal those who hit us today."

The next day, leaving Bob and Kevin to visit Rio on their own, David and Kathy went sightseeing, during the morning David stopped to buy an English newspaper and shortly afterwards when they were sitting down together drinking their coffee David quickly looked through the newspaper and saw that President John Kennedy had been shot and killed on his way to deliver a speech in Dallas Texas and that Vice President Lyndon Johnson had been sworn in as 35th President. Reading it to Kathy David said "The Americans don't waste much time do they? Because as soon as one President dies in office, the vice President is sworn in immediately." Kathy immediately said "Perhaps that is the best way to do it because there is always someone officially in power, with the authority to rule the country." David with a smile on his face looked at her and said "What a clever person you are to say a thing like that."

After another nice day together seeing the lovely sights in Rio, that evening they were making their way to the La Conchita club because they had been told it was a very good restaurant for a nice meal, and as they were not very far from the club they were looking through a large front window of a large store, looking at the clothes on show, when they heard a loud commotion coming from down the street. They turned and looking in that direction they could see four men fighting and then they heard a gun shot. Then they saw two men fall to the ground and then two men jumped into a taxi that was standing close by. As the Taxi sped by them Kathy said "David I couldn't see who was in the taxi, but I managed to get its number, it was 178." It was because there were not many people walking along the street that Kathy hurriedly said "David quick, let's see if we can help those two men who are on the ground."

When they got to the scene, quickly looking at the bodies they noticed two guns besides the bodies. David told Kathy to stand well away when two police cars arrived. A policeman began to question David, but being unable to speak Portuguese he couldn't answer. The policeman then brought forward a senior officer who spoke a little English. While David was explaining to him what he and Kathy had seen, he could see that both men had been stabbed and their throats cut, and must be dead, then he saw the face of one of the men on the ground and recognized him as one of the American agents he had spoken to in Santa Maria and he had a gun in his hand. Just then one of the policemen spoke to the senior officer and handed him two passports and as the senior officer looked at them David could see that one was an Israeli passport and the other the American's passport. After the police ambulance had taken the bodies away, the senior officer asked David to accompany him to the local police station but David said to him "My wife is Kathy standing over there (pointing) and I would like her to come with me," the senior officer said "Of course but she will have to travel in the other police car." At the police station David was asked to produce his passport and in doing so, his security service card accidentally fell out. On seeing his Australian security card, David was taken into another room and after many telephone calls had been made, the senior police officer handed back to David his security card and passport and apologized to him, shook his hand and thanked him and allowed him to leave.

When they were outside the police station David said "Kathy I had tell them that you was my wife and it was when my security card fell out, I thought we were going to be in big trouble. I was taken to another room where I was again interrogated and I told the officer that I did recognize the American dead man, who was a secret service agent and that possibly the other dead man was a security agent as well. Fortunately several telephone calls were made in Portuguese and at the end of them, the officer then spoke to me in English and said we could go. Kathy what I didn't tell the police was that I do firmly believe that Gee Gee and Cereberus were responsible for those two murders and they were in that taxi that you saw." Kathy was walking beside David listening to him as he was talking and when he had finished speaking she put her arm in his and said "Okay David let's forget about it for moment. We can't go to the La Conchita club because it's too far to go, so let's go some where near and eat in a nice restaurant." They found a quiet restaurant and had a nice meal and afterwards they slowly made their way back to their hotel. While they were in Rio, David and Kathy's friendship grew much stronger and it was on the flight back to England Kathy said to him "David you are such good company to be with and a gentleman, I do believe I could fall in love with you." He smiled and nodding his head as he listened to her and was about to speak when the air stewardess brought them their drinks. A moment later David raised his glass and with a nice smile said "Listening to you saying you could fall in love with me, reminded me of a quotation by Charles Dickens

> *O let us love our occupations*
> *Bless the squire and his relations*
> *Live upon our daily rations*
> *And always know our proper stations*

and remembering our proper stations I do believe I could fall in love with you"

Kathy was perplexed by David saying that verse and for a moment there was silence between them, then she said "Why did you say that rhyme and why are you saying that we should always know our proper stations?" David still had a slight smile on his face when he answered "Well we are in this security service and we are often sent separately to different places, but at the moment you and I are very lucky to be thrown working together and it is because we are together, we have both realized that our feelings for each other have grown very strong, however you must remember that this operation is not over yet and anything could happen." It was the look on her face that made him pause and he began to drink his wine then he smiled at her, and thought for a moment before saying "Kathy it's because the two main people got away from us during this trip, namely Gerry Giovanie and Nicholas Pitman and I do believe there is still plenty more action to come and what I meant by that verse is that something may happen to one of us and we will not be together, but our feelings for each other will always be the same"

She replied "David I think I understand what you were referring to, but since we first met on that island in the Pacific, and having worked with you on a few assignments, and ever since Tony's death, I want you to know that I have found myself wanting to be with you. Please don't think that I'm throwing myself at you, because I'm not. A few moments ago I told you of my innermost feelings and I feel that you are laughing at me by saying that rhyme. However having had it explained what it actually represents, but now I still feel perhaps you don't have the same feelings for me." He was upset by her remarks and took his time before he said "Kathy that is not true, because I have just told you that I believe I could fall in love with you When we met in London and I had told you how I felt about Susan Pitman, well it was that incident at Heathrow, when we embraced and I kissed you and you were responding that I felt a different type of passion, and when I saw Susan kissing Gerry Giovanie, in what I thought to be a rather passionate manner, I began to realize that she and I were on different social levels." He paused, looked around then he began talking again "and whenever we have been working together I have always been comparing her with you, and I also remember the way she treated me when we were together on a trip to France, and I remember she has never kissed me the way she kissed Gerry Giovanie. However with you, I have always remembered that kiss at Heathrow, and there has been several times when I wanted to show you how much you meant to me, but I have controlled myself, because I thought I would wait until you could show me the same feelings you had about Tony."

Kathy responded by saying "Don't you think I know how you feel about me. I knew it from the start when we first met. But Tony came into my life and you and I went our different ways for a short period of time. Then when we met again you began to tell me how Tony seemed to be always around you and I began to suspect that you were teasing me and I didn't like that. Anyway can't we forget the past and think of the future, because knowing what could be in store for us with the problems of the Triumvirate, we can never be sure how long we have together."

David was sitting near to her drinking his wine listening to what she was saying and was agreeing with practically everything she had said.

Then he said to her "Kathy I want you to know that I think you are a wonderful person to be with and I also do believe that I love you and I thank you for listening to me and for being so practical. But I must explain to you about Tony, because I do believe in life after death, but I cannot prove it. Then every now again whenever I am in a dangerous position    I feel he is beside watching over me, and I believe you should also know I have had visitations from a young girl called Mabel Flitch." He paused because he saw the look of surprise on her face before saying "She was a young girl who had been burnt at a stake for being a witch who during her short life had helped people during their illnesses by giving them the Lord's help through prayer."

He paused again thinking and then he slowly said "These visitations first began during World War 2 when my Canadian navigator, Jack Donoghue and I went to view a very old church near where we were stationed and after viewing this very old church, we were looking at a tombstone of a young girl when the local minister told us about her death and after he left us standing at her graveside, we thought we could feel her presence around us. It was sometime later when we were on a bombing trip and the aeroplane received very bad damage and was badly shot up, I was having trouble controlling the plane, not only through the damage we had received, but also we only had three engines that were sporadically working. I am certain she visited and stood beside me and helped me to get the plane fly safely over the occupied territory, but our troubles were then not over, because our home aerodrome was fog bound and we were unable to land, so we were told to go to another 'drome that had FIDO where we were able to eventually land safely and I am certain it was with her help."

The mention of the word FIDO brought a smile to Kathy's face and she excitedly said "So when you came to collect us from that island in

Borneo and had to land by the aid of FIDO you knew exactly what it was, and that is why you asked me how I knew how to operate it to help you land? Sometime afterwards I began to be concerned when you told me about those visitations you say have had of Tony being close to you, and it has been worrying me ever since, because I thought you were just joking and teasing me, but now I can understand why you are so interested in those visitations that you and I appear to be having and want advice about them." David was smiling and nodding his head all time she was speaking.

# CHAPTER 8

## (Back in London)

It was early on Saturday morning when they landed at Heathrow and Kevin and Bob went their separate ways, leaving David and Kathy to travel to London. David asked Kathy if she would like to say at his flat and go to church with him the following morning. She paused and said to him "Are you sure that is all you want me to do?" David began laughing and then he said "Yes that's all. Because you know that I am a perfect gentleman and I also promise you that you can have one bedroom and the other bedroom I will have, and also because I have been thinking of our conversation concerning Tony and Mabel Flitch and I thought a visit to church together may help both of us"

The following morning when they were both in church and were listening to the Gospel being read and it was when the minister said *"And the heavens opened to him and he saw the Spirit of God descending like a dove and alighting on him. And a voice spoke........"* It was at that point of the Gospel that David's thoughts went to the many times he thought he had heard Tony's voice talking to him. David turned to look at Kathy but she appeared to be listening to the minister. When they came out of church and they were walking towards a restaurant, David said to Kathy "When I heard that part of the Gospel when the minister said 'and a dove alighted upon him and a voice spoke', I immediately thought of Tony and Mabel Flitch and Kathy don't laugh because I am certain there have been many times when I have thought they have both been with us, especially when we appeared to be in danger. Now I suppose you must think that I am stupid or mad telling you that." She was smiling when she answered "No David I don't think you are stupid but maybe a little grazy at times, because I've had that same feeling." He felt much better hearing her reply and said "That's great. Now how would you like to have a meal with me in that restaurant (pointing to it) on the other side of the road?", Kathy looked across the road at a rather elegant restaurant said "Yes David I think that would be very nice." When they entered the restaurant they heard music playing and then when they were sitting at their table listening to the music the waiter appeared and Kathy said to him "That is a very nice tune would you know the name of the singer?" the waiter replied "The manager is very keen on Perry Como songs and the tune now playing is called *'Mandolins in the moonlight'* and there are more Perry Como songs coming and I hope you like them" It was during their main meal with Perry Como singing *'I may never pass this way again'* that David said to Kathy "I like the words of that song because they remind me of you and there could be a chance that you or me may never pass this way again" She was blushing as she said " I also like that tune, it has a lovely melody and I'm certain you will pass this way again and more than likely I'll be with you" as she began to eat her desert the music changed to another song with Perry Como and Eddie Fisher singing a song called *"Maybe"*

David was not eating because he was concentrating on the words of that song then he said to her "The title of that song is called *'Maybe'* and if I was to ask you a certain question I  wonder what your answer would be, I think it would possibly be the same as the title of that song."

She was blushing and smiling as she looked at him smiling at her, then as they were finishing the bottle of wine they had had with their meal, she was thinking about what he had just said and leaned across the table and held his held and with a big smile she said "I don't think you would have been disappointed with my answer to your question" Hearing that answer, he felt very happy. After leaving the restaurant they spent the rest of the day enjoying their each other's company. The following morning on their way back to Richard Crossley's office, David was reading the morning newspaper and Kathy was driving the car, when suddenly he said  "Oh dear here we go again I bet Richard and Mike Taggert are going to blame us for that" Kathy with bewilderment in her voice said "Why? what's the matter, what are we supposed to have done." very quickly David said "Kathy stop driving and park the car." Having parked the car, she sat there in the car thinking she have done something wrong to upset him and said "Have I done something to upset you." He gave her the paper and pointed to a photograph and said "Do you know who that is? It's Dr. Roberto Arias, the husband of Dame Margot Fonteyn, the famous ballot dancer, and Dr.Arias was in Panama City when we were over there and he has been shot three times and seriously wounded. Now I'm certain that Richard and Mike will think that we might be responsible for that shooting, because he told us that Mario Lorenzo was going there and Richard might be thinking we followed him and caused a gunfight. So we can expect some fireworks from them this morning."

When they were in Richard Crossley's office, it was because Richard did not ask any questions about the Panama incident that David said "Richard about that incident in Panama. We didn't have anything to do with it because we didn't go there" Richard was laughing as he said "Oh we know all about that shooting and we know it had nothing to do with you. We have had a report here from an agency, informing us that Dame Margot Fontyn was being held incommunicado in jail in Panama City in Brazil. Her husband who was a former Panamanian Ambassador in London, was being hunted by the National Guards in the hills around his country estate which is near Santa Clara about 75 miles from Panama City. This action was all to do with the Panamanian Government" Richard stopped talking went to his cabinet and withdrew a file containing a newspaper cutting that he handed to David, who looked at the newspaper cutting and saw a picture of Dame Margot Fontyn and said "I was worried when I saw that there had been shooting in Panama City and I thought you would immediately feel that as we had been chasing Gerry Giovanie and Nicholas Pitman and you might have thought it was us that did it, so I'm pleased you know we had nothing to do with that shooting." Richard took the newspaper cutting from David and put it back in the file and said "Just tell me about your escapade in Brazil" Kathy began looking at David as he began telling Richard of all the events that had taken place in Brazil, including the murder of the American and Israeli agents.

It was during their colloquy of Brazil that Mike Taggert came into the office and listened to the last part of their trip and what had occurred and when they had finished, Mike said "I can inform you that all the security services involved are very pleased with your efforts."

Then he paused, smiling as he said "But now comes the bad news, we have been informed by Henri Fouchard of the French DGSE that two bodies, one male and one female, have been found on the beach near to Propriano in Corsica. Now Propriano is near Ajaccio and

Ajaccio is where that German diplomat, who is connected to the Triumvirate, and Wendy Willowbey were last seen together." He paused to look at Kathy then he said "We feel that the bodies are of Wendy Willowbey and also of the German diplomat, but we are awaiting a call from France to inform us of the exact cause of death and the true identity of the deceased." Richard intervened and said "Since both of you have been away, several things have happened over here and also in Europe. Firstly our agents have been cooperating with the Italian security agencies and prior to you going to Brazil, we had been informed that Luigi Muraditori had been taken secretly to Israel and put in prison and charged with the kidnap of both the German diplomat and a woman who is believed to be the German's lady friend, but because of the disappearance of those people and if those bodies were found to them, he was facing life, or possibly the death penalty for murder, but to help his defence he has confessed to helping the Triumvirate in some of their operations" Mike then began speaking "The Israeli's are positive that the German diplomat and his girlfriend have been murdered, but up to this moment they are awaiting the autopsy of the bodies found and because of the confession Muraditori has made concerning their kidnap, he has been told he is going to get a reduced sentence."

Somehow Mike knew that David was going to ask him a question and told David to wait and be quiet. Mike began talking again "It is fortunate for him that Abraham Filligoti, who is the head of Mossad the Israeli secret service, has agreed to keep him isolated, and keep him imprisoned in Israel, because we are hoping that Muraditori will keep on supplying us with news of the Triumvirate movements, and we do not want the Triumvirate to know where he is imprisoned. However we can inform you now, that it was through Muraditori that we heard about the Triumvirate Brazilian plan to transport the drugs in large packets and put some of the drugs in copies of Robert Campin paintings. The shipment was going to be by boat from Porto Alegre to Hamburg docks and then those paintings were going to be sent direct to a house in Hamburg, where they were going to be stored before selling them on the European market. It was a whole shipment and would have been worth a lot of money to them." David quickly asked "Then the combined raid was a very successful one?" Mike replied "Yes it was, but it is a pity that Gee Gee and Nicholas Pitman were not caught, because we have heard that there is going to be a big shake up in the Triumvirate movement which could spell trouble for us and if those bodies that were found, is the German diplomat and of Wendy Willowbey, then watch out for the fireworks to begin. Those people we are trying to apprehend are very vicious and will not stop at anything to get the right material for the money they will get from supplying that Middle Eastern country, which is making nuclear weapons from the material supplied to them by the Triumvirate."

When Mike had finished talking, Richard looked at Kathy and said "Kathy we know it was your intensive searching into the Police at the Metropolitan Police headquarters that led to the arrest of Chief Supt. Harold Phillips, congratulations."

Richard paused then continued talking "Harold Phillips was spying for the Triumvirate and through your investigation, it was while you were in Brazil, that we put Bruce Robertson in charge of further investigation, who by the way has done a thorough good job, and because of those investigations that Commander Bryant, who is the head of the Police Special branch, has informed us that there are four other police officers, who are connected to the Harold Phillips spy ring." Kathy was smiling when she heard Richard say "and two of them are in the same Masonic Lodge as Harold Phillips, and all have now been arrested. So we are hoping that the leak from the Metropolitan police to the Triumvirate will now cease." While Richard was talking, Mike was looking through some papers in a file when he laughingly said "David how would you like to take Kathy to the Mediterranean for some warm sunshine?"

David looked up, smiled and said "I'd love to go there, but don't forget it was very warm in Brazil and as you have most likely been informed we had a nice time there, so I don't think the warm Mediterranean weather will make any difference to us. Though what I would like to have would be a nice few days rest." Mike said "Ok All four of you can have three days leave and then report back here in Richard's office."

It was after David, Bob, Kevin and Kathy's three days leave and they returned to Richards office, that Richard said to Bob and Kevin "We have had a report from the Israeli Security Service that a death threat has been put on Luigi Muraditori's life and the Triumvirate are sending men to Italy to carry out that threat by infiltrating the Muraditori gang to establish where Luigi Muraditori is being kept imprisoned. The Israeli's believe this could lead to a big gangland fight which the Israeli's, and we, do not want to happen." Richard paused here to look at some more papers then he looked at Bob and

Kevin saying "I am very sorry about this unusual assignment, but I have been instructed to send two people to Italy and therefore because of your perceptiveness I have selected both of you to go to there to keep a watch on the Muraditori gangs and by the way you could also be instructed to go to Israel" Richard again paused as he gave to Kevin a large envelope containing photographs of the Muraditori gangs. Then Richard began speaking again "Inside that envelope are also photographs that have been taken of the people of the Triumvirate gang who the Israeli's already know are in Italy searching for the whereabouts of Luigi Muraditori. I suggest that the pair of you go away and study those photographs so that you will have a good idea who you will be looking for. Now When you arrive at Milan airport, there will be a Mr Julius Silverman, who is a member of the Israeli Intelligence Agency, waiting to greet you here is a photograph of him. While working on this assignment, you will be under the jurisdiction of the Israeli Intelligence Agency and you report to them. There is no urgent need for you to contact us because we will get all your reports through them. Your plane leaves tomorrow and we wish both of you the best of luck." After Kevin and Bob had left, Kathy was told to go back and report to her group and work with Commander Bryant who was still trying to trace if there were any more of Chief Supt. Phillips gang in the police force who could be working for the Triumvirate. When all three had left the office, Mike spoke to David and said "David when you were trained in Australia to be a pilot did you have any instruction on flying helicopters?"

Knowing that Mike had been his squadron leader, David was a little perplexed at being asked that question and replied "No I wasn't, but I have had a flight in one Why?" Very quickly Mike said "Well that's solved that problem, because we would like you to go to Stampney Down aerodrome, where you will join your friend Bruce Robertson and the two of you will be taught to fly a helicopter, but before you go there, we would like you to spend two or three days with Bruce and go to the East End of London and mix with the gangs to obtain information on those who are connected with Gee Gee." David said "This is a lovely surprise, just think, I'll be joining Bruce and flying again."

It was while David was talking to Mike that Richard's telephone had been ringing and he picked up the phone just as David finished speaking. They heard Richard saying "Yes, Yes I understand. Okay, that will be very nice of you and thank you very much."

Richard turned to Mike saying "Mike that was Henri Fouchard informing us that those two bodies were those of the German diplomat and Wendy Willowbey and from the autopsy of both bodies, it was confirmed that they had been murdered. The German Diplomat was murdered by having his throat cut, and the girl died by having an injection of poison called Fentanyl." Richard stopped to light a cigarette then said "The French feel certain that the deaths were caused by Gee Gee and Nicholas Pitman, this is because since they arrived from Brazil, five days ago, they landed in Paris. Within twelve hours they both flew out to Corsica, because just before they had left Paris, they had heard that some of the Muraditori gang members had arrived in Corsica looking for Luigi and now with the arrival of Gee Gee and Nicholas Pitman, the French are now saying that things are about to hot up."

Suddenly Richard telephoned Bruce Robertson and told him to report to Richard's office immediately, then Richard said to David "When Bruce arrives we want you, without any delay, to go to the East End of London and to see if any of Gerry Giovanie close associates are there. This is because we have reason to believe that Gee Gee is negotiating something big. Oh I very nearly forgot I would like you to listen very carefully to what I am about to impart to you and I am going to ask you not to show any signs of your previous aggravation when certain names are used." Richard looked at David with a smile on his face and said "I have just informed you that GeeGee is negotiating something big in Corsica, but at the same time we have discovered something about him that could have disastrous results in our operations, so I feel I should also inform you that Gee Gee is having a serious relationship with the Jeanette the 2nd wife of Duke of Chardminster, who is as you know the stepmother of Susan Pitman."

The look on David's face told Richard what David must be thinking because David sarcastically said "Well I did know that Jeanette was Susan's stepmother, and I knew Susan's father was the Duke of Chardminster, but I am not surprised that Gee Gee is having a relationship with her stepmother, because Jeanette is a very beautiful looking lady and now you have told me that Jeanette is the Duke's 2nd wife that accounts for the little scene I saw when Kathy and I were at Heathrow and we were very surprised when we saw how the Duchess and Gee Gee embraced each other."

When Bruce entered the room Richard immediately said "Good

morning Bruce, because I am very busy, I have informed David what is expected of the work you have to do, and he can brief you while you are both searching around the East End of London. You have much work to do. Cheerio." They spent the three days walking around the East End of London talking to people who were informers who might know the contacts of Gee GEE They were lucky because they found one of the gangs affiliated to him. When they had reported to Richard he was pleased with the news they had found. The next day they were sent to Stampney Down Airport. It was because they had both been trained as pilots on piston aircraft and also been pilots of jet aircraft, and flying at great heights, it took them sometime to acclimatize themselves with the workings of the helicopters and they were finding flying them was very demanding. After getting to know of the controls they found it good fun, because they loved flying at low level and they began enjoying the three weeks of hard training and flying, and were soon passed eligible to fly helicopters. When they returned to Richard's office, they thought that they were going on a mission where they were to fly helicopters, but they were informed that they were being sent to Israel and they had to report to Abraham Filligoti and were being seconded to him for a short time. Unbeknown to them Kathy was also being sent to Israel on a similar mission and was leaving England two days before them. It was while they were with Richard that he said "By the way I am pleased to inform you that another big spy ring was apprehended whilst you were in Brazil and the accused have been found guilty. A Russian spy called Gordon Lonsdale was sentenced to 25 years, Peter Kroger and his wife Helen each received a 20 years sentence and a civil servant and his fiancée received a 15year sentence each. Luckily for us Peter Kroger and his wife Helen are American citizens and the American security services have found that their real names are Morris and Lona Cohen who were associated with Col. Abel head of the American spy ring who is now serving a 30 year sentence," he paused to light a cigarette and said "The Lord Chief Justice congratulated the representatives of the security services of British and American FBI agents and the senior representative of the Royal Canadian Mounted Police who were present at the trial. From this you can both see that our work is being appreciated by the Judicature system of all countries." David and Bruce left the Richard's office contentedly talking of the work they are doing and feeling satisfied that their hard work and results appear to be forthcoming.

In Corsica were eight members from the gangs that had been controlled by Luigi Muraditori. They were there, because one of them had asked some of the other members of the gangs to meet him there and when they had completed the killing of Wendy Willowbey and the German diplomat, and they had disposed of the bodies they were now going to a nightclub before departing for Milan. Henri Fouchard was also in Corsica and was walking around with three of his own agents when he saw two of the men who he recognized as being members of the gangs of Luigi Muraditori. He followed them down to the nightclub and immediately he called for backup to assist his men and within one hour six other French agents were on their way to him. Knowing where the gang members were, Henri used his mobile telephone for the remainder of his men to meet him outside the nightclub. When they arrived they lay hidden outside the nightclub.

It was 11.30pm when all eight members of the gangs came out laughing and talking to each other not knowing that they were walking into the ambush set up by Henri. On a given signal by Henri, one of his men shouted in Italian and calling to mobsters that they were surrounded and to stand still and lay their guns on the ground. Unfortunately some of gang members started to run backwards towards the club, while the others began to fire their guns in the direction where the voice came from and where they thought Henri and his men were. The men who had run backwards were caught by the gunfire of the French agents on that side and fell to the ground, either badly wounded or killed. Seeing that they had lost many of their men, the killers put their guns on the ground and surrendered. Henri began looking around and counted five dead killers on the ground, and he took the others away into captivity. The following morning Henri telephoned Richard Crossley of the gun battle, informing him how many men were captured and killed, Richard said he was very pleased with the result and congratulated Henri and asked for his congratulations to be passed on to the French DGSE.

The following morning in another part of Corsica, because the conflict had been seen on television and in the news, Gee Gee heard of the gun battle and he was fuming with anger and frustration. Turning to Nicholas Pitman he said "You Limies and Europeans, you call yourselves gunmen and you talk very big about what you can do, but when it comes to it, all of you are just a bunch of no-good bitches with no fire in your bellies, and you can tell that to your boss with his fancy name of Poseidon. If this had been in America my boys would have found and eliminated those agents and it would all be over. What I want to know, what plan has been devolved to get rid of Muraditori, because it seems to me that all you are doing is running around places looking for him and how are you going to find this Luigi Muraditori if these security agents keep beating you and stopping you getting to him" A few moments later he stormed out of the house with his bags.

Being afraid of Gee Gee's bad moods and not knowing where he was going, or what he might do, Nicholas waited before he telephoned Poseidon, who was in his flat in Monte Carlo. It was 10.00am and Poseidon was in bed with a lovely Parisian girl when the telephone rang. Being woken early he was not in his best mood in answering the telephone. "Hello" he growled. Nicholas Pitman rather sheepishly said "There I will make a bed of roses with a thousand posies Can I speak to Poseidon please" Nicholas heard the voice swear and growl even harder, then Nicholas heard a much more harder swear word and the voice said "A cap of flowers and a kirtle embroider'd all with leaves of Myrtle."

Recognizing Nicholas's voice Poseidon again vehemently swore and said "I'm still in bed and what are you winging about now?" Nicholas took a deep breath and said "This Cereberus here. Have you heard, or even seen the news because if you haven't, there was a big gun battle late last night in Corsica, between some of Luigi Muraditori's men and the French Secret services. Five of Luigi's men were killed and three were captured. News of the capture of those men has upset Gee Gee and I tried to calm him down but he exploded and said that we are all a bunch of no-good bitches." Poseidon began to yell into the phone.

However Nicholas kept talking then Poseidon heard Nicholas say "and he said I should tell that to the boss with that fancy name of Poseidon, then Gee Gee stormed out of the house with his bags and drove away in his hired car. However I do know that he had a telephone call from my cousin, Susan, to say she was holidaying in France with Nancy Oldfield and whether Gee Gee has gone there to see her, I don't know."

Poseidon was still very annoyed and stopped Nicholas from talking by shouting into the phone saying "So Gee Gee think's that we are a bunch of no-good bitches with soft bellies does he. Well you get your ass off over to my flat in Paris and meet up with my brother Hades because he is flying over from America and will be staying in my flat and he'll brief you, on where you are going and what we are going to

159

do about Gee Gee. You can take it from me that Gee Gee has had his day, because he is becoming a big headache to our organization. What with him having an affair with that duchess woman, he is disrupting our plans and he will have to be dealt with very quickly. Now look here, Hades will be landing in France tomorrow and in a short time he will be in my flat. I will telephone him and I'm going to tell him what you have just told me about Gee Gee and you had better be there and when you meet him he will tell you how we are going to get rid of GeeGee. Goodbye." Nicholas put the phone down and knowing he had time before Hades would be in Paris, he could telephone his uncle informing him he was flying to fly to Paris. While he was getting ready to leave he received a telephone call from Poseidon, who advised him that before he left for Paris he must contact a member of Muraditori's family and arrange a meeting with them in Paris. When Nicholas asked why should they have the meeting in Paris, he was told it would be better to have the meeting with the Muraditori family in his flat in Paris where it would be away from prying eyes. This meant Nicholas had to go to Italy, to contact Luigi's brother and bring him back to Paris.

In Italy he met Luigi's brother who insisted that two cousins come with him to meet Hades. When Nicholas arrived in Paris later than he intended with Luigi's brother and his two cousins, it was a stormy meeting in Poseidon flat with the Muraditori family speaking about the family member who had died when Luigi had been captured. Hades temper rose when the Muraditori family began to make accusations against him at not being able to trace where Luigi was being held. After many hours of conflicting accusations and bad tempers raging, Nicholas eventually managed calm things down and with Hades help they made plans for more men to go to Israel to find out where Liugi was being kept prisoner. Then he and Hades also asked for one of the Muraditori family to help find Gee Gee so that when he is found, the Mudaditori man was to shadow Gee Gee and to let Nicholas or Hades know exactly where Gee Gee goes and who he mixes with. These plans seemed to calm the Muraditori family members and they agreed to help in the search for Luigi and Gee Gee, and shortly afterwards they left Paris for Italy.

Back in England David Hogarth was with Kathy in the office of Richard Crossley who was asking them if they remembered the trial and verdict of Adolf Eichmann. Both David and Kathy nodded their heads as David said "Yes. We know he was executed but that is all in the past. Surely there are other matters you want to discuss with us?"

Richard looked a little upset as he answered "Yes there are, but the reason for me asking you that question was, are you aware that it was the Israeli secret services called Mossad, who tracked him down in Argentina? Then it was also through information from other national security services that we tracked down in England another person called William John Vassall who had been violating the Official Secrets Act and he was sentenced to 18 years in jail and it is because of that close cooperation we have with the Mossad is the reason why we want you to work very closely with the Israeli security services" Kathy and David were slightly confused by this conversation and Kathy said "Richard you do know that we do understand and realize, that having been employed by the Security Services for a number of years, both David and I are well aware of how the Security Services systems work, so what are you actually implying to us, are you saying that we are not up to the usual standards required by the Security Services?"

Richard was now very embarrassed by Kathy's outburst statement and the questions she was asking and he replied "Kathy I am very sorry to both of you if I have offended you. Yes we are well aware that you both are very good agents for the Security Services, so do not think that it is anything like you inferred. What I was trying to impress upon both of you, is that all the countries involved in this current operation, are putting the own Security Service agents on top alert and all those countries are working together very hard to try to smash this group." He paused to look at some papers he had in front of him and then said "You are well aware that the group calling themselves the Triumvirate feel very confident, therefore you are going to be called upon to work very closely with agents from all the other countries involved in this operation. This is because all the leaders of those countries, together with this country, have had many talks and discussions on how to break the Triumvirate group, because they realize they are a danger to the whole world. Information is coming into us telling us that they are very near to supplying all the atomic fuels to those middle-eastern countries, and those countries are now quite capable of making atomic weapons"

Suddenly the door opened and Mike Taggert entered the room just as Richard had finished speaking. Richard looked at Mike and said "Mike I have just been telling Kathy and David the situation as we know of it up to this present time." Mike said to David "Well that is good, because both you and Bruce must have a good idea where you will soon be going and Kathy you will be told your duties tomorrow. Everyone I have spoken to about your escapade in Brazil was very impressed with your help and its outcome. However all of us know that the real trial and test is about to start and anything can happen." He paused and seeing that both David and Bruce, together with Kathy, did not appear to be worried Mike carried on speaking "My advice to everyone is to be extra careful, so please remember that old adage, *Be careful of a wounded animal, because a wounded animal can be very dangerous.* Gerry Giovanie is a human animal and can be a very dangerous person and we have information he has upset some senior members of the Triumvirate. The Triumvirate will strike hard and it will not be long before they do so. However there is a strong feeling that their organization is beginning to fall apart."

Mike paused again to look at them, then said "Information has reached us that Gerry Giovanie has upset the top person in the Triumvirate group, namely Poseidon and there is also a strong feeling amongst our top men, that Gee Gee is living a dangerous period of his life and may not have long to live. So watch out because we could have two wounded dangerous animals to deal with."

While Mike was talking to Bruce, Kathy and David in London, Gerry Giovanie was standing with one of his bodyguards at Orly airport in France remembering the weekend he had spent at the home of Jeanette Pitman in Flimwell, while the Duke of Chardminster had been away on business and he had struck up a very amorous friendship with her. He was waiting to meet Susan Pitman and her stepmother Jeanette Pitman who were flying in the next plane to land, When their plane had landed and they had alighted from the plane and were coming towards him, Gerry could see how pretty Susan was, and he said to his body guard "What do you think of that beauty for a daughter eh? She is yours to do what you like with, but I must say though, I prefer her mother best." When the women met Gerry he went straight to Jeanette and took her by surprise by kissing her fully on the lips. Although she was very startled by that approach, Jeanette quite liked it and coquettishly said "I must say I have never been welcomed like that before." Knowing of the close relationship between her stepmother and Gee Gee, Susan was also very surprised at the welcome Gerry had given to her stepmother, but as she was standing beside her Susan was looking at the person standing near Gerry.

162

While she was looking at him she was thinking how smart and handsome that person looked, then she was surprised but felt flattered when that person began to say some encouraging and suggesting remarks to her, but at that moment she didn't know he was a body-guard for Gerry. After their brief greeting, Gerry's bodyguard put Jeanette's and Susan's luggage into the car boot and ushered them into the car, then he drove them to a very high-class hotel. When they arrived at the hotel Susan was feeling very comfortable in the company of the person sitting beside her, and after entering the hotel and they were at the reception desk and Susan was amazed when she heard the receptionist say to Gerry "Here are the two keys to your rooms Mr Giovanie and one for Mr Freeman" He took the keys and they entered a lift and went up to the sixth floor and with the porters carrying their luggage they stopped when they arrived at the doors to their rooms, Gerry said to the porter "Put those two suitcases (pointing to them) in that room and put the others in the room next door." Noticing the porters were putting her mothers suitcases into the room that Gerry had said he was sleeping in, Susan looked immediately to her step- mother expecting her to say something, but hearing no response, she began to wonder what was going to happen next. She was waiting for her stepmother to speak and was very surprised when her stepmother and Gerry went into one room., leaving Susan and the bodyguard to go into the other room. When she was in the room with the bodyguard, it took her some time before she could speak, but the bodyguard seeing the look on Susan's face said "Don't worry. Gerry has arranged everything and you will soon understand that everything will be fine."

Very shortly afterwards Gerry came into their room and said to the bodyguard "I want you to do some telephoning for me" and at that point Gee Gee went up, and whispered to him so that Susan couldn't hear what he was saying, then he left the room.

A short while later Gerry and Jeanette knocked on the door and called out "Are you ready Susan?" Susan opened the door and all three of them went downstairs into the cocktail lounge for a drink. It was while they were sitting casually talking and drinking Susan noticed that Gee Gee kept saying passionate things to Jeanette who seemed to be enjoying the attention he was giving her, and this upset Susan, who was again shaken. Seeing and hearing her stepmother behaving in such a common way, she quietly sat there and thought for a moment, then said "Mother, will you be wearing anything different for dinner this evening?" Jeanette stopped listening to Gerry and replied "Yes I shall be wearing that nice floral dress that I know you like." Susan gave her stepmother a sickly smile and said "Oh I'm glad you are wearing that floral dress, because I now know what I'm going to wear." When they had nearly finished their drinks and were contemplating retiring to their rooms, Susan quietly whispered to her mother "Mother, are you going to sleep in that room with Gerry?" Jeanette with a lovely smile quietly replied "Why? What difference would that make?" Jeanette finished her drink and giving Susan a lovely smile said "Now I'm going to my room to sort a few things out and get myself ready for this evening," then as she walked past Susan she said "I will see you later for dinner. Bye darling." With her stepmother and Gee Gee gone, and as she made her way to her room, her mind was working very fast then when she opened the door and went inside, seeing the bodyguard sitting in a chair reading a newspaper it reminded her that she was supposed to be sharing the room with him tonight. Suddenly a bright idea came to her and she said to the bodyguard "Hello I see you have finished your duties for Gerry and you are taking it easy," but before he could answer she carried on talking "I've just been speaking to my stepmother and she would like me to go to the cosmetic shop, which is just a few shops away from the hotel. Hopefully I will not be too long, and if I leave now I should be back in about 15 minutes." He put the newspaper down and nicely said "I will come with you if you would like me to?" For a moment she felt very sorry for him, but she quickly replied "That is very kind of you, but no thank you, because what I have to get her is something very personal, and hopefully I shouldn't be very long." She put on her coat, picked up her purse and after saying cheerio to the bodyguard she quickly left the room.

Outside the hotel she got into a taxi and went for short drive that ended when she was well away from the hotel where she felt safe enough to use a telephone. She telephoned her father, who was at home at Flimwell in England, and after telling him who she was and the hotel where she was staying she began crying, he immediately began asking her what was the trouble and she told him how her stepmother was behaving with Gerry Giovanie. He told her not to worry because he somehow knew that Jeanette was having a relationship with him and said that everything was being taken care of. Hearing her father telling her that news she stopped crying then said "Daddy I am very sorry to tell you that bad news about her" but he interrupted her speaking because he said " All you have done is to confirm my suspicions about her and of the way she has been behaving over the past few years."

Susan began crying again and sobbed to her father "Daddy, oh Daddy, since mummy died I have felt very sorry for you because I feel I have let you down over my behaviour. I should have seen how Jeanette was behaving and I do wish I could also have been a better daughter to you." He immediately interrupted her saying "Now don't you start thinking those awful things about yourself, because you have been a wonderful daughter and one that I love very much. You have only confirmed my thoughts and doubts about Jeanette's behaviour, and I am pleased you have telephoned. When I was in London last week I saw my solicitors and I have put in for a divorce, because ever since your mother's death and after I had married Jeanette, I knew I had made a mistake by marrying her. However I have also made other mistakes, and now you having told me that news about her, I can tell you some other news about what I intend to do concerning your cousin Nicholas. He doesn't realize that I know he is keeping friends with bad people and he is also doing some very awful things. Later today I am going to go to London and stopping the night at the Savoy Hotel, because I am going to have dinner with my old school friend Commander Bryant, who is the head of the Special branch of the Metropolitan Police and I am going to talk to him about Nicholas, and that hopefully it will take care of that little problem. Now don't you worry or say anything, because everything will be all right and will you promise me you will not tell Jeanette about this conversation you and I have had." Susan replied "Daddy do take care of yourself and remember that I love you very much and I also promise that I will not repeat this conversation to anyone. I must go now, because nobody knows that I have left the hotel or that I am telephoning you. Bye." Susan returned to the hotel and when she went into the room the bodyguard said to her "Oh hello, that errand took you a little longer than you expected." She answered "Yes it did, because I was still unable to get what my Stepmother wanted and I looked around for something else"

While Gee Gee, Jeanette, Susan and the bodyguard were in their hotel in Paris eating their evening meal, in the Savoy Hotel in London, the Duke of Chardminster was talking to his old school friend Commander Charles Bryant and explaining to him the connection he had with his nephew, Nicholas Pitman. The Duke said "Charles I must confess it all started about two years ago when Nicholas came and asked me if I would change some Bearer Bonds into cash for him. Being chairman of my own bank I couldn't see any harm in changing them and I did so. However after a period of time it began to become a regular habit and I became suspicious and I began to make few discreet enquires and I have just recently discovered that bonds were coming from Middle Eastern companies and recently one came from an American company." Charles interrupted the Duke "I do apologize for interrupting you, because I know more about this money business and I was getting very worried about you. One thing I cannot understand, why on earth didn't you speak to me earlier when all this started happening? I could have helped you." The Duke was shaking his head and was about to speak when Charles carried on speaking, "I again apologize for being unable to reveal the real nature on why I could have helped you and I am unable to explain to you in detail what I now know and why I am not allowed to tell you." The Duke interrupted Charles a by saying "Can you help me? I believe I have been used for laundering and I am very worried."

Charles said "All I am allowed to say to you, that what you have said about the Bearer Bonds is very important to me, and as you have revealed to me how you began to be involved in the exchanging of them, and yes I will do my very best to keep your name out of this business. From what you have said I can see that you are an innocent person."

Charles stopped talking and smiled at the Duke of Chardminster who appeared to be relieved with what he had heard. He was smiling as he said "Thank you Charles for those comforting words. It is always nice to know that one can depend on his friends in time of need." Charles quickly said "I would like to know where Nicholas is, can you tell me where he is?" The duke frowned and had a worried look on his face as he said "Well earlier today he did telephone me and said he was going to Paris, but where he is staying I have no idea." Charles was smiling as he said "That's all I want to know. I am sorry I have to go, because I have much work to do, I must leave you now but before I leave, I would like to say it was lovely having a meal with you again." Charles shook hands with the Duke and went immediately to Scotland Yard and knowing that Richard Crossley was at home, he telephoned him and informed him that Nicholas was in Paris. Richard Crossley said "Thank you very much for that information. It was only an hour ago I was informed that GeeGee and the Duchess of Chardminster are staying at the Ritz Hotel and I immediately sent two of our agents over there to keep a watch on him, because I believe that if we know where he is staying so will Poseidon, and that will mean that there could be trouble." Charles immediately said "Good man, because when the Duke of Chardminster told me about Nicholas Pitman I began to think of trouble brewing. Well we will have to wait and see what becomes of all this. I will come to your office tomorrow morning for an update, Goodnight."

In Poseidon's flat a telephone was ringing, Hades answered saying "Hello what" then he shouted to Nicholas Pitman who was standing nearby, "there's a person on this telephone who I am having trouble understanding what he is saying. Come and see if you can make anything of it." Nicholas took the telephone from Hades (Mario) and said "Can I help you?" The person spoke with a very bad Italian accent saying "I know where GeeGee is staying. He is in the Ritz Hotel and he has two ladies and one man with him and at this moment they are having a meal in the hotel restaurant, Goodbye" Nicholas put the telephone down and said to Mario "That person informed us that GeeGee is at the Ritz hotel having a meal and he has two ladies with him and possibly a bodyguard." Before Nicholas could say anything else Mario became excited saying "Come on we'll have to get going before he moves." Nicholas said "Why don't we take our time getting there because we have someone there watching them and if Gee Gee goes anywhere we shall immediately know." Mario was satisfied and agreed. In the hotel restaurant, after Gee Gee and the others had finished their meal, because he had seen two strange men near the entrance door peering into the restaurant, GeeGee felt uncomfortable and whispered to his bodyguard "I want you to check that our car is okay with plenty of gas in it." The bodyguard went and when he came back he said "The car is full of gas and Boss you are right I recognized the two of them." GeeGee looked at Jeanette saying "I'm sorry about this, but I think it would be a good idea if we depart and book into another hotel."

Jeanette began to worry and ask questions, but all GeeGee would say "Look. There are people who want to know where I am, and I know that I'm being followed and I have to leave here immediately. I can, and do, assure you it has nothing to do with your husband." They all rose from the table and GeeGee settled the bill with the head waiter and asked to see the hotel manager, when GeeGee explained to the hotel manager why they had to leave immediately the hotel manager said he understood and waived the fee for the booking of the rooms. It was 10.30pm when they all got into GeeGee's car at the rear entrance of the hotel. GeeGee was sitting with Jeanette in the back seats, with Susan sitting in the front with the bodyguard driving the car. As the car drove away from the rear of the hotel into Rue Cambon, two cars began following them. GeeGee noticing the cars were following suggested a detour round the Place de la Concorde then said turn right into Cours la Reine, because the two cars behind them were going very fast. As they entered into Cours Albert Jer they were travelling quite fast, they still going very fast when they entered into the Alma Tunnel. Inside the tunnel they suddenly felt a big bump at the rear of their car that caused their car to hit a pillar and swerve into the tunnel wall turning the car into a big heap. Seeing the crash the other cars managed to stop, and when people went to the wreck of GeeGee's car they saw that he and Jeanette were very badly disfigured and appeared to be dead and the bodyguard who had been driving was also dead. Susan who was wearing a seat belt was very badly injured and bleeding from her mouth. The police were called and when they and the SAMU ambulances together with the medical team arrived, they immediately tended to Susan, who was in a coma, and took her immediately to hospital where they operated on her straight away. When questioned by the police the men who were driving the other cars explained to the police that they were not involved in the accident and were allowed to leave. It was a little later when Poseidon was telephoned and informed of the accident and of GeeGee's death, he said that he was not sorry and pleased to hear of his death. Unbeknown to Poseidon, Henri Fouchard who is an agent of the French foreign Intelligence Service, known as the Direction Generale de la Securite Exterieure (DGSE), knowing Nicholas was in Paris had informed the French Elysee & Renseignements, which is the gathering arm of the French National police, with information concerning his connection with the Triumvirate and of his dealings with forged paintings and drugs The DGSE hearing of the accident and kmowing that the Duke of Chardminster's daughter was involved and was seriously injured, they sent two of their men to the hospital to stand guard and watch.

Poseidon had telephoned Nicholas and told him of the accident. The Duke of Chardminster hearing of Susan's accident booked a flight to Paris to go to the hospital to see his daughter. Nicholas was very upset hearing the news he flew into a rage and had an argument with Hades, and afterwards he arrived at the hospital just before the Duke of Chardminster. The two DGSE guards having been given a photograph of Nicholas, saw him arrive at the hospital and watched him go to Susan's bedside, but with her still being unconscious and unable to talk, he left her. On leaving the hospital the two DGSE men spoke to him "Sir, are you related to the young lady injured in that accident?" He replied "Yes I'm her cousin" one of the DGSE men said "We would appreciate it if you would accompany us to the police station to give us some more information about her."

# CHAPTER 9

## (Israel)

Arriving at the police station and before he was spoken to, Nicholas was handcuffed and taken away in an enclosed van and transported to another place where the DGSE began to interrogate him concerning his connections with the Triumvirate. It was after 24 hours of intense interrogation, and then only with the promise that he would be given a lighter sentence if he told them everything he knew of the Triumvirate future moves and of their organization. When knowing of the future movements of the Triumvirate, the DGSE immediately telephoned London, and conveyed the news to Mike Taggert and Richard Crossley immediately arranged for David Hogarth and Bruce Robertson to go to Israel and be met by members of the Mossad (The Israeli secret service) and introduced to Abraham Filligoti, the Head of Mossad. Having been told of Nicholas Pitman's arrest, Kathy Goolaburra, who was already in Israel, was also told to contact Abraham Filligotti with the latest news concerning the arrest and of the death of Gerry Giovanie (GeeGee)..

While all this was taking place, because they had been told a couple days ago to fly from Israel and go to Italy, Bob Statham and Kevin Mitchell together with Julius Silverman were in Italy shadowing a member of the Muraditori gang, when Julius received a message to say that he, Bob and Kevin were to return to Israel immediately, because a substantial number of members of the Muraditori gang had just landed at an old wartime aerodrome that was being used as a small civilian airport which was near the town of Dimona which is near Al Arish in Israel. The three of them went to Milan airport and boarded a plane to Israel, and when they landed they were met at the airport by Abraham Filligoti, who informed them that an Israeli agent had infiltrated the mixed Muraditori gang, and had informed Filligoti that the gang had were at that small civilian aerodrome near Dimona, and they had contacted a local man who gave them news of where he had been told Luigi Muraditori could be kept prisoner, and the gang were now awaiting Poseidon and Hades to get to the airport, because he was bringing some more men with him before heading to the place where they believed Muraditori was hidden.

Julius, Bob and Kevin were told by Filligoti it was essential for them to hurry and get to Israel as soon as possible and he also told them that when they arrive at Dimona to be very careful and keep alert but also keep out of sight and to await further instructions, because when Poseidon and Hades arrive they were bringing some extra men and counting the Muraditori gang, it could amount to be about 40 men in total, who were all likely to be heavily armed and hopefully landing at that civilian airport near Dimona. He also told them to be careful because a number of other members of the world's security services would be there at Dimona possibly before them. This was to help makeup a substantial force against the gang and he added because of the other security men being near or around Dimona, rooms would be hard to find and he said "I have already booked two rooms for you in a small hotel next to the restaurant, so you had better hurry and by the way I shall be with you as soon as David Hogarth and Bruce Robertson arrive. They are expected to arrive and be with me in Israel within the next 4 hours."

While Bob Statham, Kevin Mitchell and Julius Silverman were discreetly, but hurriedly making their way to Dimona, Poseidon with Hades and a group of men were on a plane flying over the Mediterranean Sea, heading for the civilian aerodrome that they believed that they we going to land unobserved and undetected.

A few hours later in Dimona, Bob, Kevin and Julius had booked into the small hotel, next to the restaurant. When they entered the restaurant for their evening meal it was practically empty and they were just about to have a cup of coffee when Bob who was earnestly looking at a dark skinned lady startled the other two when he suddenly said "Gee whiz I don't believe it. Now don't you two say anything out loud, but just look at that lovely dark skinned woman sitting over the other side of the room, doesn't she look like Kathy?" The three of them were intently looking across at her when Kevin said "Kevin I believe you are right let's go and talk to her." Leaving Julius sitting at their table, they went to the lady and as she turned round they immediately recognized her and Bob said "Kathy, we didn't recognize you dressed as you are, because you look so different. How long have you been here and did you know we were going to be here?" She looked and smiled at them saying "Yes I knew and I have been waiting for you," before she could say anything else, they called out to Julius "Come and meet Kathy." When Julius was introduced, they were all seated around the same table, their meals arrived and just after they had finished eating and were talking, they heard the sound of a large plane go overhead, flying very low. For a moment they looked at each other, then hurriedly going outside, they saw a plane with its undercarriage lowered, and its landing lights glowing, flying in the direction of the civilian aerodrome, a few miles away. They immediately telephoned and informed Abraham Fillgoti and they were told that he would soon be with them and he would tell them their instructions.

At the old aerodrome after the plane had landed and all the passengers with their equipment and stores had been quickly unloaded, the plane was put into an hanger and kept out of sight. Poseidon (Marcus) knew that some brick buildings had been built around the airfield and he told his men to go into them and find a bed to sleep, while he and Mario (Hades) went into another building that was near the control tower. Poseidon, who was still very upset over the arrest of Cereberus (Nicholas Pitman), said to Mario "Before you begin to think of going to bed, we have got to stop Luigi Muraditori from talking, therefore you and I have got to sit down and work out a plan of action to stop him and those agents from spoiling our plans for the shipment of the next big load of drugs, because we need that money to buy more Uranium and Plutonium for the Middle Eastern countries. After we have dealt with Luigi, I'm going to suggest to those countries, that their next supply to them is going to be the last supply of the nuclear stuff. We therefore will have to make sure that the Uranium and Plutonium is a big load, that is huge enough to keep them happy and hopefully we should be able to collect from them a large amount of money that should keep us happy for a long time." Poseidon proceeded to withdraw from his brief case a large map and opened it and looking at the map he pointed with a pencil to the town of AlArish and said "Mario we are near here (pointing) and I think that Luigi could be there.(pointing again at the map).

Mario could see that Marcus was pointing to a spot on the map near to the Dead Sea and the wilderness of Judea. Mario said "I disagree with you because I think where you are pointing is where those security agents would expect you to go, but I feel that Luigi could be here (pointing) in a house or a compound in Sede Boger." For the first time Marcus looked at his brother in amazement "What a bright lad you have turned out to be, I believe you could be right. I think it would be a good idea if you and I went to sleep and we can get up early and work out a plan on where he could be kept a prisoner, then formulate a plan of action when we get there and what time do we start leaving here."

Just before Kevin and the other two, left the restaurant, Hamid the restaurant owner came to their table and said to Bob "Do you know this young lady?" (pointing to Kathy) Bob looked amazed and looking at the others before replying "Yes, why is something wrong?" the owner said "Oh no there is nothing wrong, but I think you ought to know what a lovely lady she is, because a few days ago my wife was out walking and she fell over cutting her head very badly that caused slight concussion and this lady was there, tended to her wounds and then brought her home here and while she tended to my wife's injuries, she also told me my wife was suffering from *Candidiasis*, and she told me it was a fungal disease that causes itching and she said she was going to stay here with my wife until she recovers from the disease and her injuries. This made my wife feel much happier and this lady has stayed with her all the time coming in here every day and she wouldn't let me pay her for her trouble. She told me she had to survey some building work in this area, but because of my wife's injuries she has stayed close by and helped her, and I do not know how to thank her." Kathy was very embarrassed listening to him and quickly said "Hamid, anyone would have done what I have done." Hamid shook his head and smiled and he looked at the others who were also smiling then he said "There is no need for any of you to pay for your meals." After thanking him and when Hamid left, Kathy began to tell them that she had been in Dimona for 7days and that prior to Hamid's wife accident she had been touring and exploring the area and had been to the civilian airfield and was there when some of Luigi's men arrived and she had secretly met the Israeli agent who is with the Muraditori gang. Listening to her talking they realized that she was a remarkable person, who besides performing her AISS duties she had also taken the time to show compassion to Hamid's wife.

Abraham Filligoti with David and Bruce Robertson and few others arrived in Dimona in the early hours of the morning. When Bob, Kevin and Julius were in the restaurant having their breakfast they were very surprised to see Abraham, David and Bruce walk in and then very shortly afterwards Kathy came in and soon they were all listening to what they had to do and who and how many of their fellow agents there were. After discussing what next to do David said to Bob and Kevin "We would like you two to go immediately to the airfield, have a good look round but don't expose yourselves, keep out of sight and to report to us what is happening there, while the others will remain here discussing plans" Looking at Kathy he could see by the look on her face that she was unhappy because by the plans that had been proposed he could see that it looked as though she was going to be left out of doing anything.

Then he said to her "Don't worry Kathy we haven't forgotten you because what I would like you to do is to stay here and watch out to see if any more of the Poseidon gang are around." Again it was the look of dismay on her face telling she was staying behind that made David say "You will be coming with us when we know where Poseidon is, but at the moment all Abraham and me are doing is to go and see the other agents who we know are around here and talk with them about our plans and hopefully know where Poseidon is going, then we can then formulate a plan where this time he can be stopped or apprehended." It was an hour later that Bob and Kevin reported that Poseidon and a large party were leaving the airfield in large vehicles and had taken the road to Sede Boger.

Hearing that news both Abraham and David were surprised because they thought that Poseidon would have gone the opposite way towards the Dead Sea, and now they were alarmed by this news, and they realized that somehow he must have been told that Luigi was in Sede Boger and now they knew that they had to get there before Poseidon. They hurriedly left the restaurant and informed all the other agents what was happening and after a hurried discussion they all quickly arranged to meet just outside Sede Boger. When they arrived at their meeting place, which was on the borders and out of sight of Sede Boger, they quickly hid their vehicles and all gathered round to listen to Abraham Filligoti speaking. He said "I want you to know that Poseidon and his men are already here and I feel you all should know who your fellow members are in this operation. We have a senior member of the French DST (Direction de la Surveillance du Territoire), a senior delegate from the Australian security (AISS) and members of the American (CIA) as well as the British delegation (MI6). I am the senior man of Mossad the (Israeli Secret Police). Now

I have been advised by the senior members of all the countries involved in this action, that as we are on Israeli soil, this should be an Israeli led operation, so I will be the chief negotiator and therefore in charge. We will now exchange views on how we are going to operate this action." A big discussion then took place and within an hour, it was eventually agreed on the plan of operation.

It was now dark and immediately after the discussion, the American agents went into Sede Boger and cautiously went to where they knew Luigi was being kept a prisoner. When they were near the building, they could see and hear a number of men talking out loud and walking around looking into all sort of places. The Americans kept hidden and just watched, then one of them hearing the searching men speaking he realized that they were Poseidon's men, he quietly whispered to his companions that he would go back to Abraham Fillgoti and tell him the news. When Filligoti heard of the position of Poseidon's men he spoke to David, they immediately told the rest of the agents to take up their agreed positions, then David spoke to Kathy saying "I want you to keep near to me and Bruce." At first she was a little annoyed at being treated like a child, but after speaking to Bruce she understood why David had spoken to her and as they moved into their position, Bruce amazed her when he whispered to her "You do realize that he is in love with you and is trying to keep you safe," she just quietly smiled and said "I'll believe it when he says that to me."

With everyone in their stated positions, David left Kathy with Bruce while he went quietly went around to everyone reminding them of the importance of the action, and to wait for the starting signal from Abraham. Looking at his watch he saw that the time was 2.00am and he knew he was beginning to feel a little tired, then he realized that Abraham had given him some tablets that would keep him awake. He took a flask from his pocket and as he drank some water he swallowed two of the tablets, then made his way back to Abraham and with some others was discussing the plan with them when Abraham said "I think now is the time to move and start the operation," and he gave the signal.

Hearing the signal, the Americans made a dash towards the building next to where Luigi was being held, Henri Fouchard and his men who were nearby went to follow but some of Poseidon's men seeing the movement of the Americans and Henri's men to the building opened fire and everyone took cover and began to return the fire. The noise of the gunfire caused other Poseidon's men to awaken and they began looking where the gunfire was coming from. Very soon as each side became aware of the other persons presence, they began firing and everyone was engaged in their own personal battle with Poseidon's men. The noise of the gunfire had awakened Poseidon and Hades who were in the centre of the individual battles going on, and then seeing how precarious their position was, they began to make moves to get to the building where they knew Luigi was a prisoner. David however had already sensed they would make for Luigi and he said to Bruce, "I want you to stay here with Kathy and keep her safe, at the same time you deal with those Poseidon men who are keeping you penned in here, while I take a couple of men with me to get to Luigi." Then he left with the men and they stealthily made their way to where Luigi was being held. It was very dangerous going the long way round, but they eventually managed to get inside the building and they were told that one of Poseidon's men had previously managed to get into the building, who before being killed by the men guarding Luigi had managed to fire his gun at Luigi and badly wounded him. On learning of the state of Luigi injuries, David said to everyone "Luigi should be attended to by a doctor, but on no account do we let any of Poseidon's men know of the state of Luigi's injuries, we must let them think that he is still unharmed."

Inside the building they could hear of the mayhem of gunfire going on outside and they knew they had stay inside and fight it out. Suddenly terrific blasts of gunfire and explosions shook the building, which shattered the front doors and then some parts of the building became unsafe, Abraham Filligoti who had accompanied David knew that they were in dire trouble because Poseidon had many more men on the outside. They decided to move Luigi to a secure part of the building, and while some of the men were moving Luigi, Abraham suggested they plant booby traps near the stairway, David said he would take two men to plant them. He was thinking of the danger when he suddenly felt as though someone was close to him this caused remembered the wartime bombing trip to Berlin and of Mabel Flitch. Thinking of her seemed to give him comfort and strength and he felt much safer. After he and the other two had placed the booby traps near the stairway and along the ground floor, they hurriedly went to the secure part of the building and waited for Poseidon's men to enter the building.

Suddenly he thought of Kathy and was pleased she wasn't with him. When Poseidon's men came rushing into the building, the booby traps began exploding killing one man and injuring many more of them, then seeing that they had many casualties they hurriedly retired to the outside of the building. It was after the big explosion at the main doors of the building and hearing of the state inside the building Poseidon knew that going for Luigi was useless. He quickly called his men together and began to concentrate his manpower and guns where he thought Bruce, Kathy and the others were situated. Despite having many casualties Poseidon and Hades knew that they had inflicted more casualties on Abraham and David's men, than their own men had suffered, therefore believing they had more men available to carry on the fight Hades began to talk with Poseidon on how to annihilate the forces opposing them. Poseidon stood quite still clasping hands together and thought for a moment, then he quietly said "Mario in that large hanger at that civil aerodrome, we have all the antiques and drugs we have been storing and collecting and they and they are worth a lot of money. Now I have given it a lot of thought. I feel we should leave here immediately and get away with our men and go back to that aerodrome and clear all of that stuff out of the hanger, because I am beginning to believe that those security agents know we have something there and it would be better for us to get that gear to a much safer place, possibly to that middle Eastern country. We could leave Muraditori men here to fight to free Luigi if they want to, because he will not be a danger to us because we will have changed our hiding places" Mario had a big smile on his face and jumped up gleefully clapping his hands as he said "Marcus what a good idea. I will quickly go to our lads and tell them to leave singly and quietly and go to our trucks and we can get away, so that those Security agents can fight it out with the Muraditori gang." Previously Poseidon had told the Muraditori men to stay and put up a good fight and get Luigi out of the building. Mario very quickly left and told his men what was happening and to quietly to move out. However inside the building, David was getting very worried because of the heavy fighting from the Muraditori gang he knew that he and the men with him were now very low on ammunition.

Bruce thought he and his men were in a very favourable position, because besides having the big onslaught that Poseidon and his men had inflicted on them, they had not had many serious casualties, and he was wondering why things appeared a little quiet, and the situation appeared a little different, because there had been little firing then he realized the opposition towards him had got weaker and he said to

Kevin "I wonder what the ruse is now, because they have only been firing at us sporadically and I think the time has come for us to make a move." It was because there had hardly been any shooting, Kathy spoke to Bruce saying "I have also noticed the firing has decreased and I am very worried about David and the others, because they did take a huge amount of firing and don't forget there was that big explosion and I think it would be a good idea if Kevin and I went to the building where Luigi's is being held to see how David and Abraham are managing, and to help them if need be." Realizing that David and Abraham had been under a big onslaught and also remembering David's orders to him about not letting her out of his sight and realizing he couldn't stop her Bruce agreed.

Bruce looked at her then he said to Kevin "David told me not to let her out of my sight and make sure she keeps with you, so you look after her and be very careful how you go." When Kevin and Kathy were creeping very stealthy away and slowly making their way to the rear side of the building, they suddenly heard the sound of voices and many people moving around. They began to wonder what was happening, stopped and hid for a few moments listening to the movements of the people and waited to see if they had been seen or would come under fire. When nothing happened they cautiously moved further onwards, suddenly Kevin whispered to her "Kathy be quiet there's someone talking nearby" they both stayed still just listening to the voice. They waited for a few more moments and then they moved slowly very quietly forward and they saw a man lying on the ground softly crying out "Could someone please help me?" Not realizing that it could be one of the Muraditori men, Kevin quietly said "Kathy I will go to see who it is and if there is no one else nearby I will signal with my torch and you come to me." Kevin left Kathy and went forward, then very shortly afterwards she saw his torch signal and went to him. When she got there she looked at the man and saw that he was very badly wounded and she immediately said "Kevin I'll stay here and tend to him and try to make him as comfortable as possible and you go on to David." Kevin could tell by the tone of her voice and the look on her face that she was adamant and any argument against her staying would be useless, he left her and said "Kathy I know he is badly injured but he could on of Muraditori's men so be very careful and have your weapons close by."

Kathy began working through the dim light to dress his wounds from the first aid kit she always carried with her, then noticing he wasn't speaking she saw that he was unconscious. It was while she was tending to him and because she felt as though someone else was close to her that she became afraid. Looking around she couldn't see anyone in the darkness then she heard a voice quietly say "Kathy you are doing a good job keep up the good work and don't worry I'll look after you" suddenly she could feel the presence of someone very strong nearby and she thought of Tony Wright. While she attended to the injured man the thought of him being near made her feel very strong and safe.

When Kevin arrived and seeing the state of iof the building he thought that everyone who was inside would be dead. After he had managed to get inside the building, he crept very carefully and he kept calling out David and Abraham's names, then one of the men inside recognized his voice and he made himself known to him. It was after he had met and told David and Abraham everything and where Kathy was, that they heard outside the noise of vehicle engines and wondered what was happening then they heard one of Muraditori's men shouting out that Poseidon's men were leaving. Abraham immediately got in touch with his superiors afterwards he said to David "There is a sizable force of Israeli military reinforcements arriving here." It was just after Poseidon and his men had left the area in their vehicles that the military arrived and within a few minutes they had surrounded Muraditori men and took them prisoners, two doctors and medical staff went into the building and the medical staff took Luigi away on a stretcher with the prisoners. Kevin spoke to the doctors about Kathy and then he and David accompanied them to where Kathy was still tending to the injured man.

When the doctors examined the man they said to Kathy "You have made an excellent job of tending to this person, it is quite a professional piece of nursing. Well done, you probably have saved his life by being compassionate and a good Samaritan."

Knowing that the man was not going to die and was being taken away by the Israeli military and going to get hospital treatment, she began to relax but at the same time she knew she had been very frightened all the time she had been tending to him, and felt very pleased with her efforts. Suddenly she remembered that while she had been tending to him, she had heard a voice that reminded her of Tony Wright telling her he would look after her. This made her think very hard about the unusualness of it, then she remembered the church minister, Mr.Theobald, reading to her the parable of the 'Good

179

Samaritan' from the Holy book of Luke and she began comparing it with what she had been doing and this made her feel quite satisfied.

David was thinking of Poseidon's departure and said to Abraham "I think the reason why Poseidon suddenly left here was to get back to that civil aerodrome to retrieve his possessions. Do you think we can catch up with him? If so, we must hurry because we have lost a lot of time" Abraham was shaking his head and said "David I think you are right in thinking Poseidon has gone there and I know we have no chance in catching up with him by road, but if we go to the military establishment which is not far away, we can go by air." Quickly going around and collecting all their men, they made their way to the military airfield establishment, where much to Bruce and David's surprise there were a large number of helicopters. Abraham left David and the others while he went to arrange transport, when he came back he appeared upset because he said "At the moment they are short of pilots therefore we can only have the use of two of the helicopters and some of us must go by road." Bruce quickly said "But David and I are ex jet pilots and we have been trained to fly helicopters." Abraham quickly went back to the offices and when he returned he said "They are happy for you to fly two more extra helicopters so we can go as soon as you loaded and are ready." After quickly making plans where they could land and how to attack the aerodrome, it was 30 minutes later, with David and Bruce piloting two, all four helicopters were airborne carrying all of them with their equipment. They didn't fly anywhere near the civil aerodrome but landed three miles away, knowing that there would be vehicles waiting for them and then dividing themselves into groups, they quickly and quietly made their way to the aerodrome. After leaving the vehicles well away from the airfield. When they arrived at the perimeter of the aerodrome, David and Abraham could see that Poseidon's men were still loading their plane, Abraham waited until he was sure that all his men had arrived, then at a given signal they opened their attack firing at the men loading the plane. Poseidon, who was in the control tower, was surprised by this attack and said to Hades "Where is all that firing coming from? If it's those security men they have got here very quickly and we have got to get out of here as soon as possible and that means we will have to leave the rest of our gear behind." Hades was upset and vehemently said "No, we can't do that, we will lose too much money." Poseidon shouted at him "It's either leaving that stuff behind and losing money, or losing our lives. You can stay behind if you want to, but I'm going now." He quickly stormed out of the room and told the pilot to get to the plane.

The pilot and Poseidon opened the door and rushed towards the plane, but the firing was very severe and they noticed that most of the firing was being directed towards the plane.

They quickly rushed back to the control tower closed the door and stayed inside and concentrated on how to get to the plane. Hades and his men however had begun causing many casualties to David's men. Abraham knowing of the casualties being inflicted to David and his men managed to get to him and said "How do you think things are going for you so far?" It had only been few moments before Abraham had appeared that David had made an assessment of the casualties inflicted on his men replied "We have had casualties and I think we will be here for some time, because they are well protected against our small arms fire because they are using much heavier fire power against us." Abraham nodded his head saying "Well we will have to do something about that then won't we?" Quickly he left David and after Abraham had gone, for 20 minutes David's men withstood an exchange of heavy gunfire from Poseidon's forces that made him begin to get worried. Then Abraham suddenly reappeared beside him again saying "We have some military forces joining with us shortly and then we going to attack them with our heavier guns." Orders were dispatched to tell every one of their men to stay low and keep outside of the airfield wiring. After the order had been quickly passed around to everyone, the Israeli's soldiers came and opened fire with their heavier guns. David was looking at the plane standing on its parking pan just inside the perimeter of the aerodrome, and he could see that the Israeli's were concentrating their firing at the plane, when its undercarriage collapsed and the plane fell onto to its nose and its wings began to burn. Then he saw the hanger was being targeted with phosphorus bullets and because it was full of sacks of drugs and wooden framed antiques the hanger began to burn.

Inside the control tower, when Poseidon saw the plane collapse and the hanger on fire he called out to Hades "Mario we have got to get out of here now. Let's try and make our way towards the Dead Sea." Mario came rushing in and was very upset seeing the damaged plane and the hanger burning, agreed, but then he began to rant and rave when the firing was targeted at the control tower, suddenly he shouted out "Come on We can't stay here and be killed, let's go outside and make a charge and that will surprise them." Suddenly the windows

181

around them began being shattered then the shells began to take their toll of the brickwork, then amid the all the uproar the control tower began to collapse into rubble, killing and badly maiming everyone inside it. The remainder of Poseidon's men who were on the outside, seeing the hanger and the plane burning furiously and with the control tower in ruins, they knew it was useless to carry on the fight, so they stopped firing and surrendered. Hearing no more return fire from them Abraham waited a few moments then ordered his Israeli men to advance and deal with the remaining Poseidon's men. After they quickly rounded up those who were surrendering, David, Bruce, Kevin and Kathy went into the airfield and began to look at the havoc that had been made. They went to where the control tower had been situated and searched among the ruins, and after removing some of the rubble they found some bodies.

They called Abraham over, and he knowing the features of Poseidon and Hades that after looking at a few of the bodies he saw two that he recognized and said "That's them" David suddenly felt great relief that the operation was over and said to Abraham " All I can say to you Abraham is, thank you for all the help you have given to us. Without that help, I don't think we would have much chance of stopping Poseidon and his Triumvirate gang " Abraham was also very pleased that it was over, he shook hands with all of them saying "You can fly your men to the nearest Israeli military aerodrome. Leave the two helicopters they are and we will deal with them." He walked away and Bruce spoke to David about the wounded men, David replied "We will take ours with us and get them hospitalized as soon as possible." 1 hour later they flew to an Israeli military aerodrome, who were expecting them because Abraham had informed them of their arrival.

When they landed, the injured men were taken immediately to the hospital situated within the airfield, and David went and informed the station Commander of all the details of the operation, and he asked for a message to be sent to England. The Commander said "I don't think that will be necessary, because I have been informed that they already know of everything that has taken place and we are expecting someone from England to arrive early tomorrow morning." David was very surprised and said "Your means of communication are excellent. I personally didn't think that London would have heard anything yet." The Commander said "Oh we have had you under our supervision all the time and we knew how things were, and when to assist you. This

182

was because we were instructed by our highest authority to keep them completely informed of all conflicts, and when they knew of the recent conflict, they informed London and America of how the operation was proceeding." David was amazed of how organized the Israeli's had been, and after thanking the Commander he came away and spoke to the others, telling them of the excellent Israeli organization. It being evening time, it was dark and while they were having a meal they were told where they were going sleep. Everyone woke up in the morning after a good nights sleep feeling very refreshed. It was at the breakfast table when Bruce saw Kathy, she looked radiant and he laughingly said to her "Kathy, has David seen you this morning?" she appeared to blush but laughed out loud saying "No, not yet he hasn't, because he never notices me." She was standing with her back to the entrance and never knew that David had just appeared and had heard her speaking. He came in and after getting his breakfast he sat down and said "I have just been informed that after I have finished my breakfast I have to go to the Commanders office and I am now wondering what other work they have managed to find for us."

When David had finished his breakfast he went to the Commanders office and there he met Mike Taggert who said to him "David I've come all this way to congratulate you and all the men on a job well done and...." but David quickly interrupted him saying "It's women also Sir, because you mustn't forget Kathy. She has been superb and performed a wonderful job." Mike was laughing out loud as he said "David you still haven't learned when to keep quiet have you? I was just going to mention her, but that can wait until I speak to all of you."

Mike looked at the Commander and said "I think we have finished the conversation I was having with you Commander and I would like to thank you for all the help you and your country has given and the help you have performed in this operation." Mike Taggert got up and shook with Commander 0and said to David "You and I can carry on talking outside and leave the Commander to get on with his everyday work"

When they were outside Mike looked at David and said "When are you getting married? Are you waiting before you get back to Australia before you marry that girl?" David was at a loss for words and thought for a moment before he said "What girl? Anyway I don't think she will want to marry me." Mike laughing and knowing who that girl was, said "Well why don't you go and ask her. She can only say Yes or No." David now felt a complete fool and stumbled over words then suddenly feeling he had the courage he said "Okay I'll go right now and ask her." He left Mike and went to find Kathy and after walking around he saw her walking all alone going towards the room she had slept in, tand he quickly went over and asked her to stop walking. Looking at her he said "I'm sorry Kathy that I asked to stop walking but I wanted you to know that Mike has another job for me and wants me to go back to Australia and I have thought it over and I thought it would be a good idea if you were to come along and be a partner with me. If you agree we could get married and we could be a team for ever." She looked at him in amazement and then with a smile on her face she said "Are you actually proposing to me?" He was now full of embarrassment and worry replied "Er! Yes. Please will you marry me?" She was laughing and put her arms around him as she said "Yes I would love to marry you."

They kissed and they walked back towards where Mike was standing and told him the news. He congratulated them then saying "I hope I have an invitation to the wedding?" Kathy immediately said "Yes, you are invited and we will see you at Ayers Rock where the wedding will take place." David looked at Kathy with a surprised look on his face and for moment Mike was also confused, because he said with a chuckle in his voice "Why Ayers Rock? What is so important about that outback place in the Northern Territory?" Kathy was laughing and being excited she said "Oh Mike I would have thought you would have known why Ayers Rock is so important to people like me and I do believe you are kidding me, because I am sure you know that it is an important sacred monument of the Aborigines."

Mike had a big smile on his face but didn't say another word because when everyone else heard what Kathy had just said, they were all excited and happy, suddenly Bruce said to David "Now that you and Kathy are getting married I'm going to go back to Riverside in America to ask a lovely young lady called Donna Kirkpatrick to marry me. I was courting her just before I came over to England, hopefully she will still be in love with me." With everybody in a happy mood and after handing to all the English men their air tickets to England, and giving Bruce his air ticket to America. As Mike handed to Kathy and David their tickets to Australia he said to everyone present "Well folks I wish to thank you for everything you have all done. I am extremely proud of you and I wish all of you the best of luck and when another job comes up, I hope I will see some of you again."

To David and Kathy he said "I wish you both good luck and of course my best wishes for the future. Then he teasingly said "By the way, I know I will be seeing you again in Melbourne in the very near future, but before I leave, I would like to know whether you are both going to say in your marriage vows that you agree to love, honour and obey?" Kathy and David were laughing as she replied "Yes, because we know we love and honour each other. In the past we have spoken about the obey part, and we both agree that to obey, does not mean to stand to attention or obey orders. To both of us it means that we agree to abide by the law of morality, which gives everyone, whether they be male or female, and what ever colour or creed, they have the right to say Yes or No to anything, including sex."

Mike looked at both of them and said "From that statement I know you will both have a happy marriage and I look forward to being at Ayers Rock for your wedding ceremony."

Lightning Source UK Ltd.
Milton Keynes UK
UKOW050617080313

207344UK00009B/93/P